Andrew J. Davis

Views of Our Heavenly Home

A sequel to a Stellar key to the summer-land

Andrew J. Davis

Views of Our Heavenly Home
A sequel to a Stellar key to the summer-land

ISBN/EAN: 9783337373504

Printed in Europe, USA, Canada, Australia, Japan

Cover: Foto ©Andreas Hilbeck / pixelio.de

More available books at **www.hansebooks.com**

VIEWS

OF

OUR HEAVENLY HOME.

A SEQUEL

TO

A STELLAR KEY TO THE SUMMER-LAND.

BY

ANDREW JACKSON DAVIS.

"Dreams cannot picture a world so fair,—
Sorrow and death may not enter there;
Time doth not breathe on its fadeless bloom,
Far beyond the clouds, and beyond the tomb."

ILLUSTRATED WITH DIAGRAMS.

BOSTON:
COLBY & RICH,
BANNER OF LIGHT PUBLISHING HOUSE,
No. 9 MONTGOMERY PLACE.
1878.

Trow's
Printing and Bookbinding Co.,
205-213 *East 12th St.*,
New York.

INTRODUCTION.

The author has been persistently charged with "tearing down" many time-honored structures. He replied: "'Twas but the ruin of the bad, the wasting of the wrong and ill."

But he here presents a volume devoted mainly to "building up," by means of a revelation of facts and principles existing in the inmost constitution of Nature. A *new* heaven and a *new* universe are now offered in place of the old and erroneous, which, however tottering and untenable from base to turret, are still occupied by numerous talented and learned families.

"If you tear down our sacred dwellings," say the conservatives, "why don't you give us something *better* in which to live and die?" Thus you emphatically exclaim; but I ask: *Are you in earnest?* Are you ready for the question? prepared in your hearts for *re*-formation and *re*-construction? When our modest, tender-hearted, clear-eyed Whittier "woke as from a dream," during which he had witnessed the ruthless overthrow of Sacred temples, he said :—

> " I looked : aside the dust-cloud rolled,
>   The Waster seemed the Builder too;
> Upspringing from the ruined Old
>   I saw the New."

The stellar heavens have interested mankind from the earliest periods. They are, and they have always been regarded as the most sublime, the most elevating and inspiring, of all objects and questions known to the mind of man.

As much as possible the author has avoided technical terms, and employed such language and illustrations as would be most intelligible and require the least study. But he would have his readers accustom themselves to thought-ful meditation upon these ennobling themes.

The first part of this work is deemed a necessary prepara-tion for an understanding of disclosures, made in the second part; and the third and concluding portion, being an " ex-planatory discussion of important questions," is submitted as a necessary supplement to this and to parts of preceding volumes.

The telescope, as practically applied, has been in the world only two hundred years.   Seventy-five years later, which brings the time very near our day, Newton discovered Gravitation.   The printing-press is a comparatively recent invention; that is, mankind lived upon this earth thousands and thousands of years before the power to print and pub-lish a book was discovered and applied.   In fact, with this stretch of time in view, it seems but a few weeks since the first appearance of the printing-press, the steam-engine, the electric telegraph, the spectroscope, and the telephone. The religious darkness, the intellectual stagnation, and the material poverty of mankind prior to these inventions, need not here be mentioned.

Along with these material developments—in a manner, analogous to them in order and importance—came magnet-ism, clairvoyance, psychology, psychometry, and spiritual intercourse.   Just in proportion as the physical discoveries have promoted physical freedom and commercial brother-hood, so have intellectual and religious liberty, and the overthrow of despotism and tyranny succeeded the applica-tion of the above-mentioned mental discoveries.

But these mental discoveries are capable of accomplishing *more good* for mankind than is yet conceived; for, as yet, we but stand upon the threshold of the boundless domains to which they point the looking millions.

The author hopes that the readers of this volume will per-ceive at least some of these promised benefits, and be en-couraged thereby, and enlightened sufficiently to enter upon the *new* universe and into the *new* heavens of harmony and peace.

A. J. D.

New York, February 16, 1878.

CONTENTS.

SEQUEL TO THE STELLAR KEY.

CLAIRVOYANCE.

ITS ORIGIN, POWERS, AND PROGRESSIVENESS.

BLINDED by prevailing materialism, and deeply perplexed by the conflicting claims of an incoming Spiritualism, the candid and brave, yet cautious, searcher after pure truth finds himself unable to fix a just valuation upon the natural powers of the human mind. On the materialistic side he beholds man's mental attributes as so many exquisitely refined galvanic forces, or self-conscious currents and throbbing emotions, evolved by the combined action of cerebrum and cerebellum; on the other hand, on the Spiritualistic side, he beholds man's feelings and thoughts as so many manifestations of various superintending intelligences, of spirits and angels more or less perfect, who perpetually originate and feed whatever he may think or feel. The first party consign him to the bottomless pit of oblivion at the moment of death; while the party of the second part, although opening the sky to him on leaving the earth, consign him to a mixed and dubious existence well-nigh unintelligible. The first teaches him that mind is the most perfect fruit—the superlative degree of organization—upon the matter-tree of the universal world; the second teaches him that mind is at best but a medium for the demonstration of disembodied mentalities.

But is there not a third party who should be summoned to yield testimony upon this important question? Of this other group of witnesses the writer is, and from the first has been, a well-known member and illustrator.

Clairvoyance is as certainly a power of the human mind as is memory or consciousness. It is not derived or borrowed; it is innate and natural. That clairvoyance, as to its manifestations, can be simulated, I do not deny; but I do deny the doctrine, with the authority of knowledge, that the *real* power of vision can be projected by another's will into man's mind. And yet it is true, and this truth is of the. first importance in all investigations, that magnetism, or some influence equivalent, is indispensable to its origin and growth. The insistent materialism of the physical body acts like a clog to the feet of the interior spirit. The blinded eyes, behind the bodily organs of vision, must be rubbed and brightened up by magnetism. But once truly opened, once perfectly developed through the cloud of brain-matter, they can never again be wholly closed. To the eyes of the inward mind amaurosis is an impossibility; although, by the force of disease or the oppression of circumstances, the exercise of these wondrous eyes may be, nay, often is, suspended.*

---

* The condition, mental and physical, which is now most generally sought and known is, the state of " mediumship." which has

Terrestrial or celestial magnetisms, and sometimes nothing but the refinements of certain attenuating diseases, are required to originate clairvoyance. But when fully established, when it is consciously a *part* of the mental operations of the mind, and under the control of the will, which stage is the highest attainable in this world, it is a power of most wonderful scope. It has four phases, or, more properly, in different persons it is manifested in from three to five forms. The very highest is telescopic; I mean exactly what I say—*telescopic.* For example, the sun is supposed to be 92,000,000 of miles from where I now write. Clairvoyance can bring it so near that it can scarcely be seen! Its extreme nearness strikes and blurs the mind's eyes. And yet, *these eyes do not see anything of that external sun which is contemplated by astronomers.* It was a long time before I had perfectly and practically acquired this essential truth. Everything is seen from its *vital* points; thence outwardly and successively, until the outmost or matter-forms are fully discerned. Thus clairvoyance is the vision of the natural eyes exactly reversed or inverted. And here it may be remarked that the mistakes and blunders of persons gifted with clairvoyance find in this fundamental fact a complete and all-

---

many varieties of manifestation. It seems to most persons the only mental state by. which spirits and mankind may freely meet and converse together. Of mediumship there are about twenty-four differing forms. The reader is referred for information concerning these states, to " The Arcana of Spiritualism," by Hudson Tuttle ; to " The Philosophy of Spiritual Intercourse," also to " The Present Age and Inner Life," by the author ; to "Isis Unveiled," a remarkable work by Mme. H. P. Blavatsky; and to a large list of lesser works written by persons in the medium state.

sufficient explanation.   (See further remarks in the Appendix.)

Here you are invited to read an eloquent and literally true delineation of the state termed the "Superior Condition," written by Dr. S. B. Brittan, who is one of the most comprehensive thinkers and elegant writers in the new school. "When our footsteps have encircled the earth; when we have surveyed all orbs in space and all outward forms of being on their surfaces; and even looked through the last open door in the stellar heavens into the outer darkness beyond, we have yet to penetrate the *inner mysteries of being*. Then the faculties, by a kind of introversion, begin to open in a new direction. *We look inward and reach centreward;* and at every step the mind is intromitted to a new and more interior sphere of being. The shadows that float in the dim atmosphere of our earthly life gradually disappear; the translucent forms of a superior creation hover about us; and from the loftiest summits of this world, we behold the immortal day-spring!

"The grandest of all human discoveries is made when the senses are opened from *within*, and we are brought into conscious relations with the vast realm of the invisible and eternal. How does the spirit thrill with amazement and ecstasy at the grandeur of the scene presented, when the great veil that seemed to cover the world is suddenly drawn away and we are made to realize, that in the wide Universe there is nothing concealed—that *all doors are open to* MAN. Before the vision of the philosophical Seer everything is transparent as the luminous ether. He dwells in a region of ineffable light, and can know no darkness save the obscurity that depends upon moral conditions, or the existing state and relations of the soul. The solid earth becomes a crystal sphere; the rugged mountains stand out in the clear air white as alabaster forms; and the fathomless depths are discovered to be illuminated ways where the spirit may dwell in light and walk alone with God.

"If we gradually enter upon the inner life we at once begin to see those divine realities which before were only objects of faith and hope. The stormy passions of this rude world are hushed, and sweet peace soothes the unresting heart. The music of glad voices and the universal harmony are precious realities to our waking consciousness; radiant forms people our day-dreams or glide before us in ' visions of the night when deep sleep falleth on man.' Through rifts in the clouds of our mortal sphere we catch glimpses of happy faces, whose entrancing smiles are the attempered glories of God and his Angels. If by a sudden and strong development of this vision we are ' caught up into heaven,' things are revealed which the laws and limits of human speech do not enable us to communicate. But with reverent and grateful hearts we remember, that, at the approach of the humblest soul, the everlasting doors of the inner temple are freely opened."

The foregoing is a faithful description of the progressive stages which ultimate and blossom into the "Superior Condition."

The forms of clairvoyance, are, first, a glimmering perception of things as in somnambulism; second, a narrow and limited vision of disease, of personal acts, of metals, and of things terrestrial exclusively; third, a discernment of personal states and emotions; thence thought-reading, psychometry, fortune-telling and prophecy. But there is in reality no clairvoyance of much value until the higher phase is fully developed.

And yet development is one of its ever-present possibilities. The mind must be harmonious, or at least considerably self-poised and tranquil, and the purposes of the seeker unselfish and exalted. Then the will is pure and under its direction, and the eyes of the immortal may be unclosed. A steady progressiveness will be likely to characterize the spiritual perceptions, which should be systematically exercised. The temple of the starry heavens will swing wide open its flaming doors, and the gardens of the summer-land come as near as are the fields of earth to the bodily eyes. The very near worlds of matter melt away, and the very far off spiritual universes sweep into your immediate presence. This is what happens to every worthy mind a few hours after death.

------◆------

PSYCHOPHONETICS.

THEIR DEVELOPMENT, LAWS, AND WONDERS.

" HAPPY they," said Father à Kempis, " who penetrate into internal things, and endeavor to prepare themselves more and more by daily exercises to the attaining to heavenly secrets."

Among the treasures of the human mind, which are more numerous than the stars and more precious than all the constellations combined, is the power, or sense, of hearing sounds which are, and forever have been, perfectly unknown in the outer universe. These soul-sounds, so to speak, which are absolutely inaudible to the physical ear, I term " psychophonetics." Who can believe, without at least some items of private experience, that there exists a boundless ocean of intelligent sounds which is never, because they cannot be, heard by bodily organs of hearing ?

The ears of the spirit are seldom opened in this life. Clairvoyance, in comparison, is a familiar power. " Their *eyes* were opened," occurs in the most ancient fables concerning mental illumination. " The scales fell from his *eyes*," and then he *heard* a voice ; but vision came first and led the other senses ; because sight is the handmaid of intellect, and is the sunlight of the whole interior. With his open spirit ears he heard only " a voice," but with his newly-unfolded vision his understanding became illuminated, and love flowing in with the light, his whole heart and soul hastened over to the side of truth and deity.

Sounds of spirit lips disturb and vibrate through an ethereal sea as much finer than the common air as electricity is finer than the common water. The waves of these sounds can touch nothing less refined than the internal ear of the spirit. Yet, when once the spirit ear is open, the inmost of *all* sound-waves can break their music within its labyrinths. Hence the voices of the external universe exert some influence upon the listening soul. There is a telephony between stars and suns. They communicate with each other in a speech unheard and unknown to the ordinary human ear. A most exquisite insight into the laws of psychophonetics is indispensable to a correct comprehension of the wonders heard by the spiritual tympanum. Distance is seemingly no impediment to the flight of these sounds. Neither the interception of currents of wind, nor the presence of immense masses of common earthy matter can prevent the words of the spirit from entering the ear of the prepared listener. Whisperings from Mount Starnos in the Summer land have been heard by the writer, when he was tranquil and absorbingly listening, and the words from those immortal lips sounded as distinctly in his internal ear as did ever the sounds of ordinary speech. But such an experience is rare, and necessarily, because of the great and constant demands of the body and of the present world in which it appropriately exists.

Hearing of sounds inaudible to the common ear, is a truth which foreshadows the glorious ultimate life that is to be; although, unlike the power of vision, it is a part of mind very slightly under the sway of will or desire. It may be suddenly developed, and the happy or astonished possessor may receive in a few moments the voice of warning or of government for a lifetime, and as quickly it may be closed and sealed until after death. Or, it may be slightly unfolded—just enough to admit the speech of distant earthly babblers, of rollicking diakka, or of the groanings and moanings of sorrowing and imprisoned persons afar in this world —bringing to the unfortunate hearer nothing but confusion, agony and uncontrollable feelings of wretchedness and despair. This unhappy form of psychophonetics is, alas! quite too common, and inasmuch as this sense is not subject, as sight is, to the control and government of will, or reason and desire, it is exceedingly often the source of exquisite suffering and indescribable discontent.

To overcome this incipient phase of clairaudience, I recommend a persistent attention to subjects of sight, thought, feeling, reflection, and especially of *action*.

————◆————

CONSCIOUSNESS.

ITS SUNSHINE, DELIGHTS, AND STORMS.

THE counterpartal structure of the universe, even to the coarsest observer, is too evident to suggest controversy. The scales hang evenly balanced in the hand of Eternal Justice. There is as much on one side, in one bowl of the balance, as there is on the other—a just and equal distribution, face to face, on exactly opposite sides, yet in conjugal harmony with each other—of every substance, essence, property, quality, impulse, purpose and destiny. But the extent and significance of this fact in nature is great or small, according to the state and culture of the observer. The loftier and purer the spectator, the grander and holier the scene. A limited mind, which may not be open on the spiritual side, observes a fact, and is mentally impressed with it; but such a mind feels nothing spiritual proceeding from it, and hence acquires from such fact only such knowledge as is kept in the pigeon-holes of memory. With Wordsworth, or upon minds of similar constitution, the effect of a fact is something spiritual and sublime. Walking in the fields and beside streams, he testifies that he *felt* the inner life of things.

> "I have felt
> A presence that disturbs me with the joy
> Of elevated thoughts; a sense sublime
> Of something far more deeply interfused,
> Whose dwelling is the light of setting suns,
> And the round ocean and the living air,
> And the blue sky, and in the mind of man;
> A motion and a spirit that impels
> All thinking things, all objects of all thoughts,
> And rolls through all things."

The inner life of a fact, to a mind thus spiritually impressionable, is, without hesitation or controversy, the *pivot* on which its significance rests and revolves. And hereby I illustrate to you what is meant by the term "Double Consciousness," which in man is a private demonstration and revelation of the counterpartal structure of the universe.

That every fact, like every question, "has *two* sides," is, I repeat, indisputable. Human nature is built and endowed upon this principle. And it is because of this foundation and unchangeable principle, operating through a countless number and varieties of methods and degrees, that mankind make such a multitude of curious and conflicting manifestations. A man's mental wheels turn upon jewelled pivots, provided with compensating balance movements, and with every scientific perfection, so that he can make progress in all places and temperatures, and yet no "time-keeper" more often requires overhauling, cleaning, regulating, or more careful conveyance in a pocket warmed and nourished by the heart.

The sunshine of consciousness is lightest and most prismatic when the spirit is king, and rules benignly in the lower kingdom of the senses. Such a mind walks with his Heavenly parents; for his inner life throbs in sweet accord with the Infinite heart. The holy energy of Love floods his private purposes; and there are healing and happiness in the faithful exercises of his will.

But such delights cannot be experienced except for brief moments, often with painful and lengthened intervals between, because of the *storms* to which the consciousness is subject from the universe without. An interior communion, undisturbed for sixty consecutive minutes, would, I fully believe, unsettle the mind and disarrange its necessary and just relations to this sensuous life. Hence the storms which howl and break in such wild violence upon our daily and hourly pilgrimage. Of the existence of a spiritual universe we know in the delightful depths of a *feeling* (which is flooded with ineffable recollections), even while oppressed by uncontrollable circumstances, or prostrated by the energy of opposing wills and conflicting associations.

Consciousness is twofold in its constitution and manifold in its practical operations. Sensitive persons, because of this conscious doubleness in commingling and indiscriminate exercise, sometimes seem to act or speak hypocritically, or to practice duplicity and "double dealing," in ordinary intercourse with their fellow-men. Thus the very spiritual mind is not unfrequently, also, a very weak and vacillating mind, judged by the standard of an ordinary, well-balanced intellect. But the injustice, not to say cruelty and diabolism, of such a judgment, becomes most apparent and insupportable when coupled with religious prejudices and social ostracism.

The writer's experience is grounded in a long exercise of the spiritual side of consciousness. He has attempted to live in both worlds naturally and healthfully; not, however, at the same moment and in the same hours, but at different moments and in separate hours in the same day; and his attempt has been crowned with a large, grateful, delightful measure of success. But a certain and complete failure invariably succeeded every ambition to *exist consciously* in both worlds at the same time. "Never attempt to do two incousistent things at once," is a motto you will find at the foot of the altar in my experience; and need I say that *obedience* is with me an act of pure religion?

Ambitious religionists, vainly attempting to take the kingdom of heaven by violence, have brought destructive *storms* far and wide over the stretches of their consciousness. It was with a kind of psychophonic listening that Wordsworth's internal ear caught "the still sad music of humanity;" and it was with a long cultured impressibility of his spiritual consciousness that he "*felt* a presence that disturbed him with the joy of elevated thoughts;" but what think you would have happened to him had he attempted, at the same sublime moment, to have *heard* the barking of his favorite dog and *felt* the gratification of eating a tenderloin steak?

Shall I say to church people that they are culpably ignorant of human nature? And that, consequently, they do not comprehend the true foundation of the religion of eternity? And may I also say to Spiritualists that they do not obey the pivotal principle of consciousness? and, therefore, that they fail day by day in reaping a harvest of imperishable riches from the fields of their immense opportunities ? They are drifting oceanward without a chart, and many are speeding upon narrow and dangerous voyages without a reliable pilot.

The sunshine of consciousness is delightful, with " the pure in heart." Opening of the interior *feeling* to a full and free communion with eternal principles, is the only door, swinging on golden hinges, which admits the traveller to the immediate presence of the infinite Father and Mother. All outer search after the Everlasting Centre will fail of complete comfort to the searcher. Facts to the senses, or even the hidden facts of consciousness, are fruitless unless their " inner life " is seen and heard and felt. To those who thus *see* and *hear* and *feel*, the dark luxuriance of the Diakka-Land and the flowering glories of the Summer land alike seem beautiful manifestations of the Infinite Wisdom, differing sides of human experience, resting and revolving upon a twofold and manifold consciousness ; without which a personal existence and consequent progression in any world would be an impossibility.

THE PIVOTAL POWER.

ITS LAWS, SERVANTS, AND MANIFESTATIONS.

THE indescribably perfect wisdom of the Infinite is seen in nothing so complete as in the two-foldness of human nature and in the manifoldness of its operations.

> " Tell me, brother, what are we ?
> *Spirits bathing in the sea of Deity !*
> Half afloat, and half on land,
> Wishing much to leave the strand,
> Standing, gazing with devotion,
> Yet afraid to trust the ocean,
>   Such are we."

Nothing more entirely transcends the comprehending faculty of mind than this familiar ever-present fact called " human nature." The solution of the impenetrable mysteries of the " Godhead," with the completest explanation of the universal system of Nature, do not (apparently) so much strain man's reason and imagination as do the every-day questions, " What is reason ? " and " What imagination ? " The magnification by man of his own personal consciousness into infinite proportions and attributes, which immense Man he tranquilly names " God," and which he then bows down and worships, is a child's performance compared with the impossible task of answering that ever-recurring question, " MAN, *what art thou ?* " Man cannot answer this question because he cannot transcend himself; nay, he cannot ascend to the highest summits of his own attributes of comprehension. Therefore there forever remains a superior part, an Alpine peak of unapproachableness, a private height of consciousness to which the self-investigator can never attain, and which consequently forever remains to its proprietor a supreme mystery.

This private mystery in the heights of personal mental existence is rendered more mysterious by the celestial influences which hover about its undefinable susceptibilities. These touch and fill it with uncontrollable longings for wisdom and knowledge. Doves, descending from unknown arks, alight within its recesses; and they seem to tell of things far off—awakening day-dreams of the lands of immortal beauty, and enkindling the flames of love and adoration for things and persons in a higher realm.

Very few human minds are strangers to these mysterious whisperings in the heights of consciousness. But in the haste and confusion of common life it is not often that any one enters into the golden silence long enough to interrogate them. The popular method is to attempt to gratify or neutralize their celestial interpositions, by attendance upon "public worship," or by indulgence in pictures, poetry, music, and the drama. But there are always a few persons who seek to feed these longings by occasional association with spiritual natures; by consolations through favorite agents of communication with the departed; or, most rarely, by the cultivation and calm enjoyment of an "inner life."

Shall I augment the mystery, or may I solve one of the supreme problems of human nature, by affirming that there is a Power enthroned in man's consciousness, to which both the matter of his body and all the mind in his possession are servants? This power is the pivot on which his universe revolves. It lifts him superior to all ordinary ties and dependencies. He is cut by it free from every "entangling alliance," which arises from his intimate relationship to everything in the kingdoms beneath, or from the world of life which rolls perpetually around him. You are by this power made *conscious* of an existence independent of both Nature and Deity. It compels you to accept the sublime responsibility of an eternal individual life. Its two-edged energy separates you from the womb that gave you form and consciousness. You master by it all the clogs that impede your growth and progress. It inspires you with courage, strength to overcome, patience to endure, fortitude to stand, motive to spiritualize matter, and with a sort of peri-consciousness by which you meet and measure everything and all persons about you.

Am I increasing the mystery which floats over the summits of your already inaccessible mental mountains? I think that I am not. But I believe you will smile with incredulity and disappointment when I affirm that the "pivotal power" in man, to which both mind and matter are servants, is that energy which is familiarly called WILL.

Upon the diamond-point of this power turns the entire universe of mind. In the animal we behold nothing but a partial manifestation of this mystery. To a seer, the mental force and headlong persistent energy in the mind of the animal, is but a prophecy of that power which in man exalts him to the fellowship of gods. Impulse, derived from the attractions and repugnances of awakened inclinations, is all the will-energy ever manifested by an animal. And it is also true that this is the origin and quality of all the will-power that is exercised by an animal-man ; it is all the will that such a man knows anything about, and it is all he can believe in ; for such a man is naturally a fatalist, and is easily rendered helpless under a pressure of adverse circumstances ; but such a man and such a manifestation of the "pivotal power," is not meant by the terms MAN and WILL employed in this chapter.

Love is the source of quantity in a person. There is great fulness of life where there is great affection, which flows out of love's fountain ; and there is great intelligence where there is great reflection and memory, which arise from the knowing faculties ; but there are presence, individuality, self-assertion, independence, courage, heroism, self-poise, movement and *execution* where there is WILL. Both mind and matter obey its fiat ; it is the inherent evidence of the existence of God.

Human affections, flowing as they do out of the inmost fountains of Love, irresistibly cling to and climb about whatever acts upon them as a natural attraction. They have no innate power of deciding *pro* or *con*— whether they shall or shall not—because they are pure, and superior to all thought and intention. When they are attracted, they go ; when repelled, they retire in silence. They are like the angels in heaven: they " neither marry nor are given in marriage," for they flow like the life of the heart, to and fro, in and out ; obedient to the eternal laws of happiness and misery, which in usual words are called attraction and repulsion. To follow the ebbings and flowings of your affections would be living a beautiful life in childhood; but it would not be worthy or characteristic of truly unfolded men and women, who are of the peerage, coëqual with the gods who know and *do* both good and evil.

Human intelligence and memory are obedient to a different set of laws; and yet are not antagonistic with the best needs of the affections. The very perfections of infinite wisdom are displayed in the harmonious co-operation of these apparently antagonistic hemispheres. A man takes a problem in business or in society; keeps it in his memory; revolves it over and over and from side to side; thinks upon it selfishly, and reflects upon it with the lurid fires of his desires; hoping to see his way to the end of it, like a chess-player; and planning to out-general his adversaries, and to mentally overreach those who go the same way. In the animal brain the same mental processes occur upon the same laws, but in a degree very far down and inferior to those in man; and yet in the *animal-man* there is not very much difference in the quality of the thinking of the thoughtful faculties.

But what can the affections or the reflections accomplish of themselves? They may incline or decline, and they may decide or refuse; but nothing less than the "Pivotal Power" can impart movement and manifestation.

WILL is not an organ. It is a fulcrum at one moment, a lever next; but, finally it is the sovereign power which moves the lever, the central god-energy which animates and exercises all the organs; the self-conscious Jupiter, superior to all the other deities, who forges and hurls his own thunderbolts through the heavens of the inner universe.

Mind obeys the will, and matter obeys the will; for without Will, both mind and matter, which are derived alternately from one another, would be motionless, lifeless, formless, *dead !*

Man is conscious of his consciousness—although he cannot fully comprehend the totality of his superior powers—and he is therefore conscious of what is called "originating." From the twofoldness of his consciousness (that is, from the senses without and from the spirit within) man's mind derives the idea of causation. And causation implies and necessitates an exercise of the Will. If this be true of and within man, must it not be also true of that eternal organization of attributes, which is sometimes called "Omnipotence"? Will and causation are interchangeable terms. All material phenomena are the ever-varying manifestations of a pivotal energy, which is self-conscious, self-poised, independent, self-intelligent, and eternal in its own individual right. By the term "independent" is meant that which is not clinging and dependent like the affections, or rotary and helplessly self-involving like the intellect; but that degree of power which enables the mind to choose, to transform, to inspire, to act; for truly, all independence is comparative.

I would not dare to set bounds to the originating reach and sway of Will; *i. e.*, when it is pure and exercised for a pure purpose. It can overcome all forms of diabolism—diseases, sensualism in the blood, vices in the habits, appetites in the senses, weaknesses in the moral feelings, hypocrisy, falsehood, and all manner of evil thinking. All this it can do when it is pure. But an evil Will! is the highest expression of what in the religious world is called "the devil." It takes counsel of the inclinations of affection, which are the sources of desires, and it employs intellect solely to plot, and plan, and teach the way in which the pivotal power should proceed. How many fair, spiritual natures are held down to earth in bondage and in misery by the evil will-power of animal men and women!

If you would know the full happiness of the harmonial angels, let your Will do only what is requested by your highest Affections, and only what is approved by the reflections of your highest Reason.

THE INNER WORLD.

AN INTERIOR VIEW OF THE PRESENT LIFE.

THE merest mention, with becoming seriousness, of the spiritual world, suddenly envelopes the ordinary or natural mind with cloud-mists and suffocating vapors; and to such minds, who not unfrequently are great bible-believers and church-members in good standing, the use of the simple term "death" acts like the drop-scene which separates the awful stage of eternity from the weeping audience left in this world. Multiply uncertainty, obscurity, doubt, and anxiety one hundred and fifty times, and you obtain the composition and magnitude of that undefinable cloud of blackness which hangs over the tomb. The clearest-headed, most analytical, fairest-minded teacher of the Religion of Humanity in the city of New York (Octavius B. Frothingham) seems to appreciate and eulogize this so-called impenetrable tomb-cloud as an unspeakable blessing to mankind. It acts like a demon of danger, standing with beckoning gestures upon the brink of an unknown sea. All men hesitate before death, and most men, because of the great mystery beyond, settle steadfastly into this world, resolved to live in it as long as possible, to squeeze all the happiness possible out of it, to perform their parts as well as possible, and at last, reluctantly, to die when they must.

On the other hand, from 1747 to 1770, the most spiritually-minded, most intellectually and morally endowed, least enthusiastic, wholly devoted man in Europe, Emanuel Swedenborg, by revelations and reasonings almost innumerable, taught that the ordinary (or natural) mind in this world could experience or accomplish nothing glorious and worthy unless the spiritual world, by influx, was permitted to make itself fully manifest in the affections, will, and understanding. He made the most complete and comprehensible affirmations, by means of indispensable repetitions, of the composition of the spiritual world, its internal government, and explained what he understood to be its exact relations to the natural world and to individual men and women. The spiritual world, he insistently repeated, consists of three heavens, one within the other

—the natural, the spiritual, and the celestial. The first, lowest, is the region of fraternal (or neighborly) love; the second, or middle heaven, is ruled by fraternal love, which is characterized by the love of truth; and the third, or the highest heaven, is called celestial, because it is altogether a realm of most divine love, being essentially in the love of the Lord. But these triune heavens give you to comprehend only one half of the spiritual world, as Swedenborg explained it; for the other half consists of three hells, one within the other, which in every particular are exact antagonists of the heavens; instead of love to the neighbor, the inhabitants of the first hell are in the miseries of self-love; instead of being governed by love of truth, in the second hell, they exist in conflict with each other, through falsities, evil devices, and horrible practices: and in the inmost hell, instead of divine, fraternal love and essential love of the Lord, the people give themselves up to the most infernal hatreds of one another, insanities of diabolism, and indulge in the most distracting blasphemies and enmities toward the Lord, and oppose constantly whatever is celestial and heavenly.

But immediately after death every person first enters the vast "world of spirits," which is intermediate or between the three hells on the one hand and the three heavens on the other. The final destiny of each is fixed subsequently, under the freedom of the will, which the Lord everlastingly maintains, and gives to each soul at every hazard, and regardless of the cost to infinite system. Our author also discerned what he termed an exact correspondence between man and the supernal structure—three degrees, or the natural mind, the spiritual mind, and the conjunction or subjection of the first to the second, called by him regeneration, which unfolded the third degree corresponding to the celestial or inmost heaven. In this state, or degree, the individual is conjoined to the Lord—a perfect representation of the "Essential Divinity and the Divine Humanity."

Degrees, says Swedenborg, are of two kinds—discrete and continuous; neither of which can, by any possibility of intimacy or refinement, ever become the other. Thus the natural or external world is divided from the internal or spiritual world by the impassable barrier called "a discrete degree." It is only by influx, or "permission," that the love or life, and truth or light, of the spiritual flow into the receptacles of this world.

The explicitness of the foregoing is to the end that what is to follow may be more readily comprehended by the reader.

You are aware, doubtless, that in these later days, more than one hundred years after the illuminated Swedenborg retired from the external world, a greatly modified conception of the relations of the two worlds has taken possession of the common understanding. And now it seems that even his revelations demand a further revealment; just as, by the great law of progress, all modern revelations will require the more illuminated commentaries of the seers of 1976. Receivers of Swedenborg's revealments as *final* statements will, I am well aware, turn from this assertion with august disdain, and explain all attempted discredit of his claims as the direct work of evil spirits. But will they not sympathize with the receivers of the last book in the Bible? In 1764 Swedenborg wrote an explanation of what John meant in his visions on the Isle of Patmos—a great many hundreds of years after the visions had been experienced and recorded, not to be disturbed or changed under penalty of eternal death—which, nevertheless, Swedenborg did in a masterly manner, under the title of "The Apocalypse Explained," and which he subsequently undertook successfully to improve upon, being himself moved by the spirit of progress in 1766, when he published his superior revealments of John's revelations under the appropriate title of "The Apocalypse Revealed." And now, as an unavoidable consequence, Swedenborg's own apocalyptic utterances call for analytical commentaries. The step from what is called Apocalypse to what is really Apocryphal is so short that even the lame and halt can take it. And be it remembered that what is here said of others, our revered and most noble predecessors, we expect and hope will be as freely and truthfully said of us.

In this chapter, which must not be too extended, your attention is called especially only to the correspondential method of interpreting properties and qualities, with reference to their degrees and states of being. And first I remark that the *method* which a mind adopts instinctively and, as it were, irresistibly, as by an involuntary natural election, is to be explained in only one way, *i. e.*, by the structure, rather than by the superficial inclinations, of the mental organization. Thus a mechanic by mental structure does not interpret the objects and qualities of nature musically;

neither does a naturally religious and poetic mind see
and explain things like a mathematician or scientist;
but, by the force of an inherent law, each mind is
bound by the necessities of its own organization and
condition, to interpret what it sees and feels by a
method natural to itself, but which would be arbitrary
and a cruelty when forced upon another mind to which
it would, by the same law, be as naturally unnatural.
Take, for example, the case of Origen, the faithful
Christian teacher of the third century, who in his
"Hexapla" and "Octapla" rendered the meaning of
the Scriptures by the most persistent and cohesive employment of the allegorical method. He invariably regarded the literal meaning as secondary. In like manner, with the same headstrong profound earnestness and
logical cohesiveness, Swedenborg discerned a spiritual
sense within the literal texts, and a celestial or heavenly
sense hidden at the core of the spiritual meaning.
Clouds, for example, denote the literal sense of the
Scriptures, and the spiritual sense floats in with power
and glory. Thus the Lord (or the spiritual and the
celestial signification) is seen coming "in the clouds of
heaven with power and great glory," etc.

In this place I will not introduce any of the important explanatory conversations which I have enjoyed
with the illustrious author of the "Apocalypse Revealed." But I may be permitted to relate how I have
taken lessons from him, for purposes of solving his own
method of observation and interpretation of things
spiritual which are truly within the external, and to
record what were the effects resultant. It is not natural
to my mind to indulge in fables, in tropes, symbols,

2*

figures, hidden meanings, signs, secrets, &c.; hence whatever I did, or can do, by the "language of correspondence" must be from the effect of lessons and a determination to apply them. For a long time I practised the method of associating in my thoughts "innocence" with the sight of the word or object "lamb," thus trying to see a quality, and reading its full signification, whenever I saw the name of an object or the thing itself. When I looked up and saw a *cloud*, or read the word in the Bible, I must instantly associate it with the "literal sense;" in which enormous *cloud* the sceptic is often wrecked, and from which one extremely rational mind evolved "one hundred and forty-four contradictions." So I must think of "strength" when I see a "lion"—of "courage" as the meaning of an "eagle"—of a "cow" as the good of "use"—of "wine" (in the Scriptures) as the "interior truths of the word"—of "bread" or flesh as "divine goodness"— and of water "baptism" as the "regeneration" of the mind, &c., &c. It was long before this method became possible for me to employ in interior investigations. But at length I could apply it, and I *did* on several penetrations of a city in the outer world.

Swedenborg said the spiritual world is within the natural world, as the spiritual man is within the natural man. After a long experience I agree with him perfectly; with this understanding: That by the "spiritual world" is meant a vitalizing, governing, developing world of forces, essentially divine and omnipresent with divine love, will and wisdom. But as to the "discrete degree," I find that we must, with the best feelings, part company and walk in different paths.

One day, not long since (but it was only one of many similar experiments), the city of New York, as it looks in the spiritual world, was subjected to the telescopic process I have already explained. You will remember that Swedenborg taught that a correspondence runs throughout the universe ; that all things in the natural world (for example, in the city of New York) have their likenesses or prototypes in the spiritual world. In a word, just here let me remark that I never could find this statement exactly true, except in the general sense —that all things spring from spiritual centres of forces and principles which are, of necessity, dwelling *within* the outer forms and worlds which are visible to the bodily eyes.

But this is what was visible to the inward organs of vision : I beheld a city of living, throbbing, rainbow-tinted beauty. The streets and the buildings on either side, the trees in the parks, the water flowing through the pipes, the very air—all was perfectly represented, down to the minutest detail, as plainly as any of these things ever looked to my external eyes. I could see the shape and location of furniture in the rooms every-where, and the appearance of the occupants, and their situation and circumstances, whether sick or well, whether rich or poor ; and often I could even discriminate as to the color of their garments, but especially the affections and thoughts which were occupying their feelings and brains and time. It was like stripping New York of its material vesture, peeling off its coating or shell, so to speak, and viewing its actual, vital, spiritual existence. Even after so much of this kind of experience, I could hardly guard my mind from believing and my soul from exclaiming : " Why, truly, this is New York in the spiritual world ! " That is to say, it was so difficult to keep faithfully to the fact, which for the time was totally obscured and forgotten, that what I was witnessing was actually and locally *within* the familiar city on old Manhattan Isle.

But I must apply my acquired method. Therefore the people in the streets and stores, in the saloons, hotels, habitations and hospitals, began to assume appearances according to their ruling loves, desires, qualities, conditions and occupations. It would consume pages to relate what I saw in particular instances. One gentleman's shoulder was loaded with the head of a certain horse, upon which his thoughts and affections were set ; another presented the face and head of a lamb, although he was awaiting the day of execution for a crime " proved " against him ; another's right arm and hand looked like a vicious serpent ; a blackbird rode on the head of a gentleman high in office ; a man seemingly great in control wore a dog-collar around his neck, with the initials of his office engraved upon it; a handsome-faced man in a beautiful residence had the hind legs and hips of a goat ; a quiet, very modest person, in a great store, had the bust of a lion ; a ministerial look-ing man walked like a beetle, which was an Egyptian symbol of the world ; a splendid ram's head surmounted the face of a public character, which corresponded to intellect and pride, destitute of love and good will ; a medical gentleman carried a dove upon his shoulder, which meant pure affection, while another doctor had the facial expression of a nighthawk ; and yet another wore upon his bosom the image of a wolf ; a lady, beautifully organized, was covered with sores and repulsive colors ; a very ordinary appearing woman had the most attractive crown of white lilies upon her brow; a procession of persons intent on deeds of charity for the sake of their faith, looked like a flock of ravens ; a cluster of thorny vines enveloped the head of a dealer in cheese and butter; a man in the attitude of prayer, in a church, had the top of his head covered with a cap of gold coins ; a dealer in gold and silver was all over perfectly black, except his hands and forehead ; another man, in the same place, had a few violets and the most beautiful tiny flowers growing out of his shoulders, showing that it was only the force of circumstances that made him a money-changer—his affections and aspirations being far different. And thus I examined the city of New York as it is in the spiritual world, leaving, as you may well imagine, hundreds of thousands of important observations unrecorded. It was a city of lights, clouds and colors. But it is not true that the internal or spiritual city is separated from the external or natural city by a " discrete degree; " for in very truth the outer is not only an evolution and continuation of the forces and principles and individualities within, but it is through and through one and the same, a legitimate growth from seed to shell, from the prime-causes invisible to the full blown effects which constitute, in totality, what is commonly called " New York." And yet, if you will adopt the correspondential method, accustom your thoughts to think through pictures, allegories, symbols and secret signs, it becomes as easy as " second nature " to look into the internal city and see it to be (what, alas! it is too truly) a hell, where the spirits (the citizens) are in the evils of selfishness, in opposition to the "good of truth," refusing to accept truth itself, and persisting in living in antagonism "to the love of the Lord," which makes the most wretched hell that Swedenborg's insight brought to the understandings of mankind; and it is my conviction that Swedenborg was not often enabled to employ the faculty of clairvoyance, but instead, that it was his belief (as it was his experience) that when the spiritual degree of the mind is opened and conjoined with the spiritual world, which is *within* the external or natural world, whatever by impression or by correspondential interpretation forced itself, as to its qualities and uses, upon his understanding and into his will, became thereby and fixedly a vision of heaven or of hell, even into detail, as I have illustrated by what was distinctly visible in the interior of New York.

SKEPTICISM.

A CAUSE OF TRUE PROGRESS IN KNOWLEDGE.

EXEMPTION from doubt would prostrate enterprise and destroy the mainspring of imagination, whose first-born is curiosity, whose handmaidens are investigation, experiment and achievement, resulting in universal progress. All that man can know for *certain* is what has been, and what is, and of these only items and fragments; for his mind is not capable of comprehending the whole of either past or present, even in his own little world. "I know that I know that I am," is the Alpha and Omega of certainty.

Doubt, which means uncertainty, is the mind's prime incentive to activity. The uncertainty of life keeps the soul revolving very near the orbit of its just equilibrium; it is the ballast in the hold, which saves the vessel from going over in a storm.

Absolute, unquestionable certainty—the self-demonstration and incuriosity of sleepless omniscience—abolishing all reasonings, crushing all research, destroying all possibility of surprise and emotion, is happily impossible to human nature. Some Orthodox poet (Pollok, I believe) professed to find comfort in *certainty* at the Day of Judgment. "The good man," he wrote, "*knew*, in very truth, that he was saved to all eternity, and feared no more; while the bad man had proof complete that he was damned forever; and believed entirely, that on every wicked soul anguish would come, and wrath, and utter woe." But then, we must remember that Orthodox Christians have a genius for drawing comfort from wells into which a reasonable and refined person would not even let down an "old oaken bucket."

What shall we say? Do not spiritual communications make *certain* the immortality of the soul? Does walking a mile into the country give you certain knowledge of the contents of every other mile around the globe? Of future existence for you, let us agree that spiritual intercourse is a demonstration. But can immortality of your own special memory and private consciousness be rendered *certain* by any proof short of the absolute living of an immortal life?*   Doubt, at this juncture, is the mother of fresh thought and investigation.   Imagination, which is the seer of the intellectual faculties, now spreads its wings for another flight into immensity.   From the realm of *uncertainty* will now come back a flock of birds of paradise.   Hope, Aspiration, Yearning, Prayer!   These are faithful life-preservers for the groping millions—while to the thinking few, there are the faithful safeguards of Nature, Reason, Intuition, Philosophy.

Thus, in a universe of doubt and uncertainty, the great army of fools and philosophers jog along side by side; no one quite knowing exactly in his own mind the critical spot where the fool ceases and the philosopher begins.

EMANATIONS.

AN ATMOSPHERE AROUND EVERYTHING.

EVERY principle wears appropriate garments.   The life within the blood, like the sensation within the nerves, puts on an armor of many-colored atmospheres, compounded of particles derived from the constitution within, as grass grows out of the soil, or hair upon the head.   These particles, which form an atmosphere about a person, are pleasing or repulsive, and can be detected by animals like horses and dogs, and more especially and certainly by impressible sensitives called mediums.

* I have treated the question of " proof " fully in the Gt. Har., vol. v., part iii.

It is this *aura*, going before a person or trailing along the path the feet have pressed, which makes it possible for the bloodhound to track the slave, the fond dog to find his master, or for you to realize when a particular acquaintance is near your house, or for two silent persons to think the same thought at the same moment. There is a great reality in this atomic emanation about a person, which, in progress of science, will lead to great discoveries and social revolutions. It may do far more than the ten commandments to regulate the marriage relation and the production of children. Real individuality and spiritual status can be accurately ascertained by the aural atmosphere which, in spite of either wish or will, surrounds a person, preceding and following him everywhere he goes and under all circumstances, indicating and analyzing him as completely as words can impart an idea to the mind.

———◆———

APOTHEOSIS.

THE ELEVATION OF MEN TO THE ESTATE OF GODS.

FROM time immemorial, because taught instinctively by the indwelling oracles of Intuition, mankind have believed that actual *death* was impossible to any wise and good man. The early Christians (*i. e.*, the Roman Catholics, and afterwards their lineal descendants, the English Episcopalians) believed that the great and good, both women and men, went to dwell in Paradise with

God.   But ages before the Christian Era it was a common faith that above the skies, in the temple and before the throne of the Deity, the noble, the wise, the heroic and the virtuous lived and watched over the great family of man, and especially worked in behalf of those on earth, who believed and worshipfully regarded them.

Christians of to-day profess to regard all this as so much superstition; and yet they have a religion that teaches exactly this "superstition;" which is only a doctrine in the Churches, but which is a demonstrated familiar *fact* among Spiritualists.   The time was, says a writer, when "it became common among superstitious and passionate people for lovers to raise altars to their mistresses, and parents to their children."   But it may, with great logical propriety, be asked: What mean these monumental displays in our modern cemeteries? What is a church but an altar erected to and named after some departed good man, or beloved woman? Yonder is a holy establishment called "St. Paul's." Just up the avenue you see "St. Ann's Church."   Who does not fancy the old apostle, with a possible degree of ungodly pride in his heart, looking over heaven's high wall at "St. Peter's, in Rome"?   All around you are costly and beautiful altars dedicated to personages who have experienced what in ancient times was called *apotheosis.*   There is "St. John's Cathedral," which is a graceful architectural monument.   But what do you think of that immense structure called "The Church of the Holy Redeemer"?   More ambitious altar-builders, who dislike being on the fence in the expression of their preferences, come squarely out and say, this is "Christ's Church."   Very uncertain disciples concerning the

" apotheosis " of their favorite saints, with one bound jump the mystic chasm, give all inferior deities a respectful slip, and christen their sanctuary " The Church of the Holy Unity." Imagination alone can reach the possible feelings of " St. Thomas " under this slight.

But Spiritualists, although accepting the whole truth of apotheosis, yet save themselves an enormous expenditure of labor and capital. They rationally regard the circumstances of the other world as quite as comfortable as this; that persons, who have experienced the celestial promotion, do not need material altars erected to them, nor religious ceremonies performed either for their benefit or ours; and, lastly, that the virtuous and the truly great, who as spirits and angels dwell above the earth, are chiefly interested in aiding mankind's growth toward universal peace and harmony. Thus a rational religion is not only practical, but it is also just as to the requirements of the past and the present, and with respect to the future an unparalleled economy !

PRIMITIVE BELIEVERS.

SPIRITUALISTS OF THE FIRST CENTURY.

An Oriental Spiritualist, or (as some writers prefer) Pythagorean Philosopher, named Apollonius, lived about the commencement of the Christian dispensation. He was actively engaged in disputing with the learned doctors, in performing (so-called) supernatural cures among the people, and in teaching Spiritualism like one having heaven-ordained authority. He ate no animal food ; discarded woollen clothes ; wore very long hair, and combed it ; washed his face ; kept his body sweet ; refused to associate with women, lived single, therefore, like Jesus, and the Shakers and Catholic Priests ; opposed all sacrificial offerings as evil and corrupting ; did not think much of oral prayer ; proclaimed the perishableness of all material possessions ; was an original teacher in religion, loaded with eloquence and attractive free speech ; in short, he urged the precepts of truth, honor, equity, personal purity and universal education.

In those days, a spiritually illuminated mind was understood to be *a miracle.*   An Apollonius, a Pythagoras, a bright Spiritualist who lived in a superior mood, who could suddenly perform a magnetic or a psychologic cure, was believed to be either a god, or the son of a god, or else a veritable Beelzebub, the prince of devils. But, happily, we live in an age which is more of a miracle than all the mysteries of all the religions of the world combined—an era of Reason and Liberty, opposed to superstition, but hospitable to what is deemed the universally *Natural,* which is found to contain everything that is good and true in every creed that ever existed inside or outside of Christendom.

MISSIONARIES.

THE APOSTLES OF A NEW GOSPEL.

THE phrase *apostle* signifies one who is sent, like a delegate or missionary, to perform some special service. It is usually employed in connection with the system called Christianity.

This mixed system was originated by the apostles; and *not*, as is so generally believed, by the spiritually minded son of Joseph and Mary. Christianity, for this very reason, has been, from the first, an inconsistent compound of elements spiritual and temporal, a curious admixture of the supernatural with the simple and common; with teachings both attractive and repulsive to Judaism on the one hand, and to the Gentiles on the other. It was the desire of the apostles to render Christianity comprehensible and congenial to both sides of the world—to the Jews, who were looking for a Messiah in the line of David, and to the Gentiles, who wanted to start free of Moses and the prophets. Paul was the most influential " apostle to the Gentiles." The earlier apostles were anxious to Judaize the teachings of Christianity, or rather, to compromise enough to convert the Jews. In order to throw the gospel net around the hard-headed Israelites, it was important to preach and exalt Jesus as the real, originally promised Messiah. But the spiritual illumination of John enabled him to perceive and to render Jesus in a new light. In continuation of Paul's philosophical interpretation, John's spiritualized perceptions caused him to conceive the idea that the crucified One was an intimate of God, that he was the very " Word that was made flesh ; " which conception, to both Jews and Gentiles, as well as to people generally, even to this hour, is an incomprehensible mysticism. This conception of John, in its very essence, is nothing but a reappearance in religion of the Messianic idea—another manifestation of " the Arabula ; " which is the saving Principle from the Most High ; the anointed in the spiritual sense ; the spirit of holiness, goodness, and purity ; a religious mystery known only to and by the spirit, a transcendental, spiritual consciousness, taught as a cardinal truth from God by the Essenes, a sect of pure believers and celibates, among whom Jesus spent some of the best years of his life. (It will be remembered that he was preaching and healing the sick, or practicing his precepts, only about *three* years before he was executed by the Jews.)

There are, however, apostles of the Spirit, and truly inspired missionaries of the Truth, in all countries and among all sects. But by this I do not mean exclusively apostles of Christianity, or of any other system organized into a form of dogma and doctrine. For it would be easier to show that a matter is perfectly consistent with Christianity than to prove it to be the truth. I would rather have one truth than a thousand texts to establish its identity with Christianity. So should we welcome and sustain the apostles of progress and reform—the advance guards and heroic pioneers of any new statement or discovery—for, by so doing, we take sides with humanity as did Confucius and Jesus, and as do all sincere natures who see and love truth as a revelation from God to the understanding.

------•------

AUTHORITIES.

FOR THE GUIDANCE OF THE INDIVIDUAL.

WHEN there is too much familiarity and fraternal equality between officers and soldiers, there is a proportional amount of laxity in the discipline, and a very general disobedience of orders. An authority inspiring respect and insisting upon prompt obedience to the word of command, is absolutely indispensable. The individuality of the men—their personal pride, their private tastes, their great individual respectability in social life, their superior education, their dignity and weight of character—all is totally immersed in the supreme authority. Without such authority, and without such total self-abnegation of the persons voluntarily associated for a purpose, there could exist no effective coöperation. Without it, no ship could ever be sailed, no factory run, no government founded, no church organized.

But the philosopher detects the evils which accompany this necessary obedience to centralized chieftainship. The integral rights of individuals are more and more trampled down. The supremacy and success of *the organization* are exalted and proclaimed as of paramount importance. Individuals exist and die for the institution; not the institution for individuals. Outraged and enslaved individuals, with their private sensibilities disregarded every hour, and their most sacred desires and aspirations systematically offended and crushed, at last discover that "corporations have no souls." Revolt and revolution, resulting in a new organization, and regulated by new forms of authority, are natural historical developments. And so, for a period, the constituents are satisfied, and the new departure is victorious.

In religion, men call these changes "a new dispensation." Think of the progress of mankind before the era of Moses! Arts, agriculture, science, society, morals, governments—all wonderfully flourishing under the sun in Egypt, in Persia, in Babylon, in Chaldea. And yet, with the authority of a heavenly sovereign, Moses, with the exception of the book of Genesis, rejected all the religious authorities and all the sacred Scriptures which existed anywhere in the world at his time. He seemed to perceive enough cosmological and historical truth in Genesis to entitle it to a place in the new collection of Scriptures which would in time be written.

This was a radical revolt. It resulted in revolution, in wars, in horrible conflicts between the Pagan nations and the Jewish followers of Moses and the prophets. Who authorized the great lawgiver to reject and accept? Who gave him power to invalidate one popular authority, and to enhance and augment the authority of that which was unpopular? Was Mosaism a finality? Did that one dispensation under him comprehend and embody for all future ages the intentions and ways of God to mankind?

Let us see. The Jews had among them many very learned doctors of divinity. Their sacerdotal scholars, their divinely appointed prophets, their chief scribes and God-ordained rulers had written many sacred scriptures. Things were getting into shape to stay forever. The whole body of doctrine had been declared. All laws, all ceremonies, all things good and acceptable in the sight of Jehovah, had been with infinite labor written down in books, and were possessed of transcendent authority.

But just at this comfortable hour a man called " Jesus " was announced. He entered at once into the wholesale business of a new dispensation. He treated the Jews according to the principle which they had applied to the Pagan authorities. He authoritatively accepted (*i. e.*, he did not peremptorily reject) the few books accredited to Moses and to the foremost prophets; but he repudiated without compromise all the Jewish sectarianisms and all the religious writings of their highest sacerdotal authorities!

This was repudiation on a grand scale. It was revolt in the religious world; it brought not peace, but a sword; it was radical revolution; another new dispensation. Conflicts countless have resulted; and sects swarm throughout Christendom. But there is a Bible! Here (in the Scriptures) you think you find the whole body of doctrine. Here you think you read all the heavenly laws, all the essential commandments, all that is necessary for mankind to know of God, of immortality, and of the way of salvation. Indeed! Are

3

you quite certain that nothing more is needed? Has an unchangeable God, who has from the first been manifested successively in new and still newer dispensation—has *He changed?* Has he reversed the order and method of His unreversible mind? Has He altered in the very heart of immutability?

We shall see. Spiritualism was suddenly announced. It enters, and at once begins business. With unquestioning authority it repudiates all sects and all systems; Pagan, Jewish, Christian, together with the authorities they claim for their sacred books—all equally rejected and invalidated! This is exceedingly hard upon the Christians; even as Jesus was hard upon the Jews; even as Moses was hard upon the great authorities of Paganism. It means revolution—a revolt in the camp of sects; it means another new dispensation. But the war will continue. Spiritualism cannot be the final statement; not the complete authority. Phases of religious truth are lights set upon the hills of human progress; beacon-lights to humanity, embodying great accumulations of inspiration and experience: but the same beacons cannot always burn; new lamps will be lighted in newly-constructed towers upon the walls of Zion.

CEREMONIES.

OLD FORMS IN A NEW COUNTRY.

It is because Nature is system, order, rotational and repetitional, that mankind find themselves inclined to forms and systematic proceedings. " We come honestly by it."

But many formulas and ostentatious ceremonies never appear among the refined and truly cultured, either in society or religion. A commanding intellect and a noble heart have little fellowship with artificial distinctions and high-sounding titles. A deep thinker soon finds the limitations of speech. A thought that is not too profound for ceremony is superficial, and of little account. A profoundly grateful and loving heart is slow in verbal prayer and exquisitely delicate in professions. Manners are superior to ceremonies. The first flow out of the spirit; the latter from education. Ancient nations were nothing unless ceremonial. Chinese and Japanese continue to this day many of the extreme social and religious demonstrations practised hundreds of generations ago. Mahometans, Brahmins, Buddhists, Roman Catholics, and Modern American Episcopalians, are brim full of dignitary titles and contemptible distinctions. They can do nothing without precedent and ceremony. A certain circumlocutory service, a barbarian genuflectional etiquette, is deemed solemnly attractive and indispensable. Religious chieftains can do nothing without mysterious forms. The creed of their institution the ministers gladly leave to the theologians to analyze and quarrel over; but the traditional rites and ceremonial observances of their church they maintain and obey with pomp and circumstantiality; knowing full too well that the ignorant multitude is drawn and held by empty show, parade and display, however cold and unfeeling, while intellectual substance and real spiritual merit would be unrecognized and passed by in stupid silence.

All this is characteristic of countries with titled no-bility, where there are castes and arbitrary distinctions, plebeians and patricians, poor and rich, goats and sheep, subjects and kings, the common people ruled by aristo-crats. Religious organizations and ceremonial obser-vances correspond, in all such countries, with the structure of government and the form of the social organism. Because, to tell the truth, the Church of any country is a *reflection*, not the leader and the instructor, as it should be, of the social state and legal conditions of the people. But *here*, in free-thinking, progressive, pre-eminently democratic America! *here*, in the beautiful Utopia of mental freedom and free schools! *here*, in the paradise of peers and self-supporting sovereigns! *here*, in the land of religious liberty unbounded, and of political progress without end! *here*, where the arts and sciences prosper, where philosophy is blossoming into spirituality, where poetry and general literature have inspiration and readers without measure—*here*, in such a country, and amid this equal distribution of every essential blessing, how absurd, how uncalled-for, how backward-looking and criminally weak, to surround true Religion, pure and undefiled, with the services and ceremonies derived from the age of mythology! And yet, notwithstanding the absurdity and criminal weakness, look about you; see, in all the wealthy, aristo-cratic churches, the memorial services and parade of processions peculiar to ancient periods—" customs gray with ages grown," causing the philosopher to stop and ask, " Where am I?" " Is this fair Utopian America?" " Do I live in the nineteenth, or in the ninth century?"

And yet we can do nothing without manners and forms. If these are bad, how repulsive; if graceful, how attractive and pleasing. What is the law? Here is the answer: The more the substance, the less show; the greatness of Truth renders the littleness of forms contemptible; downright reality and substantial merit drive out the devils of dress and display; just as a true diamond is most beautiful when set in plain black, with a fine thread of pure gold running round the edge of the ring.

True refinement in religion, as in the civil realm of life, will wear the fewest possible forms.

CHERUBIM.

MEANING OF THE WORD.

THIS was the name given by the ancient Jews to any guardian influence belonging to the celestial system of government. Sometimes it signifies a spirit, next to a seraph in importance; but in general use the term stands for an emblem of hierarchical authority.

Let us take a like liberty, and employ this word to signify wisdom. Let us put into his hand a flaming sword, and station him at the entrance of society.

Do not the gates of our Eden need watching and guarding? Within them you behold a corpulent, selfish Eve, manifesting grossness and cruelty to her servants, stupid indifference to the development of her children, spending her vitality on dress, novels, parade, and a pampered appetite. There, too, you see a rotund old Adam, bringing on premature decrepitude, accumulating wealth in every land, exhausting his great energies in laying the foundations for protracted lawsuits among his heirs, and in destroying what little happiness circumstances may perchance bring within his life. Let a cherubim be stationed at the great garden gate, with flaming sword, instructed to drive out these fallen parents, and to preserve the paths and fruit trees for the good angels who are surely coming.

THE PHYSICAL ORGANISM.

SIGNIFICANCE OF THE HUMAN BODY.

The human body is the perishable chariot of fire by which the spirit is individualized, and in which the spirit rides through the world. Fire in the lungs keeps the blood boiling; fire in the heart keeps the blood throbbing; fire in the blood keeps the passions and appetites bubbling; fire in the nerves keeps the brain blazing; fire in the brain keeps the whole house warm and inhabitable, in all climates, and preserves the whole establishment against the ten thousand fire-extinguishers which continually threaten individual existence. The only genuine fire-proof armor is health. A sick person is liable to combustion and sudden destruction from fevers, inflammations, and corruptions, which are only different consuming fires in different parts of the house. All persons who are thus slowly burning to death in the presence of their dearest friends, may be said to be paying a high rent for a poor, dissolving habitation. No blasphemy is more ungodly than a conscious transgression against the laws of rudimental life and health. Such a person is irreligious, although he may fulfil all the rules of his church as to prayers, Bible-reading, and obey every known formula of piety and worship.

CHEERFULNESS.

AN ALL-HEALING MEDICINE.

SOME one has well said that "cheerfulness is a duty." The discharge of this essential duty should be obligatory upon all mankind. The existence and inculcation of a "religion of despair" in the world will account for a vast deal of human sadness. For who can smile, yea, who *dare* so far forget the true sympathies of his heart as to be *glad* for a moment about anything, when the preacher positively tells him that only about *one person* in a hundred millions ever reaches the kingdom of eternal bliss? How *dare* an Orthodox minister wreathe his mouth with smiles? In his Christian scheme he teaches that, since the "tidings of great joy" were first heard, countless hosts of human hearts have died without being "converted;" and that each of these thronging millions has gone under the everlasting "wrath of God" into a hell of endless suffering! *He* smile? Yea, how *dare* any sincere believer in such a "religion of despair" venture to be glad, or indulge an emotion of joy even for a brief moment? For the credit of human nature, let it be recorded that those who sincerely believe these unutterable doctrines are never cheerful, and do not, because they have not sufficient indifference of heart to, smile from morning till night. They are always sad, because they are partially insane!

But while writing these few sentences, the birds of the air sing cheerfully, and the whole earth is throbbing with gladness. Cheerfulness is a cardinal principle in true religion. Not frivolity, not silliness of conduct and idiotic gabble, but cheerfulness, thankfulness, and robust happiness. The setting sun, the beginning of winter, the decline of rudimental life, are, to the truly religious and healthy, as beautiful and cheerful as are the rising sun, the opening of summer, or the birth of a babe in the beautiful morn of spring-time.

Cheerfulness, believe me, is an *all-healing medicine* prepared in the laboratory of the gods. Disease, Adversity, Death—these fertile sources of human suffering vanish under the magic spell of cheerfulness. It illumines and sends gladness through the darkest chambers of the solitary heart. But beware of persons who can be jovial only when stimulated and magnetized by excitement; beware of those who continually assail you with flippant tricks and interrupt you with small talk; for such know really nothing of true cheerfulness. They are given to hours of that terrible wretchedness and despair which is the lot of the unredeemed, and may at any moment ruthlessly break the golden bowl at the sacred fountain of your happiness.

ORIGIN OF FAMILIES.

FOLLIES IN GENEALOGICAL TREES.

GENEALOGICAL trees usually flourish most luxuriantly in poor soil. It is hazardous to sound the stream of families. The source is frequently too near the discoveries of Darwin. Family and personal pride, resting on the foundation of ancestors, is destitute of principle. It is well, for scientific ends, to look into the past, as it may be justifiable in order to settle property questions in dispute, but never to establish one's title to respectability. Let blood "tell" in present merit, not in reputation and success of a long-departed progenitor.

The investigations of anthropologists have already exposed the flimsy foundations of family genealogies. Manhood is preceded by youth and childhood, and the whole superstructure rests on infancy and the protoplastic cells of yet earlier months; so the present races of the human family come from barbarians and savages, our only ancestors in the far past, about whom the least that is said the. better, except for the advancement of science and the equal distribution of common sense.

The time is coming when to be known as the descendant of so-called "nobility" will be as much of a disgrace as to be known as one who "never worked." To be received in society as worthy because of those who bore you, is as false in principle as to expect a

3*

situation in paradise because of your belief in the catechism's definition of a redeemer.   False foundations are
crumbling before the Darwinian army ; and woe to all
family pride and ancestral trees which pray for recog-
nition and fresh fertilization.   There's a long spine
within the constitution of animal life—an extension of
vertebræ far down in the back of human history—which
is too remote from the head of the race to admit of
fashionable adornments.   This great rear organization,
to speak candidly, is the main root of your ancestral
tree.   Humility begins with this fundamental discovery,
made partially palatable by the scriptures of Wallace,
and subsequently strongly enforced by the facts of Darwin, that

> " There's a divinity that shapes our ends,
>   Rough hew them as we may."

Ancestral halls begin to smell mouldy, because the
minute animal formations of progress are creeping out
from the stale blood of royal families.   It will soon be
more essential to have a character than to have had a
regal grandmother.   I think personal excellence will
pass for more than the received opinion that you are
really the son of your own father.   It is now vexatious
to proud persons to be referred to as the husband of the
celebrated Madame G—— T—— ; or as the wife of the
distinguished General W—— J—— ; because individualized existence and intrinsic *merit* have steadily
appreciated in value, until the long-looked-for right has
come " uppermost," compelling the pride of ancestry to
die " amid its worshippers."

MORALS, ANCIENT AND MODERN.

STOICISM.

EIGHTEEN hundred years ago, one of Nero's guards, Epaphroditus, had a slave whose name was Epictetus. His cruel physical circumstances acted upon his intellectual and intuitive faculties as the wine-press acts upon grapes. " Patience, perseverance, brotherly kindness and charity "—these four cardinal Christian virtues poured out from his entire life.

Plato, Socrates, Seneca, Epictetus, Antoninus, although not engaged in prophesying of and clearing the way for the popular religion (which was developed by the Apostles, not by Jesus), were nevertheless remarkable teachers and practitioners of every important principle or precept that can be found in Christianity. The Romans were not philosophers ; they were only intellectualists ; fond of *knowing* all that could be known in metaphysics. They were constitutional eclectics in their independent philosophical inquiries ; and by temperament wilfully stoical in all matters pertaining to religion. How to get best and justly and triumphantly through the world, was the ethical and philosophical question in the Roman mind.

" Bear and forbear," replied Epictetus ; and his life was a complete illustration of his doctrine.

" Learn to be one man," said he ; and the absence of all doubleness in his own character and conduct was remarkable. "No man can serve two masters," is another way of expressing the same idea. The Roman intellect was inevitably fatalistic in religion and morals. Their distinct perception of *law* in everything impressed their judgment with a belief in inexorable Fate. Epictetus had spiritual illumination superior to his era, but his chief desire was to teach the Romans how to live. Duty was never surpassed by the pride of personal rights. Every one's duty was to strive to love virtue, truth, honor, and to daily practise what he knew to be required by these radical precepts and principles.

This system was perfect as a rule of faith and practice; but it lacked what a beautiful landscape lacks in a cloudy day, namely, light from the sun in the heavens. In our century this light, emitted by a resplendent sun in a sky far more interior, is shining upon mankind. Let us live and love, in harmony with our superlatively superior advantages. It will be a wonderfully happy and pure epoch when mankind shall practically embody the immortal teachings of Epictetus.

INNATE JUSTICE.

A PRINCIPLE IN THE MENTAL CONSTITUTION.

MEN take a natural pride in being in the *right*, or rather, they wish to be believed as though they were true and reliable, even if the facts be otherwise. This innate passion for accuracy is prophetic of the coming excellence in human nature. The non-fulfilment of a prediction, as in the case of Jonah, even when the prophecy covers great disasters and suffering, is a source of vexation and disappointment. Such a prophet is angry and mortified, first, because the information communicated was inaccurate ; next, because the prediction was in its every word erroneous ; next, because the people would laugh at him for making the proclamation : lastly, because the failure throws a doubt over the entire profession of foretelling future events. Few men can bear the imputation of ignorance and dishonesty. They would rather be knowing and accurate than kind or good. This state is savage and cruel. But there is in time coming a sure progress into truth and right, founded upon a sincere love of what is intrinsically just and permanent.

Self-made men, as the saying is, are persons who have " worked their own way," through greatest obstacles to a position of equality with the best. They are usually possessed of a sound article of conscience—self-made, like the rest of the character—which is not often obedient to popular standards. These are the minds who promote the world's progress. They institute new laws, inculcate new morals, generate new maxims, and fill the air with new revelations of truth and principles.

But all manufactured men inherit consciences to correspond. Their ideas of right coincide exactly with the prevailing definition of right. If they be Jews by birth, it is right to under-rate the Christians ; if Christians by birth, it is equally right to oppose and berate the Jews. If they be born in slaveholding countries, it is right to perpetuate slavery ; if freedmen by birth, it is right to pronounce eternal condemnation upon slaveholders. If born into the lap of Roman Catholicity, it is right to curse and destroy all dissenters as enemies of God ; if born among hot-blooded Protestants, it is right to slander the ancient church by calling it the " whore of Babylon." Thus, all through and through the world, what men call " conscience " is a manufactured article, an inheritance, like the color of their hair and eyes, and as blind as learned ignorance always is as to what is in reality right and wrong.

And yet, deeper than all transmitted qualities and bias, is *intuition ;* of which Washington said : " Labor to keep alive in your breast that little spark of celestial fire called Conscience." This innate wisdom is beneath every man's inherited ideas of right and wrong. It is a dangerous power in the spirit. You cannot reason it down to death. After a prolonged silence, it arises in its own might, and by its internal condemnation makes a strong man feeble. When inspired by its approbation, one man can put ten thousand to flight. One man with a clear intuition of Right on his side is sustained as by the strong arm of Omnipotence. It is important, therefore, to know whether your views of right and wrong arrived with your blood, or from the fountain of all spirit—the infinite source of every good and perfect gift.

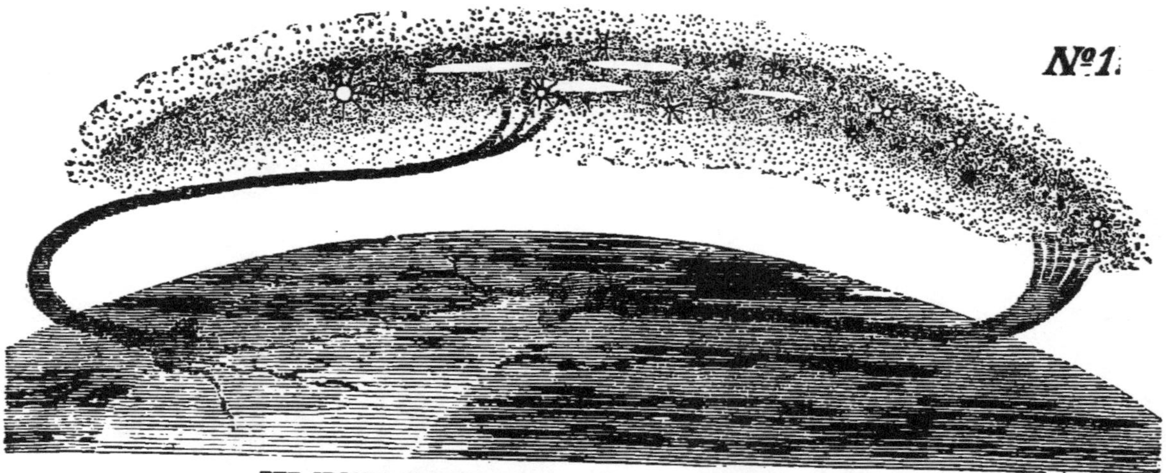

THE SECOND SPHERE WITHIN THE SIXTH CIRCLE OF SUNS.

VIEWS OF OUR HEAVENLY HOME.

CHAPTER I.

A GENERAL STATEMENT OF THE SYSTEM.

> " My Father's house is built on high,
>   Far, far amid the starry sky ;
>   When from this earthly body free,
>   That heavenly mansion mine shall be."

A SUBLIME and beautiful theme appropriately seeks to clothe itself in sublime and beautiful language.

A powerful temptation to write in " an unknown tongue" upon a theme unknown to the senses of men, is upon me ; it feels like a necessity pouring through the wand of an enchanter. And yet, lest I should not be distinctly understood by the reader, who may not have access to a dictionary, I press back both the necessity and the enchantment ; and thus I proceed to use the plainest words, or at least such phraseology as will most naturally convey the sublime and beautiful realities under contemplation. And I will also, which will soon come, disregarding all temptations to the contrary, add to my intentional plainness as much as possible of the sweet grace of brevity. Inasmuch as in the " Penetralia," p. 167, in the " Stellar Key," but particularly in the little volume " Death and the After-Life," the reader may find that already I have reported or described many of these celestial scenes ; therefore it will be with me a principle to avoid, as far as is practicable, when treating an obscure question, a multiplication of words and all vain repetitions.*

That there is a general correspondence between man and the earth, is admitted by all analogical thinkers. Like the globe, man is full of revolutions, seasons, changes, periodicities. In his wakings and sleepings are incorporated the days and nights of the planet ; its light and heat are repeated in his phosphorescent brain and magnetic heart ; its rocky framework is perfectly represented in his osseous structure, and its great waters reappear in the miniature seas of serum and tiny oceans of blood in which man's physical constitution rides like a freighted steamer.

In more interior parts the correspondence between the human individual and the great globe beneath him is a million times more amazing and complete. In his physiological inception, as well as in all the stages of his subsequent progressive advancement, he repeats the entire organic history of the whole animal world ; and in his social, moral, and intellectual progress, from youth to maturity, he consecutively reproduces the entire social, political, moral, and intellectual history of mankind. All this, you observe, transpires in the universal, not in the very particular sense. For in

---

* These references to other volumes, for the purpose of avoiding repetitions, may possibly entail some *obscurity* on the points too briefly treated in these pages. The industrious reader will therefore seek the passages referred to.

specialties, in the details of experiment among variations, all deductive correspondence ceases and the inductive philosophy begins; and the latter is commonly called "scientific research and demonstration."

Upon the primordial principle of correspondence, thus briefly illustrated, there exists a general resemblance, a similarity of order and appearance, between the Winterland (earth) beneath man's feet and the Summerland (heaven) above his head.

In a certain sense there is no more distance between a man's spirit and the earth than there is between his spiritual body (now elemental) and the suprasolar sphere to which he personally ascends after death. And as to the localities, sceneries, social gradations, moral spheres, love circles, intellectual distinctions, wisdom brotherhood, seminaries of learning, hospitalities for the worn and weary, unfolding nurseries for the innumerable little ones, all of which is distinctly visible as natural belongings and institutions in the Summerland; the correspondence (the analogy) between all this and man is seen to be perfect when you carefully investigate and classify the internal structure of the human brain, and thence gather inductively knowledge of his organs, faculties, attributes, affections, the degrees of his various interconnections, and the laws of his immortal necessities, his absolute needs, not to mention his wants and energetic impulses, which constantly and forever characterize and govern his indestructible nature.

The underlying principle is the unchangeable principle of "like producing like"—illustrated, broadly, in the likeness which exists between man's external structure and the globe on which he lives; which likeness is repeated, on a scale at least a million times more perfect, between man's internal nature and the external of the Summerland wherein he is certain soon to journey and reside.

There is also some very faint resemblance between the external surfaces of the superior inhabited planets in our solar system and the geographical and topographical facts of the great Second Sphere under consideration. But it is an error to suppose that the Second Sphere is but a repetition of this exceedingly rudimental world, even on a higher and far more extended scale; because it is in the first place impossible that Mother Nature should exactly repeat herself, and, in the second place, it is even more impossible that the infinitely superior should be a likeness of a most rudimental inferior, except in the most universal sense, which truth I have heretofore attempted to plainly set forth.

The foregoing is properly an introduction to the fulfilment of a promise long since made, to write a sequel, or Part II., to the volume entitled "A Stellar Key to the Summerland." The reader is urgently requested to consult Part I., for a more *intellectual* and extended consideration of questions which will be only inspirationally awakened in these chapters. In this sequel, the whole subject will be presented as revelational Views of Our Heavenly Home; thus, of necessity, referring the reader to other volumes for philosophical reasonings and special explanations.

As in Part I., so also in this Sequel, it is deemed beneficial to introduce *drawings*, so that, in the first place, the reader can obtain a conception of the actual situation of the great spiritual universe to the visible Milky Way; also, in the second place, so that his intellect can form some reasonable views concerning relative positions, magnitudes, and distances.*

The accompanying diagram (No. 1) supposes the reader standing far, far in the fields of space. From that remote point, and being gifted with the telescopic power of observation, he is supposed to be contemplating the immeasurable magnitude, the unutterable grandeur, the overwhelming glory and absolutely indescribable harmoniousness of the scene. You must employ your natural telescope from the crown of a glittering observatory situated in an abundantly rich star-field millions of miles from the earth and the Sun. On your journey you should stand for a moment upon Herschel's great discovery, Uranus, which rhythmically rolls in its silvery orbit, more than eighteen hundred millions of miles from its progenitor. Still farther you must journey to obtain a knowledge of the field covered by the subject before you. Extend your observations millions of league into space. Go forth into the boundless wilderness of cometary matter, yea, into the realm of unformed and yet perpetually forming suns and planets beyond the sixth circle of suns, infinitely far

* The Milky Way is often referred to by the author as the great sixth circle of suns. Strictly speaking, such is not his meaning. Mankind can see but a few of the universes which belong to this infinitely expanded outmost system of suns and planets. Speaking strictly, then, the "Milky Way" is an irregular and fragmentary integer of the sixth system. But owing to the fact that the heavens are beautifully and conspicuously decorated by the *light* of the great systems which constitute the "Milky Way," therefore the author has figuratively employed it as a visible sixth circle.

beyond wondrous Neptune, the discovery of Leverrier, which sweeps through the star-strewn immensity nearly three thousand millions of miles from the productive sun.*

From this astronomical station you will observe something entirely *unlike* anything you ever witnessed or imagined on earth, when at night you may have contemplated the stellar universe. In ordinary language you will now obtain a " bird's-eye view " of that vast universe of suns, stars, earths, moons, and comets which constitute what would be commonly called a " Milky Way." Like a universe of clouds this mass of worlds and systems of worlds appears to swim over our heads (when seen from the standpoint of earth), whilst very far *below* the nebulous galaxy seem to burn our particular sun, around which revolve all the bodies of the special isolated universe to which our earth belongs.

Viewed from earth the Milky Way appears to be an endless belt. But seen from a remote point in space it becomes a member of a group of successive systems of solar and stellar universes; and in that one group of systems is located our sun and its harmonious family of children, grand-children, and great-grand-children; which by the most ancient astronomers were named Mercury, Venus, Earth, Mars, Jupiter, Saturn; to which must now be added all the various satellites, including the teeming fields of lesser and yet younger bodies known as asteroids, comets, and meteorics.

You will now caution your mind concerning actuali-

---

* In regard to these distances astronomers do not agree among themselves. A reform is now in process. The author gives only approximate distances in round numbers to aid the mind.

ties or verities; not to confound them with mere *appearances*. For it was owing to the influence of "appearances" that mankind for so many centuries believed the earth to be a flat, stationary, immovable mass of matter; around which the entire universe rolled as so many servants obedient to the fiat of their centrally enthroned sovereign. The revolution of the earth on its axis causes an *appearance* which, but for the strictest application of mathematics, logarithms, and fluxions, would to-day impress everybody to assert that all the bright bodies in the firmament rise in the east and set in the west. And the revolution of the earth around the sun develops an appearance—the reverse of reality —that the sun is travelling in and out among the stars. Against appearances I am constrained to affirm that our sun and our earth, which seem to be detached and far removed from fellowship with the Milky Way system, are in reality members of that endless sixth circle of suns, which circle is outmost of the present development of the physical stellar universe.*

Overwhelmed by the vast grandeur of the solar and astral universes, the author of the "Celestial Indicator" exclaims: "And what shall we say of the countless millions of stars, of which number our sun is but one,

---

* Readers will recall that the author, in previous volumes, has used the term "fifth" for the circle of suns that now he numbers as the "sixth." The reason is: The Great Central Sun, which heretofore has incorrectly been counted as nothing, being equivalent in every particular to all the infinite systems exterior to it, must now be called the FIRST; thus, there are six circles *within* the measureless realm of embryo worlds, or the cometary sphere which will henceforth be known as the seventh. The *sixth* circle of suns, therefore, includes our sun and its planets.

all with their respective solar-systems, and then all grouped again into star-systems, wheeling *probably* eastward around remote central points of their own groups, our system moving, perhaps, around Alcyone (one of the Pleiades), but in periodic times too great for our comprehension? Then again, what if these groups are combined, and moving around other points in the universe, and this is only the threshold of the Great Universe! How vast, then, the creation, and how numberless the spirits may be in the spirit-world! And who can tell what countless glories in this science will yet be unfolded to us, in the new life, for endless ages to come?"

The bird's-eye view embodied in the accompanying diagram, drawn with reference to imparting an idea of the greatest magnitude, involves the necessity of impairing the impression of a *circle* of suns and stars. And the same remark is applicable to the appearance of the Summerland Belt in the diagram. It is represented (or should have been represented by the artist) as a slight light strip stretching through space horizontally across the sky, and beneath the universe of nebula called the Milky Way. This appearance, as before said, is a necessity of the attempt by diagram to impart the fullest and most lasting impression of positions and magnitude. It is only possible to represent a strip of the Summerland; and also only a very small section of the sixth circle of suns. But the inconceivably immense magnitude of the golden belt of our Heavenly Home may be imagined, somewhat, by comparing what is seen of it in the diagram with what is therein represented of the vast stretch of the numberless constellations which compose the sixth circle of suns.

You can understandingly and truthfully estimate the relative importance of the little *dot* in the Milky Way called "the Earth," by looking to the right, where it is located, and contrasting it with the surrounding universes of suns, stars, earths, moons, comets, etc., which seem to fill infinity itself to repletion. Mankind, in their pride and sacred mythologies, have called this obscure *dot* " the mighty earth; " to which the Eternal Mind in his great mercy once delegated his " Only Begotten ! "

The belt of immortal beauty and harmony is, I repeat, *within* the sixth circle of suns; because whatever is spiritual is of necessity *interior*, approaching nearer and nearer the great central fountain of All; while the material is external, sweeping out farther and farther from the source of all Spirit.

In the diagram No. 1, you observe the cosmical and cometary (or world-building) bodies are represented in their aphelion—that is, in a position farthest from the sun-centres about which they circulate; thus signifying as well as if some of them were in their perihelion, the subordinate and superficial part which they perform in the grand epic of the Stellar Univercœlum.

The bodies called " cometary," etc., are represented in the diagram by the outermost dots and points.

You observe vast openings among the constellations— airholes, so to speak—in which no bodies are visible. These are unlimited seas of celestial magnetism and electricity. These will be fully explained in succeeding chapters. Interstellar spaces and abysses of emptiness are atmospheric cushions between the great solar systems, whereby all unnecessary planetary friction is compensated, and whereby all impedimentation is rendered impossible ; while, as great vital reservoirs, a constant supply of celestial electricity and magnetism is fed into and perpetually flooded throughout the stupendous whole.

In succeeding chapters I will endeavor more particularly to illustrate our sublime and beautiful theme, giving more spiritual information in detail; to the end that the unspeakable glory and overwhelming grandeur of our Heavenly Home may be intellectually comprehended as well as intuitionally anticipated.

It is of great consequence that we learn all we reasonably can concerning the present and the future. For the silent and sacred hour is fast approaching when you, friendly reader! will be called by a supernal voice to cast aside all your earthly possessions, and to "embark upon the glittering streams;" to sail forth into the vast infinitude with the angel commanders, and with officers you may not know, possibly forced to take the humble position of a deck hand, or to go "before the mast" in the lowest angelic service ; compelled, by the beneficent force of a sublime necessity, to rise above all terrestrial belongings as "on wings of living light," and tranquilly or reluctantly to glide onward and onward and *inward*, until your feet press the silvery shores of the Summerland—which is a Sphere so great, so grand, so glorious—glowing with the heat of love and with the light of wisdom—that you cannot but bow down and worship, and yet it is a world whose appearances and bestowments and adaptations will be in exact accord with what you may be in a condition spiritually to perceive, to impart, and to appropriate.

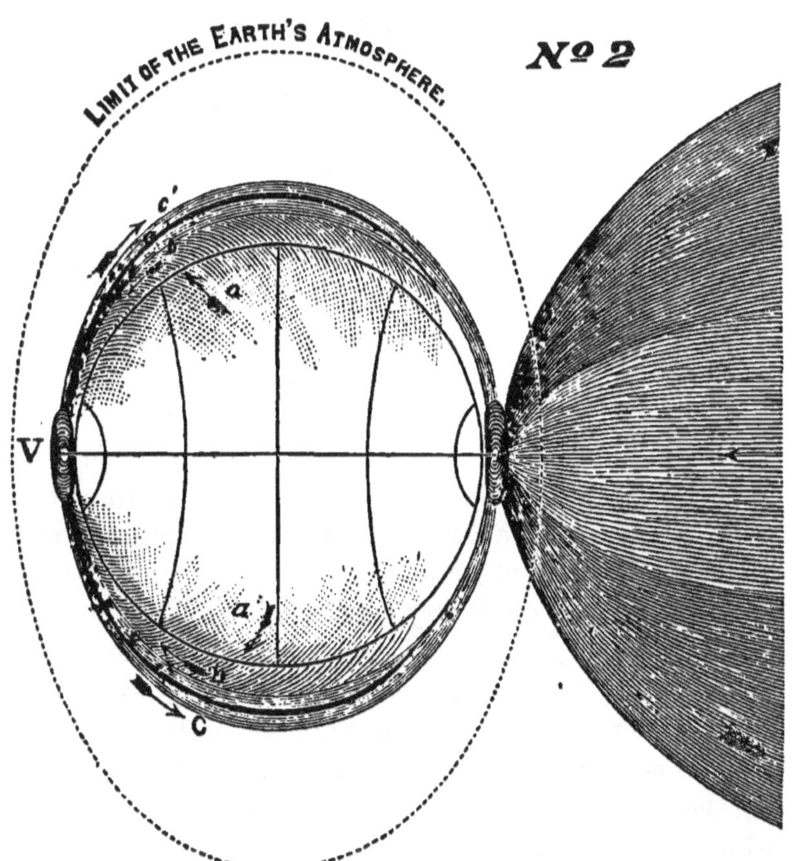

FORMATION OF THE MAGNETIC RIVERS.

CHAPTER II.

> " We'd sail across thy silver seas,
> We'd hear thy streams and murmuring trees,
> We'd feel thy gentle, fragrant breeze,
> Summer-Land, sweet Summer-Land ! "
>
> —*Song by Love M. Willis.*

IN this communication it is purposed to treat plainly a subject full of celestial effulgence and overflowing with harmonious beauty, which has been quite briefly alluded to on p. 38, "Death and the After-Life," in "Stellar Key," p. 157; also in the "Great Harmonia," Vol. V., p. 414, et seq., namely: Concerning the streams and rivers of immensity.

No science of chemistry, no theory of electricity, no philosophy of geological development, no system of meteorology, no explanation of planetary revolution and harmony, can be even approximately complete without some definite and practical knowledge concerning these invisible, yet substantial, elemental circulations which exist and labor in the vast upper spaces.

I have several times observed that, from each of the earths in our system, great electrical and magnetic rivers flow out and in, to and fro, like a ceaseless tide; on the soft, golden bosom of which all death-emancipated men, women, and children float into their celestial home; and by means of which they and all other voyagers may, and do, return again and again, personally, or by representation, or by telegraphic contact, or by cerebral and mental impressment. And I have also observed (and most of my present statements and facts are of recent date), that the flowings and ebbings of these elemental Gulf Streams—those Amazonian rivers, which sweep through the upper atmospheres and onward far away among the interstellar spaces—correspond, in a general way, to the forward and backward movements of the blood, which floats upon currents yet more vital, from its governmental centre, the heart, to the finest and most remote points, the outermost of the human body. Let this perfect analogy, based upon a fact inseparable from your daily life, impress itself distinctly upon your mind. As the crimson fluid of your heart, which is both positive (*arterial*) and negative (*venous*), and which with corresponding reciprocations pulsates to and fro, in and out, throughout the arteries and veins of the human body; so, and upon like principles of motion, and with similar functions, the magnetic and electrical streams of the upper regions start from geo-centres (earths) and from helio-centres (suns) and flow with every conceivable form of beauty through the heavenly atmospheric fields. The directions of these streams are as various as are the radial lines from a globe, and in numbers they are strictly countless. These great living currents promote the refinements and assimilations of atoms among the organs (globes) of the infinite body of God. They form and flow forth between all the solar centres and the inhabited globes in space; and thence they stream onward and inward into the next great sphere of human existence, which we now call the Summerland.

Your attention is now asked to a brief consideration of this transcendent fact, which is one of the greatest wonders of the starry universe, which no astronomer has yet seen, because it belongs to the so-called invisible ocean of imponderables—a fact, hidden in the physical constitution of Nature, which no investigator can afford either to neglect or underestimate. For are not all men pilgrims? Are they not stopping on earth over night as at a wayside inn—their home not being the house they for the season occupy? Nor can any man among you afford to underestimate or ridicule your fellow-pilgrims. In your scholastic pride, in your majestic assurance as fact-adoring scientists, you can neither afford to bandage your eyes nor to stuff your ears to spiritual facts; nor can you afford to be absorbed by, nor affectedly satisfied with, your own special theories, cogitations, and discoveries; because you have already acquired sufficient culture, and because you possess enough limited knowledge, to impress your judgment with the boundlessness of your ignorance concerning things and principles which animate and govern the surrounding universe of matter and mind. In visiting a country for the first time you consult maps drawn faithfully by stranger hands, and you also read guide-books written by primitive pioneer travellers who have braved and shunned the dangers and enjoyed the beauty, sublimity, and goodness of the remote region which (now that the pathways are all cut and cleared for you) you heroically set forth to explore. Incalculably more natural and more honest is it, that, not knowing anything absolutely essential concerning the splendid sublimities of infinite, you should consult the diagrams and read the guiding chapters hereby submitted to your serious investigation.

Chemists recently have enumerated sixty-eight elementary substances—meaning bodies which are simple, not containing anything beside themselves—not capable of either alteration or decomposition ; such, for example, as the *solids*, called gold, iron, sulphur ; the *fluids*, known as bromine, mercury, etc. ; and the *gases*, oxygen, hydrogen, nitrogen, etc. But with the development of scientific knowledge, is gradually being born the idea that there are a very few elementary substances—not less than two, nor more than five—out of which the stupendous system, with its infinite details, has been and is constructed. Thirty years ago the writer of these chapters was in a condition, intellectually and spiritually, to affirm that Fire, Heat, Light, and Electricity (see Nat. Div. Rev. Part II.) were and are the essentials from which the universe, as it now is, was unfolded from least to the greatest. " Fire " being the name for both a condition and an effect ; so, also, of the other three successive terms. Electricity was evolved from Light ; light from Heat ; heat from the central, primordial condition, Fire. If the language of scientists would better meet the popular necessity, I would affirm that Matter and Motion, or Substance and Force, are the eternal twin principles at the origin and foundation of the universal whole. The primitive or lowest form of motion is angular ; hence, as the first legitimate effect, Fire ; the next advancement in the form of the motion, ascending out of the angular, evolved Heat ; when the perfect circular motion was developed, then Light flowed throughout infinitude ; the next step in the progression of motion unfolded the spiral, and forthwith, as from an inconceivable vortex of substance and force, a boundless ocean of Electricity overwhelmingly floods and enchains the systems of immensity.

Let us now confine our observations and reflections to our own planet; the round earth beneath our feet, with its atmospheric envelopment over our heads. Minerals constitute the body of our globe; vegetation succeeds and crowns the mineral compounds; animals succeed the vegetable empire; and the human world, mankind, succeeds and covers all, and is the proprietor of all predecessors—minerals, vegetables, animals. This truth is not only clearly demonstrated by the actual manifestations of nature, but it is as easy of comprehension as the simplest proposition in arithmetic.

The earth is an immense chemical laboratory. The four or the sixty-four elementary bodies—solids, fluids, gases, etc.—are in its constitution, and the indwelling laws of development are everywhere the same; therefore, whatever can occur in our Sun, in Arcturus, in any helio-centre in space, can be and is repeated, on a scale more or less limited and perfect, under our very feet, over our heads, before and within our very eyes, day by day and hour by hour.

Electricity is the name of one of our omnipresent servants. But his relatives are numerous, some obscure, all honest, and they have travelled all over the world, with various names and aliases—Galvanism, Voltaism, Electro-Magnetism, Electro-Dynamics, Lightning, etc. Mankind have known something about electricity ever since the Arabians and the Greeks evolved it by means of silken ribbons or frictionized amber. Hence it is

no stranger, it is accepted as a *fact;* but its origin is
yet entombed in mystery.   Franklin invited it from the
clouds, and his successors have evolved it from their
chemical compounds and improved batteries; but its
true cause and fountain source are yet unknown to
men of science. It is, however, well enough known
that electricity may be and often is developed by mechanical action; also by rapid changes in temperatures;
by the disengagement of confined gases; by the chemical activity, and by the vernal and autumnal transformations of the leaves of plants and trees; by the decomposition of animal or vegetable bodies; by changes
in the atmosphere; by warm spring rains and by cold
wind and snow storms; by rapid condensation and
evaporation; and by the sudden compression and discharge of oxygen, nitrogen, hydrogen, and magnetism.

The earth is literally a perpetual motion; it is really
a revolving electrical machine; it is practically an immense magnetic battery. From its vast mineral mountains beneath the sea—from its great beds of iron, copper, zinc, silver, antimony, potassium, bismuth, platinum, gold, tin—an unceasing rain, sometimes a terrific
storm, of electricity ascends like the breathings of lightning into the atmosphere. It is an incessant electrical
storm, literally speaking; and the great enveloping
volume of atmosphere is its receiving and distributing
reservoir.

The motion of electricity, as before said, is spiral;
in this connection I mean the electricity of space.
With a swiftness beyond imagination, it streams in
great ribbons, and winds itself upon its own natural
spool at the north. The north magnetic pole of our
4*

earth, you will remember, is not the same in location as its axis of revolution. The north-centre is an immense helix, an atmospherically coiled receptacle, for the multitudinous electrical currents arising from all parts of the globe. The simultaneous and incessant rush of terrestrially evolved electricity to this great north spiral centre, results in the instant formation of a never-ceasing self-illuminating vortex. The luminous lightnings evolved by this great battery, and from the inconceivably rapid motion of the collected electric storms within the polar vortex, make those wondrous manifestations known as the aurora borealis, which especially characterize the northern hemisphere.

Immediately on its arrival at the north helix, electricity is instantaneously transformed into a more refined form of motionary and motive force, which I have been deeply impressed should be called " Etherium ; " but for all ordinary purposes it may be very properly denominated *celestial magnetism*.

This wondrous elemental evolution from the electric coil is a substance as warm as a breath of August; and this, too, at the extreme north, where the light and heat of the sun do not exert any great influence. Mountains of ice and a continent of snow surround this *warm*, vivifying, magnetical centre! In certain years and centuries birds and vegetation, also a few animals, come up and subsist for a time beneath this boreal magnetic sun ; but, in other seasons and centuries, when the north helix is vitally changed by solar and atmospheric causes, the warmth and radiance become suddenly too diminished to invite or sustain life, either vegetable or organic. It is unnecessary that I should refer to geological discoveries, or to the testimony of Arctic explorers, to confirm the declarations herein made. Neither is it necessary to remind mankind of the polar phenomena — those tremulous lights and changeful colors which are frequently seen at night in our northern sky. But there are other evidences to which your attention may be attracted in future chapters.

At this point, and before direct explanatory reference is made to the diagram, No. 2, you might do well to glance at it and study it for a moment, or until its outline import makes a mark upon your imagination. ("Imagination!" you exclaim, "ah, yes—that is the unreliable faculty which must be appealed to by the writer." My reply is, "If you really wish to learn what I mean by 'imagination,' read the true explanation of this inward power in either the *Penetralia* or the *Fountain*.* From this digression we pass on to the subject under consideration.)

The incessant formation of countless streams of ribbon-like rivers of electricity in the air, and from three to ten miles above the heads of mankind all over the round world, is in itself a scientific wonder, and is the cause of "more things (sights and signs) in heaven and earth" than is written down in any philosopher's volume. It is an invisible, natural fact at the basis of all atmospheric motions; it causes all electric variation; and explains the dipping and fluttering freaks of the magnetic needle. It is the primal cause of climatic alterations in the far upper strata of the atmosphere; the cause of the formation of banks of auroral vapor,

---

* *Penetralia*, New Ed., p. 87 ; the *Fountain*, p. 139.

and of certain boreal clouds of unrivalled brightness and beauty; the cause, in a word, of almost all the remarkable auroral and boreal splendors—the magnificent waves of prismatic light in the North, in the Eastern horizon, and sometimes brilliantly centering and unfolding like a blossomed rose at the Zenith; the cause of flashes of blood-red flame in the sky, or of undulations of various colors at prodigious altitudes, forming a corona of orange, green, blue, purple, terminating in a centre which *seems* to rotate like a wheel; the cause of the fearful development of floods of light resulting from the flight and ignition and sudden precipitation of cosmic atoms a few miles above the earth's surface, which flight occurs in a method somewhat periodical; the cause, in connection with the voluminous streams of terrestrial magnetism, of a certain proportion of the motion of the tides, of the alterations of the zones and of changes in inhabitable regions; and finally, and most remarkable of all, these mighty streams and rivers of electricity and magnetism, which are evolved from the inexhaustible fountains of the globe, have as much to accomplish in promoting and maintaining the *revolution* of the globe itself, regulated by the universal law of compensation or equivalents, as the vital forces, generated in and by the nerve-centres of the heart and brains and lungs in man's body, are compelled to accomplish in sustaining the involuntary motions of these organs by which they are energized with streams and rivers of life and animation, not to speak of the elements of the future spiritual body which those same organs and forces are constantly attracting, evolving, and refining.

But you must not, because of all this overwhelming newness and beauty in the organization of Father God and Mother Nature, lose your mental sight of the subject just now so interesting—namely: the formation at the same moment, and in all seasons, and on all sides of the earth, of the great streams of electricity which speed, with a thought's celerity, into the spiral electric helix at the great north centre; whereby is generated and evolved a flood of magnetism, which is positive and warm to the negative and cold volumes of electricity; which positive golden Amazonian river, like a warm Gulf-Stream tending toward regions far, far among the stars, first rises high in the air, and, flowing above the South-pole, pulsates onward and outward and upward and *inward*, until it breaks like a note of immortal melody upon the welcoming shores of the Summer-land.

The accompanying diagram, although imperfect in giving relative proportions, is nevertheless a fair outline representation of the formation, emanation, and counterflowings of the chemical and electrical atoms which are popularly known as the *forms* of a motion. These eliminated and ascending particles are indicated by *a a;* which atoms (some of which have a cosmical destiny) are, as before said, incessantly evolved from the earth's chemical laboratories—rising, like unparticled rain or universal perspiration, from every pore of the earth's body, to a height differing from three to ten miles; here forming a northward flowing stream, *b*, which proceeds to the great polar swirling whirlpool or electrical vortex, *V;* from thence, having been repolarized and attenuated, they disappear in a great belt of celestial magnetism, which perfectly surrounds and engirdles the earth like an elastic ribbon—a beautiful, warm, currental river, which streams rhythmically like an epic into the vast infinitude. This might be called " the celestial highway"—leaving the earth and all entanglement with its axial revolutions at the central point of the exceedingly rarefied atmosphere, which forms an egressive opening at and beyond the South-pole—blending with itself in the bosom of space, augmenting its energy more and more by inherent attributes, and from the incidental contributions of force; and thus wholly freed from the attractions of earth, and responding to the gravitational invitations of an interior universe, this royal road of surging elements continues its inconceivably swift flight onward and inward to the beautiful shores of our Heavenly Home.

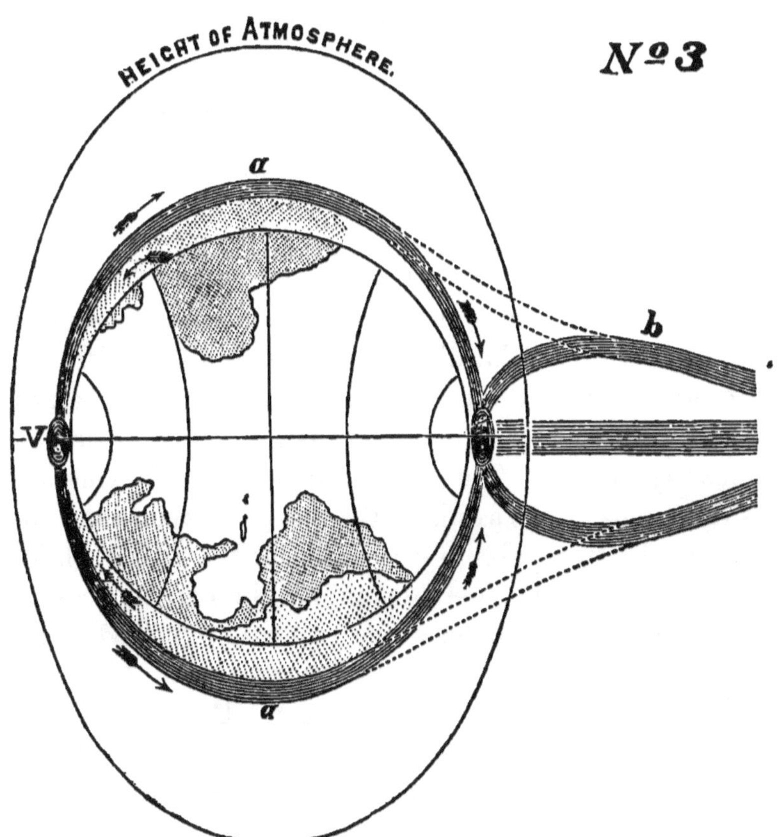

FLOW OF THE MAGNETIC RIVERS INTO SPACE.

CHAPTER III.

"Now with swifter, swifter motion,
Swaying with the swaying tide;
Onward, to the shoreless ocean
Of eternity, we glide."
—*Sarah Gould.*

OF the hundreds of thousands of Christians living in this world to-day, hardly one seems familiar with the supreme facts of the physical universe; not to speak of the heavenly spheres, to which their attention is hereby sincerely invited. These celestial facts, not fancies, are as numerous as the sands of the sea. Between the centre and the two poles of the earth lie the whole philosophy of mineral, vegetable, animal, human, and angel existence. We need no other revelation of God; and no other teacher than reverent Reason.

Let us now resume our subject. It must be remarked, in the first place, that the south-pole of the earth is destitute of elemental polarization. Strange to relate, it is neither positive nor negative, owing to its intimate relation to the great equalizing solar-power; and, consequently, the south-pole is a neutral ground, and therefore perfectly favorable to the interflowings and counterflowings of the electrical and magnetic currents.

Although in the southern hemisphere these celestial currental floods are constant, and far more abundant than at the north-pole, yet the southern sky is seldom illuminated by them.   One reason of this is their great height; another is, the position of the spectator is seldom favorable.   There are, however, as several modern scientists well enough know, certain states of the tropical atmosphere, which will admit of observation; at which times the southern horizon, also the expanse of eastern sky away up to the zenith, is gloriously decorated and overspread with many-colored illuminations. In Australia, and in the palm-growing zone, the inhabitants can recall several such displays.   (In diagram No. 2, the volume of outgoing and incoming elements is not correctly represented; for it therein is exhibited as being larger in diameter than that of the earth itself.) The mild, magnetical radiance of this vast ocean is reflected upon the earth in tropical nights, rendering every object and scene far more than ordinarily beautiful.   This immense volume of outflowing elements is inseparable from the Zodiacal Light, with the particles of which river these elements perpetually intermingle at their fringed edges, receiving and imparting heat, light, electricity, magnetism, and dynamic energy.

Let us not, however, in these chapters, repeat what has been written concerning these celestial wonders on pp. 415–16 Gt. Har. Vol. V., and in other works of the series; to which (for a differing flow of considerations) the investigator is referred; but, to make clearer and more explicit one or two points, I now ask attention to the accompanying diagram, No. 3, giving another and more accurate representation of the aerial streams as they operate in the southern hemisphere.

It will be remembered, by the studious reader of the volumes referred to, that I have affirmed that there were electrical rivers setting toward earth and toward the various planets in our system from different sections of the Spirit Land. By the above-mentioned diagram, which was drawn with stricter reference to relative proportions, your attention is called to the diameters and relations of the central channel of these currents. The arrows at the earth's surface indicate the atoms flowing from every part of the earth to the north pole, V; thence, above in the atmosphere, a, a, streaming southward to the south pole; from which, frequently like an inverted pyramid, but more resembling the half of a hollow sphere, the magnetic rivers rise and flow out into the planetary spaces. Between these twin-rivers, as you observe, is indicated the *returning* magnetic stream, which conveys constant pulsations to the life of mankind from the great central sun of spirituality and intelligence in the Second Sphere.*

Before leaving this subject, however, there is one fact more—viz.: the geometrical principle of right lines giving the shortest distance between the earth and the Summerland, which inherent principle perfectly explains the truth about the directions of these interstellar rivers. But here arises a natural question as to the revolution of the planets, comets, etc., whose orbits come near or cross the path of these celestial gulf streams. The answer is: The materials composing these rivers render them either positive or negative to the approaching planet, and *vice versa;* consequently, as an elastic

---

* See Nat. Div. Rev. Part I., wherein is given a true explanation of the method and source of the author's "impressions" concerning the realities of things, laws, essences and ideas. Also see the Appendix to this volume.

ribbon would be repelled by an electrified ball presented sufficiently near to its surface, so these rivers float away, either bending downwards or else ascending into a grand prismatic arch, thus giving ample room for the passage of a planet.   But immediately afterward they resume their customary direct courses.   The composition of these currents is such that they swing and flow like the waves of sound and light, with vibrations and straight lines and with pulse-like throbs unceasingly; thus harmonizing under all the conditions of space with planetary revolutions, with the flight of comets, and with the stupendous movements of the immeasurable Univercœlum.

Departing now from a further detailed consideration of this subject, not being consistent with the primal purposes of these chapters, I pass on to answer a large flock of buzzing interrogatories, which have been recently generated.

An impression is now beclouding the reader's mind to the effect that all personal communication and all spiritual commerce between earth's inhabitants and the population of the higher spheres, is possible only through the aerial rivers—that every one, either going or coming, must first find these particular currents, and then sail, float, or glide upon them, in all voyages undertaken through the heavenly expanse.

This supposition is based in error.   For have I not already many times affirmed the great fact, which was most completely described by Swedenborg, that the world of spirit is omnipresent?   He records over and again, "Wonderful Things seen in the World of Spirits," which is one thing; but he means, and very truly means, something totally different when he gives "Relations of Things seen and heard in the Spiritual World." By the latter terms he meant the Divine side of the universe—in three indwelling divisions—the natural, the spiritual, and the celestial or heavenly. Against these three divisions of the Spiritual World, as you will remember, Swedenborg offset and balanced his three hells, one within the other; the most interior and remote hell being the exact opponent of the most perfect and inmost heaven. This antagonism to exist to all eternity; which theory, outside of Swedenborg, has no foundation.

But however widely and absolutely we may differ with Swedenborg when expounding his theological hypotheses (by which he was, for so many serious and busy years, psychologized both day and night), we yet agree with him when he affirms, what common sense and intuition and science concurrently confirm, that, on a principle of correspondence, just as the soul is within the natural or material body, so is there a world of spirits or a spiritual world within the natural or material world. In this essential we agree with Swedenborg.

Accordingly, when a man dies to the external world, he very soon becomes alive to the existence and the things of the world internal. Without leaving the chamber of death—which is not an uncommon occurrence with persons of a certain earthly constitution and unaspiring mind—the individual is, or may be, in a position to take immediate note of many "Wonderful Things seen and heard in the World of Spirits." He observes what was before the *inside*, but which has now become the *outside*, of every person, object, event, etc. He can discern (or see) exactly what is occurring in the very room wherein " he died " only a very few hours previously. Persons who thus naturally, or by affectional preference, linger near and hover about the " place of their birth " (which is usually called *death*), are frequently mentally and spiritually disqualified either to receive or impart light and happiness. But they are *in* the omnipresent " world of spirits," and this is the only point we now desire to impress upon you.

Swedenborg described, under psychological dictation, and by force of the logical requirements of his biblical system of correspondential revealments, the situation of " the world of spirits " as intermediate, or as a sort of hadean neutral territory, between the three eternal heavens on the one hand and the three eternal hells on the other. But accepting the truth that the spiritual is *within* the natural, as the soul is within the body corpo-real, it follows logically and scientifically and truthfully, that whenever and wherever a man dies, *then* or *there* he becomes forever an inhabitant of the interior uni-verse ; and it as logically and naturally follows that from that time and from that place the death-emanci-pated man may and does ascend into the air, and, either by volition or involutarily (for do we not all speed away, on the earth both night and day at the fearful rate of sixty-eight thousand miles an hour ?), he can thus and he does thus, sooner or later, enter his appropriate place in the Summerland. For there is no space in the fields of infinitude which cannot be traversed by beings whose existence revolves upon that wonderful pivotal power called Will. The fields of earth can be crossed from any point and to any other point; even so the celestial streams can be forded—the aerial oceans navigated; and thus the very rivers of paradise may be made subservient to the eternal unrest of mind.

And yet the orderly method of travelling between the earths and the interior universe, is by means of the currental rivers already described; and these are therefore the recognized royal, celestial highways intertwining and connecting spheres and globes, which revolve at incalculable distances from one another. (See Distances, etc., in the *Stellar Key*.)

Amid the sad scenes of this rudimental world, and amid the overpowering hardships of our common physical and social life, what a relief it is to contemplate the wisdom, the loveliness, the grandeur, the uplifting love, the boundless beneficence, which exist for us under our very feet, and all the way round the earth, and over all our heads! All mankind are by necessity great travellers, and restless; because all our eternal life is a progressive and endless journey. If we halt by the way, if we attempt to take a brief needed repose in the lengthening shadows of our sunset days; then forthwith the spinning earth, like a steed at his highest speed, runs away with us; and very soon he ruthlessly destroys everything we hold in the arms of love as most sacred. Driving, driving—drifting, drifting—onward and inward every moment, whether sleeping or waking, whether good or evil, whether obedient or transgressing, whether in the mystic charm of love or enveloped in the blackness of despair — onward and inward through birth into life, through death into life again, rapidly or slowly, yet with the certainty of resistless fate—upward " Where the glorious arch is lifting," speeding with the swiftly, softly, sweetly flowing river of transparent and glittering beauty, which glows with the effulgence of liquid gold, which reflects the stars around and the suns above like a ribbon-mirror composed of purest diamonds—still onward we go, floating through scenes more resplendent than the hallowed dreamings of angels; and thus we arrive upon the dimpling margin of the Summerland—to form new associations, to grow by feeding on new surroundings, to unfold in the warming and illuminating atmosphere of the divine love and wisdom, instructed by the past, thankful for the present, and hopeful for the future which shall be everlasting.

And now we may rest. Listen ! Did you say " rest ? " What! you an everlasting pilgrim, *rest?* With a combination of elements and with a living battery of attributes which embody the activities of all dynamical principles; which are empowered to outlive and to comprehend more than all the belts of inhabited stars that beam with splendor all over the bending heavens—to you inaction (miscalled "rest") will be forever impossible! And the reason is this: you take beautifully into yourself the live wine expressed from the experiences of the whole history of mankind. Its inwrought pleasures fatigue you; its evils in your fluids harass you; its ambitions in your brain-matter push out into the most rapid express trains; its drudgeries in your muscles disgust you; its great labors in your very marrow drive you into the invention of labor-saving machines; its rattling and jolting and jarrings outrage your ears, and they force you to study and to evolve the system and the instruments of consoling and healing music; its dredgings and drainings and tunnelings put you out of temper, and they suggest to your reason and hope a world after death, which shall be all beauty and all perfection; and, presently, overcome with the oppressions of an abounding materialism, you hasten gladly to lie down upon the couch of beautiful, restful death. Your friends bend tenderly and weep over your cold body. They draw what they call "consolations," with the old bible-buckets, from the same old wells of faith. At such a time they even reach over and encroach upon forbidden ground; yea, even appealing to Spiritualism, but only as it is given to the world in the gentle lines of Whittier:

> " With silence only as their benediction,
>   *God's angels come*,
> Where, in the shadow of a great affliction,
>   The soul sits dumb."

And you? They say that you have gone to "your *rest!*" What? With the fire and frenzy of the world stored in your very life, with the experiences of all the hosts of your predecessors mixed with the elements of your affections, and inseparable from your attributes of thought? Do you know *who* you are? And do you know *where* you are? You *are* what the whole past universe of effects have made you. And you have ascended (having first died) to a more commanding summit of experience, which is flooded with infinite possibilities. You are essentially *the same man* you were before you died away down there on the rudimental earth. All your spiritual looking-glasses reflect the well-known disposition, character, and countenance. The angel spectators about you plainly see you through and through; you are by them weighed in a new balance; and love and justice, not appearances and circumstances, are now and henceforth to be your judges. Whatever you are *really* worth! *that* is the price the angels will stamp upon you; and then they will point out to you the unbroken pilgrimages of eternity. And then, moved forward in your own orbit, like the globe itself, by the inherent principles of revolution, and progression, you enter "into heavenly rest," through the wide-open gate of love and wisdom and *work*. You will build altars, and erect monuments, and set up a tabernacle to endure forever. But as surely as generation follows generation, so surely will truth crumble your altars, overthrow the monuments, and consign all your tabernacles to the ever-shifting sands of time; and thus your religions, your governments, your schools of thought, come and go, just as *you* came and went, and the universe is and will forever be all the better for it.

But we are admonished not to fill our intellectual sky with too many clouds of Nature's great system, so replete with grandeur and magnificence.

A man's great, self-important and strutting individualism becomes fearfully and wholesomely diminished in the presence of that which is irresistible and eternal and sublime. His strength is displaced with a profound feeling of helplessness; and his experiences, and his very existence, seem like thistle-balls drifting in the unknown winds of destiny. These feelings are spiritually wholesome to you; for such an honest humiliation may augment your growth. So long as you do nothing

5

to merit a loss of your own self-respect, and so long as your self-abnegation is occasioned by your devotion to what you esteem as the best truth, so long you are a safe and a truly growing man.   Your feet will ascend upon the golden rounds of a Jacob's ladder, which is daily let down from the Summerland; and the gleaming meadows beyond the sunset will blossom for you; and upon your pilgrimage you shall hear the soft footfalls of loving guardians; while your hands shall touch those whose inmost hearts beat faithfully in unison with the truth you love and worship.

CHAPTER IV.

A GENERALIZATION OF THE WHOLE SYSTEM OF NATURE.

" No boundless solitude of space,
Shall fill man's conscious soul with awe,
But everywhere his eye shall trace
The beauty of eternal law.
Sweet music from celestial isles
Shall float across the azure seas,
And flowers, where endless summer smiles,
Shall waft their perfume on the breeze."

—Lizzie Doten.

Detailed examination of the harmonious system of
the physical universe, although indispensable to the
largest practical development of what is popularly
called "inductive science," would be far easier to the
studious reader of these chapters *after* contemplating
a generalization of the system.   There is, also, a deeper
mental enjoyment experienced, not to speak of the intense spiritual enthusiasm which is invariably awakened
by viewing a subject from the highest and most comprehensive altitude of observation.

The hastening multitude, superficial in most matters,
and upon this subject indifferent to the very verge of
thoughtlessness, exclaims (when a detailed accuracy is
instituted), " Oh, you are too scientific!"   " Abstrac-
tions and technicalities are awfully tiresome," etc.
This is true, especially to an impatient inspector of, and
to a wholesale dealer in, ideas; but this is not true of
one who is profoundly and correctly impressed with the

sublimity of an eternal principle; for such a mind loves to follow truth into its minutest ramifications—at once a radical and a fruit gatherer—one who is certain to receive a rich happiness by patiently examining into the minutest roots of a subject, while plucking the delicious results which cluster upon its visible branches. It is, for example, very spiritualizing to one's superior sensibilities, and love of beauty and harmony, to ascend some enchanting elevation above the highest tree-tops, and from that lofty solitude contemplate and absorb the impressions imparted by the soft, hazy, indefiniteness of a vastly extended landscape. And, to be accurate, this is the only knowledge of natural beauty which the great human multitudes of earth have any desire to obtain and possess.

But if *all* minds were so constituted and thus governed, if there were no under-working and insistent radicals, no sub-standers within the inner vestibule of the secret centres, no interior and minute investigators into the fine lines of light, and into the well-nigh invisible shadowings which really compose the great landscape of indefinite, dreamy beauty—if all minds were generalizers, then, we ask, where would be those great, living pictures which now bring the skies, the fields, the flowers, and the musical streams into our private parlors and public institutions? A true artist is one who is compelled to deal with the definite, the explicit, the stern, the severe, the ugly, the grotesque, the painful, the discordant, the despairing, the self-sacrificing; and thus, and from these facts separately impressed upon his devoted, self-torturing imagination, he slowly and faithfully evolves the unity and the beauty, and the usually unseen enchantments of Nature into harmonious lights and shades upon a canvas, which is called "a picture;" which (alas! as too often happens in this world of haste and thoughtlessness), long years after the true artist died of despair or starvation, is given by his unpaid landlord in exchange for many thousands of dollars, which sum is gladly paid for it by some true and wise lover of Nature. So, too, the true music artist works into and out of excruciating discords—unfolds from the fatiguing details of common sounds, and from the horrible depths of jargon—the grand symphonies, the marvelous orchestral combinations, the wonderful music of surrounding Nature. The more perfect and analytical the master, the more true and enchanting are his synthetical interpretations of the universe of sounds which exist without and within him; because he knows his subject to its very roots, because he is faithful to the facts and laws of his knowledge, and because he can impart both his inspirations and the grand results of his knowledge to mankind.

"But first," exclaims the reading spectator, "let me see your picture, let me hear your music, let me behold, at one sight, what you term the 'Harmonious System of Nature!'" After the exhibition is realized in the form of a generalization, "then," you say, "I will examine the subject in detail, if I have the time to spare."

With this understanding between us, then, I will presently proceed to impart the required generalization. But let me entertain the pleasurable hope that, after you have sufficiently feasted upon the immeasurable greatness and divine beauty of the system, you will clothe your eyes with a pair of microscopic glasses, and occasionally also with a telescope, which will open to you two new universes, now almost totally invisible to you, which will demonstrate the truth of what is now imparted both by observation and revelation.

A true seer of the secrets of the material system was the spiritual philosopher and gentle teacher, Pythagoras ; whose clear, analytical vision, and far-reaching synthetical imagination, discerned and combined the rhythmical harmonies of the infinite. Had he declined all social mysticisms and all ordinary political fellowship, and been at all times only an ethical and philosophic teacher, it is probable that his revelations of the causes and effects of matter and force would be to-day as much quoted as is Shakespeare, or as are the authors of the New Testament. But his great personal popularity in a brotherhood overwhelmed his greatest possibilities as a seer ; and the consequence was, that the inductive thinker and energetic worker Aristotle walked boldly and victoriously in where the deductive and gentle Pythagoras had hardly dared to touch the least toe of his foot ; and to-day the result is, that the spiritually-minded of the world intuitively *think* of Pythagoras and quote Plato, while their vigilant critics, the materialists, instinctively appeal to Aristotle and Bacon, but demonstrate by Euclid, the Oriental, who wrote and taught over two thousand years ago.

Fact by fact, step by step, mankind have been steadily progressing out of the so-called Orphic " dreams " and subjective " speculations." And yet, in the face of it all, it might be profitable to inquire what more does the world know to-day than in the era of Plato and Ptolemy? The answer would be universally educational, and especially important to future investigators. We must turn away from neither the inspired "ideas" of Plato, nor the "rhythmical order" of the universe disclosed by the illuminated reason of Pythagoras. Scientific progression is intrinsically materialistic. It does not deal with spiritual qualities nor with the origin of things ; but it does increase in quantities, and it grows in becoming more and more accurate in detail. Thus scientists have enlarged the boundaries of human knowledge, and also of human ignorance. They have obtained much wisdom along with more systematic foolishness. And now, with the self-sufficient complacency characteristic of youth, they strut about among their club acquaintances, pronouncing *this* "absurd," and *that* "impossible ; " and, on many questions of spiritual import, it is remarkable how new scientists and old theologians play into each other's hands ; while at the same time, relatively, they are mutual antagonists.

Having prepared our minds for a more comprehensive view, I will proceed now to our promised generalization. My thoughts were led toward Pythagoras, because he was a seer of the qualities and principles of things, as Plato was by the eyes of his illumined reason. They each had vast insight concerning the essential causes and universal harmonies of Nature. Neither of these minds, however, had knowledge of the extent and operations of all the great systems of stars, nor did they discern much concerning the inhabitable planets of space ; and yet they possessed very great wisdom concerning the divine grandeur of truth, and they taught profoundly concerning the great inherent possibilities of the system.

What a deep lesson in psychophonics was taught by Pythagoras! "The music of the spheres," said the golden-mouthed teacher, "can be heard by abstaining from the food of animals; by bodily purity; by meditations; and by presenting to the elements the internal faculties of mind." Than this, nothing since has been more wisely uttered.

* * * An hour has elapsed since the last sentence was written. (This is the 15th of January, 1877.) * * * A few words have come to me psychophonically from Pythagoras, who is now one among the great hosts of the ascended: "*My lessons of numbers were wrongfully appropriated by alchemists. . . . Animals were sacred as expressions of the Supreme life akin to man's. . . . Jupiter represented the central Sun-power. . . . to harmonize with all was human happiness, a duty.*" * * *

After a prolonged waiting in silence, nothing more is heard from the inner world. And now, having long reflected upon these few detached sentences, my conclusion *is :* that, notwithstanding the lapse of so many centuries, the lover of truth thus seeks to impart a few corrections of doctrines with which historians have coupled his name. This record being duly made, I return to our subject.

In geometry the most natural and simple figure is the circle. By the use of the sphere, the cylinder, and the circle, Euclid, and afterwards Archimedes, made true progress toward solving many of the sublimest mysteries of the stellar universe. But the ellipse is a more fruitful figure than the circle,* and we find it introduced,

* "A more *fruitful* figure," seems to be an almost fantastic expression. What do I mean? This: An ellipse is a geometric form

with the hyperbola, by Apollonius; who thus aided Hipparchus in his conception of epicycles and eccentrics, as applicable to the motions of planetary bodies.

The progression of intuitive philosophy, and of practical mathematical knowledge—which moved together side by side, like the first pair in the garden—was very wonderfully advanced by that old wise Egyptian, Ptolemy, whose doctrines faithfully served the world for nearly sixteen centuries; or until Copernicus introduced the idea that the sun, and not the earth, was the centre around which all bodies in the heavens were harmoniously revolving. Then came the larger idea that each of the planets, as well as the earth, might be an inhabitable world, for which wholesome suggestion the world is indebted to Bruno. Thus, in spite of all organized theological opposition, which was intense and tragical, the sun as the centre of the planetary system, and the conception of a plurality of worlds, came into mankind's thought. And these thoughts came to remain, and to act as the germs of infinitely more important knowledge in the same sublime pathway. Galileo and a telescope now came to augment the world's growth. But these great aids came, let it be remembered, in spite of the prisons and death-racks of the so-called Christians. After Galileo we behold Kepler, with his three great discoveries or laws, demonstrating the elliptical orbits of the planets, and going far into the secrets of celestial magnitudes and distances. Then

---

with two centres in one envelope, so to say; that is, an ellipse is double-energized, positive and negative, a male and a female, which fruitful fact is made practically manifest in every chemical compound or organism where the perfect ellipse exists.

5*

came Vinci, Borelli, Newton, Laplace, Herschel, and the score of great students of the stars who now live and labor.

A universe means a revolving unit. This unit turns over and over, perpetually. And this conception antedates all inductive reasoning. It is natural to contemplate the earth as a body in space. To infantile minds the world is formless; to the youthful it is not very far to the horizon; to the strong young mind it is very large and definitely shaped; but it is only with maturity of years that the complete idea of the immeasurable *sphere* is implanted, and fixed as a reality upon the human understanding.

The intuition of the spheral form of stars and planets is very ancient. It came into the world vaguely at first, and it was rapidly mixed with clusters of gods and correlative mysteries. But time has eliminated Oriental mythology, as it will annihilate old Orthodox theology; and the truth, pure and sublime, will shine fully and freely into men's more receptive minds.

Then, too, will be seen the ineffable harmonies of the system of Father God and Mother Nature. Wheels within wheels; universes within universes; revolving units within revolving units; everywhere, beautifully and rhythmically, throughout infinitude.

It is asserted that light would consume twelve years in its flight from the nearest " fixed stars " to the human eye. (Upon this question of light " more light " is imperatively demanded.)*

---

* Readers who may not have access to Part I., of the " Stellar Key," will fail to understand what is here meant by " *light*." In that volume a carefully prepared scale is presented ; wherein " Light"

The perfect ellipse is the form of the orbits in which all fully developed suns, earths, and satellites move through space. They all rotate in the same general direction: and all the bodies move in the same general plane.

The glory and harmony of the system become more and more apparent as you study and familiarize your mind with the stupendous whole. The most fruitful form already mentioned, called an ellipse, is the geometrical figure naturally unfolded to the prepared understanding. Comets, like the fractional notes in music, manifest eccentricity; but they, like all the full notes and all the octaves embodied in suns and planets, are attuned to the master key-note, which is the innermost Sun; which Sun is, so to speak, the cerebrum and the cerebellum, *the brain*, of the Great Positive Mind.

The marvelous combinations of music are beautifully revealed in the flow and formation of all the systems of space. Seven spheres in the spiritual universe *within* seven circles of suns in the material universe. Behold in them the seven notes in music ! When the eighth note is sounded, it is but the reproduction or reappearance of the first note—acting, so to speak, as a bridge of vibrations for the formation of another series of sounds attuned to a still higher key. Thus no originally new sounds are evoked ; but rather the fundamen-

---

is seen as the first manifestation of Infinite Being, called "God." Thus the very existence of the Great Positive Mind is primarily demonstrated by the development of LIGHT. The light is treated scientifically as an ether or fluid; having a rate of motion which can be measured. But there are other attributes to which present science is blind.

tal sounds on differing scales, or in varying degrees of motion.

Thus also in the structure and among the sounding motions of the universe may be heard the pianissimo, the fortissimo, the crescendo, the diminuendo, the sforzando, all the half-notes of the chromatic scale, and all the perfections of sounds which constitute the diapason of the vast systems of immensity.

Numbers lead into all the secrets of harmony. In the eternal perfections of the spiritual universe, which is a revolving unit, the seven notes are eternally sounded. This sublime scale is orchestrally responded to by the seven grand circles in the material universe, as anthem answereth unto anthem in the vast cathedrals of eternity. But the key-note to the spiritual universe is the *interior* Central Sun of love and wisdom, and the key-note of the material universe is the *exterior* Central Sun, which surrounds and clothes the potential Centre.

Here we find the *original* of Beethoven's symphonies, the essentials of Mozart's orchestral interpretations, the spiritual richness and fairy delicacies of Weber, the sacred beauty and natural sweetness of Mendelssohn's oratorios, the affectionate energy and inspiring ideality of Wagner—in a word, in the fundamental principles and in the soul-sounds of the harmonious system of Nature are found all the existing and all the possible musical developments of mankind.

The only perfect musical instrument is the manifold perfections of the twofold universe. The universe is the harp of all the impersonal principles; the silver-tongued trumpet for the use of all the gods; the perfect-toned organ played by the Eternal Master of all grand music. The spheres musically roll through the star-peopled depths like the songs of "the morning stars." No known æolian sound is so delicate but that it is a thousand times more perfectly repeated in the Summerland. And the sweet music of eloquent thoughts is heard by ears which are open to the "breezy anthems" that incessantly breathe themselves through the interstellar spaces.

Mathematics are at the bottom of all system and order in music; and music, in its perfect and full expression, is a revelation of the whole system of nature.

And this last one sentence shall go on record as the promised generalization. It shall be to you like a voice speaking to your very heart from the sky; a melodious revelation of the everlasting truth concerning our Heavenly Home. You shall prepare yourself to hear the orchestral "music of the spheres." It will come sounding sacredly round about the temple of your interior life; like the rhythmical pulsations of Love's infinite sea. It will baptize you in its harmonious waters. And your discord and your false notes shall return to you sounding in your ear like a warning call —"Repent ye." In the silence of your listening heart you shall also hear the sorrowful sobbings of the great rivers of human life in this world. And then, when in your better state, the anthemnal songs of the angel singers shall be to you a further revelation—namely: That Father God is one universe, and that Mother Nature is another universe—that these twain are perfect counterparts in heart, in brain, in essence, in spirit— that this duality is a living oneness which is truly called ETERNAL HARMONY.

CHAPTER V.

> " Away, away, through the wide, wide sky,
>   The fair, blue fields that before us lie,
>   Each sun, with the worlds that round him roll,
>   Each planet, poised on her turning pole ;
>   With her isles of green, and her clouds of white,
>   And her waters that lie like fluid light."
>   —*Wm. C. Bryant.*

THE grand system of the universe may now be contemplated from another point of observation.

We have presented it as constructed upon the principles of pure *music*, and as an instrumental *organ* for the expression of eternal harmony.

Swedenborg presented the heavenly universe as " One Greatest Man ; " in the spiritual organs (or kingdoms) of which dwells the " Lord Himself," as a man lives within his physical body. But this anthropomorphitic representation was a natural consequence of his theological and psychological diathesis. God, he affirmed, was a Divine *Man*. In the heavens, said Swedenborg, God (*the* Man) is constantly visible—at all times perceptible to the highest angels ; but the immediate appearance of God to the spectators is that of a Sun, from which proceed love and wisdom which operate as heat and light. Anthropomorphism is, therefore, the basis and the superstructure of Swedenborg's teachings an hundred years ago; because he was at that time a profound believer in the spiritual and celestial sense of the Bible as the Word of God. But *now* does he not read Nature as the only bible?

The most ancient star-students, with far more figurative reasoning than intuitive imagination, regarded all the heavenly bodies as *wanderers*, which is the original meaning of the term "planet." Every planet, they said, is like a bird without a nest; like a fish out of water; like a goat lost among the barren rocks; like a victim-seeking scorpion without his power to inflict injury; like a prowling lion strayed from his native forest; like a master bull that must forever look for, and never find his herd; like a ram separated from the fold; and thus the Oriental star-students, aided by the science of numbers, finally developed the chromatic scale of constellations known as "The Twelve Signs of the Zodiac." In this arrangement the earth is regarded as the centre, and the planets as so many wandering divinities, good and evil; and that grand galaxy of mysteries the Milky Way, as the primordial pathway over which the great unapproachable Sun-God rolled his magnificent chariot, when his majesty had accepted the eternal crown and sceptre, as the King of kings, the Lord of lords; henceforth to act as ruler over the earth and moon, and all the stars in the firmament.

The geocentric (or earth-centre) doctrine, nevertheless, held its place firmly in the minds of all ancient astronomers—not even emancipating so great a mind as that of the learned Ptolemy; and, with the exception of several side-glimpses by Thales and Pythagoras, and by a few of their successors, the earth-centre theory prevailed until Copernicus suggestively opened the way for the inspirations of Bruno, who was eventually burned at the stake by the Christians of that day and genera-tion. Bruno and Galileo lifted the world by their great ideas. They perfectly overturned, in the face of all church-opposition (which is always ignorant and there-fore *cruel*) the venerable hypothesis; and, instead, they established the heliocentrical (or sun-centre) explana-tion of all planetary relationships and movements. Thus this new truth, that the sun, not the earth, was the pivot, entered into and expanded men's minds. But the dominant theology, as it always does, scowled blight-ingly upon all the new teachers; and when possible, the church imprisoned and burnt them; and why? Be-cause, first, the new astronomy deprived theology of the pet and profitable doctrine that *the earth* was the *chief object* of God's sleepless attention and anxiety; and because, second, the new astronomy fatally impaired the church's most vital belief concerning the supernatu-ral coming and going of God's only son; for, if the earth was *not* the most important centre, then the im-pression was implanted among men that the earth's inhabitants were hardly worth the sufferings and igno-minious death of the only child of the Infinite God. For what were the human family when compared with the countless myriads of larger human families which literally swarm on the great planets which revolve about the measureless sun-centres of space?

But the planets, those brilliant wanderers through the unfathomable stretches of sky, were reverently contem-plated by the early thinkers; and, to accomplish several ends, the stars were counted and gradually gathered into constellations. Birds, fish, serpents, animals, men, women, gods, implements, and musical instruments, were accepted as appropriate figures. Within these significant figures the ancients mapped out and systematically classified the wonderfully bright bodies, which only midnight darkness, and a transparent, unclouded sky could bring out and plainly reveal to the human eye and mind.

Astrology very naturally originated from the irrepressible suggestiveness of this very ancient Chaldean and Egyptian plan of mapping out the star-peopled heavens. The figurative and the symbolical terminology employed, soon developed the hypothesis of stellar influences as inseparable from individual human birth, life, and destiny. Mars stood for war, Venus for love, Mercury for intellect, Jupiter for power, &c.; and the constellations very soon became celestial houses of various forms and degrees of good and evil. Astrologists had a scholarly and mathematical basis. In other words, they perseveringly evolved a real astronomical system of accurate calculations concerning the relations, positions, and movements of the stars and planets; and thus, although the superstructure loomed imposingly up among the clouds of mystery and error, the so-called science was adopted and advocated as truth by some of the best minds before the dawn of better days through Copernicus and Galileo.

Unlike the anthropomorphitic revealments of Swedenborg, by whom the figure of the "Grandest Man" was given as the true form of the superior universe, the ancients filled the heavens with representatives selected freely from the kingdoms of fish, bird, reptile, animal, human, and deities; not neglecting musical instruments, implements of husbandry, arms of warriors, sceptres of power, and various signs of pride and passion. All these images conspicuously decorate, or else disagreeably detract from, existing maps and popular books on descriptive astronomy. The groups of stars, or the systems of groups, called constellations, are correctly placed in the sky by astronomical geographers. And thus we can follow the earth's path under the heavenly bodies all the way round the year. But the names adopted from the ancients, like most of the popular theology which is advocated by Evangelical Christians, both of which are derived from ages equally remote and superstitious, would be far better for mankind as simple *history* than as forms and methods of thinking.

The unspeakable vastness and holy grandeur of the Univercœlum are faintly intimated by the accompanying diagram, No. 4. No books on astronomy either contain or even suggest the figure *here* presented. All these constellations, or all of which astronomers have any knowledge, are confined to the topmost belt (M, in the cut) of suns and systems. These bodies are fed by the outlying infinity of cometary substances, which swarm in the outermost fields of the material universe. These world-building bodies are represented in the diagram as moving simply above the star-fields or universes, M. It should not be forgotten, however, that this diagram represents the different sections of immeasurable, innumerable, and inconceivably vast systems of circles of suns and planets; each circle having a silver or golden lining, so to say, indicated by those arcs, giving the positions of the succeeding spiritual zones, called

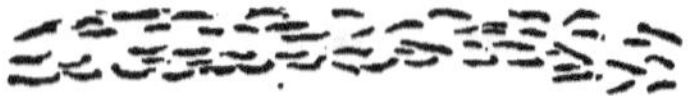

M

S.L.

No. 4.

SECTIONAL DIAGRAM OF THE UNIVERSE.

Summerlands, which become finer and more celestial as they approach the Central Sun—the relative position of which Sun, to the entire system, is intimated by radial lines at the very bottom of the diagram.*

Here let us reverently pause, and yield our interiors to profoundest contemplation. Let us not hasten, bird-like, superficially and flittingly, over and around these immeasurable, these ineffably divine and vast, these multitudinous and unchangeable realities of eternity. Your most sincere feelings, your finest thought-powers, your deepest intuitions, with their brightest illuminations, should be wholly and prayerfully concentrated upon the subject, otherwise it were far better that you should close this volume and resign yourself to indifference, or give your fancy the flattering assurance that the school-books and the august professors of the colleges have taught you far truer and wiser concerning the natural sciences and the unnatural metaphysics of philosophy. Nay, thoughtful reader! You should pause *here*, and seek to enlarge your perceptions of these sublime realities of immensity by

---

* Our astronomical universe is confined to two groups of dots in the diagram, No. 4 : that is, astronomers, with their greatest telescope, have never seen beyond those two star-fields indicated by two clusters on the left hand ; our own entire solar system being indicated by the smallest dots in the next to the last left-hand group.

The Central Sun is equal to all the infinite systems of boundless space. The Summerland zone nearest the star-belt M, is the youngest, and is therefore the first Heavenly Home after death ; but, because we, as spirits, begin here our first step in life, so the after-death world is properly termed " the second sphere." Concerning the inhabitability of the inner Summerland zones more will hereafter be remarked.

yielding yourself to a wider and profounder association (in your thoughts) with the ethers, essences, laws, and principles, upon which the Univercœlum in its harmonious perfection exists.

Have you granted this most reasonable request? Do you this moment profit by this counsel? If so, then with most pleasurable emotions you will yield yourself, free of the catechism and untrammelled by scholastic prejudices, to the contemplation and possible comprehension of the arcanum about to be disclosed.

The Central Sun! These three words are easily written and spoken. But what inconceivably vast universes, what unfathomably deep foundations, what perfections of unchangeable principles, exist in that Central Sun! It is no idle use of language to affirm that this radiant Central Sun of the Univercœlum is boundlessly vaster and infinitely richer in Divine perfections than the highest angel-intelligence can ever hope to comprehend. Yet it is possible to comprehend the constitution and functional operations of this Centre by comprehending correctly the constitution and essential workings of some corresponding Centre *nearer* our own present situation, in the outermost sun-circle of the stupendous system.

Emanations, I repeat, constitute the covering of, or the ephemeral peri-spirit to every physical organization. Things not yet organized, like simple elements in the mineral kingdom, are also clothed with an appropriate atmospheric garment, the particles of which gradually oozed from within and formed themselves as an aura closely around the surfaces; upon the same principle as the skin and the hair are pushed out and organized externally upon the body of every animal structure, or as birds are clothed with feathery garments. Upon this universal and unchangeable principle the external of every sun is surrounded with a sphere of Light (which is *not* the light by which we see with bodily vision)—a *solar fluid*, strictly speaking, which is energized with the properties of all vitalic principles; it is the magnetism of the sun-laboratory, pure, flaming with fiery radiations; it is brighter in its brilliancy than the ineffable shine of the sun itself; a solar peri-spirit, so to speak, which flows swifter than lightning far and wide throughout all that portion of space which is occupied by all those planets and satellites which belong to that particular sun.

The external function of our visible sun—to take a literal illustration, nearer to our present existence—is visible ordinarily as " a ball of fire." But this appearance is an appearance only; for a revolving and float-ing ball of fire through the cold ether of space could not long continue; while the perpetual flaming of its magnetic and elemental emanations is an inevitable con-comitant of the performance of the sun's constitutional functions. And yet it is true that our sun is a central source of one of the planetary and man-bearing systems; and, as a Centre, the sun is of necessity still in a condi-tion of uncondensation similar to the centres of the globes which noiselessly roll around it.

Comprehending the fact of a physical sun by which all around it is originated, actuated, governed, sustained, and progressively developed, you are measurably pre-pared to comprehend the existence of a Spiritual Cen-tral Sun, which, in each Summerland, is visible in the lofty heavens above; each sun being the Focus of the accumulated Love, Will, and Wisdom of that particular sphere of individualized existences. Swedenborg testified that the Lord *appeared* " like a sun " to the eyes of all who reside " in the spiritual world," which he sometimes designated as the " celestial" and most " interior heavens;" where this Lord-luminary was perpetually visible, shining with the Love (heat) and Wisdom (light) of the infinite maker of the universe.

There is a greater arcanum to be divulged, namely : that there is a Sun, shining like " the Lord of Heaven," in the pure sky over *each* Summerland ; and, moreover, the more interior the inhabited zone, the more brilliant and beautiful is the spiritual sun in the upper firmament. Wherefore, it might be said, with literal truthfulness, that *there are as many Lords as there are spheres inhabited !* Here the term " Lord " and the words " spiritual sun " are used to mean the same fact.

The great focal positive power or sun of the mental possessions of the adjoining Summerland, is, therefore, the Lord whose Love and Wisdom will flow into and nourish your love and your wisdom; and who will enfold you and strengthen you, and who will fill you with light and liberty and happiness, if you will but enter that superior condition which puts you into closest sympathetic relationship therewith.*

---

* The reader's attention is asked to Nat. Div. Rev., Part I., wherein, in other language, all this is foreshadowed. See pp. 38, 40, 41, 42, 43, 44. On the last page named, it is written: " My information is not derived from any persons that exist in the sphere into which my mind enters ; but it is the result of a law of truth, emanating from the Great Positive Mind," etc. See Appendix.

A luminiferous ether floods infinite space. It is within and without all things. Shall we call this pure life-ether the "*wine* of God?" It fills all things; it is the fire of suns; the force of stars; the purifying presence in all mineral structures; the links in the life of plants; the power which circulates the blood in animals; the bridge by which man materially is connected to man spiritually—what name, I ask you, shall we give this shining, fiery, purifying, conjugating essence of the Univercœlum? Among the stars it is an astral-emanation; among the suns it is a solar-emanation; over each Summerland it is the absolute "Lord of Heaven;" in each human heart it is inseparable from affection, and in each head it is allied to intelligence—what shall we call it? Until a better term is given, we will name this Omnipresent luminiferous ether, *the spirit of God.*

Scientists have interrogated the imponderables of space. The gases, until recently, have been called "the imponderables." But it has been discovered that a solid body may be elevated in temperature and liqufied, even etherealized; and, the reverse, that the so-called imponderables can be reduced progressively down to the fluid state, by the persistent application of *cold.* Four thousand one hundred and ten pounds of atmospheric pressure upon hydrogen, as an invisible gas, forced it to become a materialized and visible fluid. The cold of space was estimated by Herschel as two hundred and thirty-nine degrees *below* zero; and yet this enormous *cold* would not be adequate to the reduction of hydrogen to a palpable fluid.

Thus the freezing cold of space would seem to be something frightful to contemplate. But we do not go out after death with these chronothermal nerves; hydrogen is not our after-death envelopment; the spiritual body is impressible by nothing less fine than that omnipresent solar-influence and astral-ether which we have agreed to name *the spirit of God!* Neither heat nor cold, nor the changes of time, nor the decomposition of countless universes in eternity, can disturb the body of the spirit. And the spirit itself is susceptible and obedient only to the irresistible principles of progression, which are the will-emanations of the Centremost Great Positive Mind.

There is another arcanum to be made manifest in this connection.

The Summerland within the sixth circle, and also the next approaching the Centre of All, resemble the inhabited planets in this general particular: they are constituted, heated, lighted, beautified, diversified, and clothed upon with perfections adequate for the presence and sustenance of mankind, only upon their most external surfaces. In the fertile valleys and abroad over the expanded fields, Nature (the earth, for example) develops and entertains her human offspring, while she is parsimonious and barren upon her most majestic mountains, and equally so upon the elevations and beautiful hills which, at a distance, look so enchanting to mankind. But in her hidden warm places, closer to her interior bosom, so to say, she welcomes her children and feeds them with every beautiful and sweet perfection.

What we have for so many years designated as the " second sphere " and the " third sphere " must be

understood as inhabitable only upon their outer surfaces. But it is a principle that the material universes
become more refined and more highly organized as they
recede from the Central Material Sun ; even so, and in
the same relative proportion, that the spiritual universes
(the Summerlands) grow more celestial and become
more heavenly in their perfections and glory as they
recede from the circumference, or as they approach
toward the inmost Central Spiritual Sun.

Now the arcanum already mentioned is this : That the
fourth, fifth, and sixth spiritual spheres are inhabited
on both sides !

For years I have known, by psychophonic communications and by sympathy with the principles con-
tained within the luminous centre already explained,
that these more interior Summerlands are, both within
and without, inexpressibly beautiful with every divine
perfection, and that they have been for countless ages
of eternity, and are, now, populated by those heavenly-
minded and truly celestial personages who have been
thus gradually advanced in their progressive march
toward the All Perfect Sun of the Univercœlum.

Thus there is a perfect analogy between the human
spirit and body and the spiritual and material universes.
By means of logical reasonings, and not less certainly
by the testimony of your intuitional teachers, you can
satisfy your own mind that these affirmations are true.
For illustration, man's body is saturated by the soul-
elements which eventually (at death, or soon after)
assume a perfect form, which is thenceforth and forever the body of his inmost, which we call SPIRIT—
meaning the whole mental being of the individual.

Now you observe that our present material body is finest and most perfectly organized in beauty near and upon its external surfaces; but, reversely, that the more interior and central you investigate man's personal existence, the closer you approximate to the best and most divine in him, called spirit. Centrally, therefore, man is most perfect *spiritually;* while he is more perfect *materially* as you reach the circumference of his being.

Having made known these essential truths concerning the spiritual and material suns, the nature of the ether of infinitude, and the inhabitability of both sides of the three innermost zones, we are now prepared to intelligently resume a further consideration of the harmony of the whole system.* Here the thought must be urged that no telescope can possibly bring to the eye of man a point of light *beyond* the sixth circle of suns. In the diagram these systems, of the sixth circle, or rather the groups of our visible constellations, including the Milky Way, are represented as reposing just beneath the world-building comets.

Our sun, our earth, and all the planets of our own special system, exist and have their being in one of those clusters. The first Summerland zone is *beneath* this belt of suns and stars; for, being spiritual in its constitution, it approaches the Central Sun ; while the belts of suns and stars, being material in their constitution, are situated externally, and have moved outwardly.

In that one uppermost belt is the entire *corporeum celestium,* so far as is yet known to mankind, excepting

---

* Estimates by astronomers may be found in the Appendix.

as clairvoyantly revealed. The indescribably stupendous girdle or galaxy—the *Via Lactea*, or Milky Way—is visible as a part of this outermost organized sixth circle. Keep in memory that our earth-position necessitates an edge-wise perception and impression of the Milky Way. It is the light of a part of our special star-field. Standing within this field, and looking outwardly and side-wise, we see only irregular clouds of light, which clouds are in very truth whole systems of suns and planets. The constellation supposed (erroneously) to be nearest the earth, the *Canis Major* or " Great Dog," contains that star (the erroneously supposed cause of pestilence, in ancient times), *Sirius*, whose pure light consumes many years in its flight to the human eye! Herschel supposed that solar light would require millions of ages in travelling from some of the most remote stars to the earth ; and this supposition, too, is not unmindful that that form and degree of motion called "light" moves with the inconceivable celerity of one hundred and ninety-three thousand miles every second! Some astronomers have estimated the flight of light per second to be about one hundred and eighty-six thousand miles. Such magnificent stretches through immensity, implying such remote sun-centres of stupendous magnitudes, and so many millions of millions of ages, as we measure " time," well nigh overwhelm and vanquish the most expanded imagination. The healthiest human mind, unless its possessor occasionally gives it vigorous exercise upon these sublime themes, is simply appalled and stunned. And yet such contemplations are wholesome—invigorating, ennobling, exalting ; and you are therefore *urged*, because you are a spirit, and because you are destined to live an eternal life, to think upon and familiarize your reason with questions of eternity.

By impressions imparted, as I have before explained, from the sun-fountain of intelligence in the Second Sphere, we learn that the measureless sweep of the more distant universes through space is regulated upon a principle of double motion, which is perfectly illustrated by the circulations of globules and fluids in the human body.

Principles of progressive and (apparently) retrograde or backward movements—which principles are both positive and negative—apply to and fully explain all solar and planetary motion. The first is an expansive and forward (or centrifugal) impulse and movement; the second is a contractive and inward (or a curvilinear) and centripetal movement; then there is a general forward oceanic flow of the whole circle of suns, as one solid, massive universe. The whole movement is like an endless or almost perfectly circular ocean. Thus in man's body we behold, first, the outward, rotary and vibratory motion of the fluids and globules of the blood from the heart; second, the return motion of the same minute atoms and fluids to the heart; and, third, then all the movements in man's body, together with his body itself moves (unconsciously to the man) upon and *with* the earth through space, at the appalling rate of more than a million and a half of miles every twenty-four hours.

Now take the earth, for example, which originally, or at first, moved like an immense spheroidal mass of fire, heat, light, and electricity. This great mass moved at first centrifugally around the parental sun-centre. In appearance, excepting the electrical, trailing streamers, it was a vast cometary accumulation (as it *really* was) of all the essential elements and qualities which were destined to ultimate into what it now is and will become. Then as soon as it had sufficiently developed into the globular form, it forthwith made a " declaration of independence " of the maternal bosom, and immediately turned inwardly, or upon its own axis centripetally ; and thus was established, and thus are invariably established, the two eternal motions of all planetary and solar bodies. First, outward, in a rectilinear direction, terminating centrifugally ; second, inward, in a curvilinear direction, terminating centripetally.

But do not astronomers generally know or believe, that the earth has also a *third* motion ? The enlightened Russian investigator, Mädler, supposed that he. discovered a profounder motion. He declared scientifically that our sun, and the earth (of course), together with the entire planetary system, is journeying harmoniously around a mighty and far-away centre which is located in the brightest of that wonderfully brilliant group of seven stars, called the Pleiades.

For a sacred moment let us contemplate the refulgent centre about which our system is said to be rhythmically revolving. (Let me here say that while I know that our whole system is drifting toward Alcyone, I do not yet certainly know that Alcyone is the centre.) Alcyone, for example, is the mother of our ever-faithful sun, the grandmother of our earth, and the great-grandmother of the little moon which *plays in* and *out* about the orbit of the earth like a boy around his affectionate mother. But there are many mighty and majestic sons and daughters, together with a countless host of grandchildren and great-grandchildren, playfully circling around their august maternal ancestor. These pilgrim-children are great pedestrians! They all move forward with a cheerful regularity toward the great ancestral constellation, at the delightfully exhilarating rate of about eight miles in every second, thus making extra express-train time (always " on time," and never once " jumping the track "), and yet going ahead *over* and *under* and *around* and *between* the tracks of other trains, speeding to other destinations at the safe rate of twenty thousand miles in every sixty minutes !

Now just here it must be written, and not be forgotten, that our feminine Sun has been on a visit to her mother, who lives among the " Sweet influences of the Pleiades," *only twice* since her birth ; and it must be further affirmed, that, since she (our Sun) bore these later children (viz., the Earth, Venus, Mercury, and the inner asteroids), she has " not had time " to take them to see their effulgent grandmother ! For, let it be recorded that our prolific solar mother produced these later little ones when she was in the perihelion of her last journey. And it has been estimated that it would consume about eighteen millions and two hundred thousand years for our sun, although constantly travelling twenty thousand miles an hour, to carry her splendid great family back to the Pleiades, so that they might all see their gorgeous, royal, star-crowned grandmother, Alcyone !

CHAPTER VI.

THE BEAUTY AND GLORY OF THE PLANETS.

Kepler's Vision, by Lizzie Doten.

WE will now return to a consideration of the philosophy of planetary motion. I think it is safe to say that the secret of all diurnal and orbital movement is out. But, before proceeding with this subject, it is necessary to repeat a little.

At first, as I have said, the earth rolled into space as a formless mass: and thus moved in an eccentric orbit around the productive sun, its mother. Then, second, as it became more self-centered, and more steady relatively to its own heart of fire, it began to turn upon its own axis. And then, third, with its mother and the whole family, it floated and yet floats like an atom in the endless oceanic flow of the entire combined unity of the sixth circle of suns. And here we affirm that what is true of our earth and of our solar system, is equally true, and, upon the same unchangeable principles, *must* everlastingly continue to be true, of all other similar bodies and systems which exist in the surrounding infinitude.

Motion is at the bottom of all material phenomena; and motion explains the weight as well as the rarity of bodies. An increase of centripetal motion in a body increases the weight of everything attached to that moving body; but the levitation or lightness (of the same things) is increased in proportion to the increase of the body's centrifugal motion. And here, also, is another law: Slow motions among moons, and planets, and suns, arise from one of three causes, either their extreme youth, or their old age and decrepitude, or their relative position to the sun. Let us apply this law to our moon.

Our satellite, we here affirm, is in its extreme youth, a bright faced little boy, the first and "only son" of our earth; although there are enough earth-born materials afloat without and within the lunar orbit to develop in time another good sized moon. That the moon is in its infantile stage is demonstrated by the fact that, thus far in his history, he has been capable of performing but *one* revolution "on his own responsibility." He turns over only once in one of his years, which is just four of our weeks; which is the exact time he consumes in travelling all the way around his mother, earth. All satellites are latest children of the body about which they roll and play in a kind of waltzing or wavy motion.

Our especial solar system, the sun and its large family of earths and moons, is comparatively a *young* formation. Many of its operations, like the surfaces and climates of the earth, are yet crude and deficient when

6*

contrasted with some of the other and similar systems which musically move through the firmament. Nevertheless, as the satellites of Jupiter and Saturn perfectly demonstrate, by moving around with their mothers on the same direction and on the same plane, the eldest born among them is just entering upon the era of an increase in the number of their revolutions. Jupiter's outermost moon, like Saturn's, has been long showing a self-centered tendency by departing from the plane of the primary (or from the old-time door-yard and play-ground obediently observed by each of the younger children); and, also, by becoming attached to other congenial bodies, not members of the family, and thus at certain times developing a new form of eccentricity in its revolutions. Astronomers will be richly rewarded by taking new observations of Jupiter's fourth and Saturn's eighth satellite; also by making a new estimate of the sun's mass as compared with that of all the bodies known to revolve about her; and thus reach two conclusions, first, that a true balance necessitates the addition of three new planets, not less in magnitude than Uranus with satellites to equal the mass of Neptune; and second a reconstruction, if not a total abandonment, of the popular doctrines concerning the nature and effects of fire, heat, light, and electricity, whereby many planetary operations, now invisible owing to prolonged occultations and the rapid motion of neighboring bodies, will be discovered, greatly to the enrichment of astronomical science.

Our familiar, bright-faced moon illustrates at once both the primordial condition and the first grand centrifugal motion, through which all solar and planetary bodies pass, on their way from youth to extreme maturity, coldness, and decay. He cannot be trusted yet to take more axial exercise out doors ! He is now, and has been, through many of what we call " ages," permitted to make himself perfect in turning over once a month on his own strength ; but when he is older, stronger, and more self-centred, he will surprise his mundane lovers and scientific admirers by changing the programme of his performances. He will begin to have three days and three nights of his own in a single year ; for he will then take more axial exercise, making out for himself a year of revolutions in one of our months; enlarging the sphere (orbit) of his operations, and opening a place for another brother to be born out of the far upper atmosphere, which is now pregnant with flowing rivers of world-building bodies. Even now parts of the moon could sustain animal life as it does vegetation of the most primitive and gigantic proportions. Thus the moon will imitate and repeat the life and conduct of his mother. He will make three revolutions where now he can perform but one ; and, with an increase of his strength, finer vegetation will come forth, and animals and human beings will be evolved upon surfaces which are now, in sections, covered with mountains of mineral formations, glittering with electrical and magnetic emanations, which could not be appropriated by anything having lungs, a heart, and warm blood to circulate. An increase of centripetal or inward motion, developing more axial revolutions, will change the moon and everything upon its surface. It will, in a word, cease to be a satellite (except as the earth is one, and as the sun is), and thus, by the law of progress, the moon will become a fruitful planet of modest proportions.

Behold now, thoughtful reader! the figure of the universe which I have acquired by telescopic observation illuminated by impressions from the essential centre in the Summerland.   It is not, as you will naturally remark, the figure of the "Greatest Man," it is not the mythological history of past races tattooed upon the sky in the fantastic shape of constellations composed of aimless wanderers (planets) through the dreary abysses of space ; but it *is* a harmonious system of universes, of units within units, of belts of suns and systems within more remote and perfect suns and systems ; each moving musically, with almost lightning swiftness, in an orbit around its parental centre, and each also turning upon the axis of its own responsibility, so to speak ; and, finally, the whole resembling a perfect flower of measureless magnitude and filled with eternal fragrance, rooted in the loving soil of the infinite Heart, and blossoming perpetually into innumerable lesser flowers (or worlds) freighted with every conceivable possibility, destined to unfold progressively into every variety of life and animation, and to build "better than they know" by introducing upon each flower (or planet) that consummation of all organization—the human immortal mind, a miniature reappearance in image and likeness of the central productive Brain and Heart, called by all of us who are their offspring, Father God and Mother Nature.

*   *   *   *   *   *   *   *

What a memorable day was yesterday ! (the 15th of

January, 1877.)   It was the first time since the autumn of 1846 that I have enjoyed telescopic (clairvoyant) observations of many portions of the royal planets.   I saw many of their inhabitable surfaces and a portion of their populations; and the result was, the unexpected acquisition of some most important knowledge.   I have at length obtained, quite incidentally to the main purposes of my observations, a few facts which explain a remarkable record published on page 189, "Nature's Divine Revelations;" wherein, after a few generalizations concerning Jupiter's inhabitants, this statement is made: "They do not walk erect, but assume an inclined position, frequently using their hands and arms in walking, the lower extremities being rather shorter than the arms according to our standard of proportion. And by a modest desire to be seen only in an inclined position, they have formed this habit, which has become an established custom among them."

The writer has received since the publication of that work of sweeping generalizations, not only hundreds of letters from very candid persons urging the desirableness of some explanation of this passage; but, in consequence of its absurdity, which is much intensified when viewed in connection with other and inconsistent statements on both sides of it, he has also received an enormous amount of ridicule, not to speak of the actual loss of valued readers as a further result.   His inflexible rule has been, however, never to expunge or alter any word or paragraph which he has ever uttered or written, until he had acquired some explicit and comprehensible reason for so doing.   But now, after a whole generation of men has passed away, or after more than thirty years, he is unexpectedly enabled to shed a ray of light upon the passage, and for this he is deeply thankful.

The chief object of observations made yesterday morning was to obtain additional information regarding the inhabitableness of those three glorious exterior planets. A promise to this effect, you may possibly remember, is recorded either openly or by implication on pp. 183, 192, 202, of the great volume already mentioned. But the special ultimate uses and benefits to be derived from such additional information, will become apparent further on.

While observing the effulgent spirituality and personal beauty of Jupiter's various populations—embracing differing brotherhoods and special nationalities, and widely distributed far on either side of her immense equatorial belt, and also over portions of her great southern hemisphere—my attention was suddenly attracted to a massive assemblage of men, women and children, walking about beneath a bright sky and performing peculiar acts; the majority of the host walking in an inclined position, and very many of them actually using their hands also in accomplishing locomotion. And yet, compared with the bodily appearance of many tribes on earth, their physical forms were exceedingly handsome, and their intelligence was quite spiritual and commanding. At this moment I recalled the paragraph already quoted; which, very naturally, induced me to seek further light. And immediately it was made plain that I had given a general description of the religious ceremonies of a peculiar brotherhood, and then proceeded with the other generalizations without stopping to ascertain that this was a remarkable exception. It was a singular coincidence, too, that these peculiar people were engaged in their religious ceremonies on the two occasions of my observation; and it is not less remarkable that, on each occasion, the first sight of them stamped the notion that they were the aristocracy of Jupiter, and that they characterized correctly the manners and customs of all the inhabitants.

Before proceeding to the question as to the *spiritual* inhabitableness of those three exterior earths, I am admonished to ask your attention to the preliminary question concerning the possibility that Mars, Jupiter and Saturn *can be* inhabited by persons clothed as we are, in the physical habiliments of bone, flesh and blood.

It is asserted by astronomers, as a deduction from careful calculations, but which will not bear the test of a severe analysis, that Saturn does not receive enough heat and light from the sun to develop and sustain human life. And the same remark is made respecting both Mars and Jupiter. Saturn is said to receive not more than one-ninetieth, Jupiter not more than one-seventieth, and Mars not more than one-fiftieth, as much heat and light from the sun as does this inhabited, because thus inhabitable, earth of ours. And there are *other* objections suggested and urged by the fearfully religious, who only want " God's earth " populated—so that the tragedy of a supernatural scheme of salvation may be appropriately magnified—and materialists with their spectroscope contribute consolations to the trembling party, until " horrors upon horror's head accumulate." For with the ruthless hand of an exact science (?) they depopulate our three majestic planets, and freely consign the planets themselves to an existence of either twilight or total darkness, while furnishing them with perpetual mountains of ice, and with vast continents of snow; at the same time they as freely dissolve the remoter bodies into globes of exceeding lightness and of elastic flaming fluids, surrounded by a garment of perfectly unrespirable atmospheres.

These remarks are not made to reflect unfavorably upon the new form of chemical investigations by the employment of the recently invented spectroscope. The constituents of substances never before known have been brought to light by it, giving us several most valuable new metals; and many of the elements of our sun and of the active gases of stars in some of the very far-off constellations, have been recently revealed by what is called "spectrum analysis."

By this method the light proceeding from a white-hot and flaming substance is admitted to a prism through a slit only one thirty-second of an inch wide: the light, thus decomposed and shed beyond the prism, is microscopically examined; and then, by comparing the lines that are visible with those invariably derived experimentally from the combustion of known elements and substances, the properties of the particular flame under examination are reliably ascertained. An experienced spectrum analyzer can, at a glance, read the properties of a metal under examination; because it is found that the number, the position, and the color of the transverse lines obtained from the combustion of a substance are invariably the same. Thus, for example, the lines obtained from white-hot gold, silver, soda, zinc, iron, copper, calcium, potassium, platinum, oxygen, hydrogen, etc., always appear exactly in the same position and with the same number and color; and thus, by employing telescopic as well as microscopic instruments, the spectrum analysis of the sun and of the remote stars can be exactly obtained.

Just here let me remind you that thirty-one years ago, in oral discourses, which were literally recorded at the time, the writer explicitly unfolded *the fire-mist origin* of all suns and worlds in the abysses of the universe.   And now, to-day, by a recently discovered spectroscope, what "confirmation strong" do we unexpectedly and involuntarily receive!   The spectroscope has demonstrated, (1) that *the same elements* enter into the composition of the earth, the sun, and of all the infinite ocean of suns which float through the stellar systems; (2) that the clouds of nebulæ are in reality world-building matter in a state of flame, and not yet in a condition to be cooled off and rolled out into rotating worlds; (3) that the primordial condition of the solar system—that it was originally in a fiery, molten state—is fully confirmed by the spectrum of the measureless masses of gaseous matter visible in portions of the Milky Way; (4) that the most remote stars, twinkling and burning in the appalling brightness of their own light, are actually just like our sun, both in their constituent composition and as to the fact of perpetual combustion.

All the foregoing demonstrates our philosophy of the origin and present condition of the physical universe; which, substantially, was suggested by the noble Herschel and boldly advocated by the inspired Laplace as, to say the least of it, a most rational hypothesis.

CHAPTER VII.

THE INHABITANTS OF THE EXTERIOR PLANETS.

> " Beautiful home of love divine,
> Our deepest hearts around thee twine ;
> Unto thy summer bowers we come,
> Home of the angels—beautiful Home."
>
> —*Song by Mary F. Davis.*

WE return now to consider the inhabitableness of planets beyond the earth.

With this question uppermost in the mind, I proceed to ask, with special reference to Mars, Jupiter, and Saturn : Was there not a time in the history of a planet when its *internal heat* was infinitely greater in volume and more intense than any solar heat received by the earth from the sun ? Can any heat or light be lost ? What is this new *lesson* which scientific investigators have derived from the correlation and conservation of force ? If a great body in space is first equatorially cooled off, then broken up and rolled out into revolving planets: what becomes of *the heat* that is necessarily evolved and poured into space ? Is heat, or is its chemical equivalent, *lost ?*   If the sun is a fountain of heat, what do you think of Saturn's liquid girdles of perpetual magnetic flame ? What function as to warmth and light, think you, is incessantly performed by the invisible rivers of world-building or cosmical bodies, which have not yet become asteroids or satellites ? The storehouses of heat in the solar system—where are they ?

and what of them? Is there not a law of compensation? Are there no provisions, in the planetary larder, adapted to a planet's bodily appetite and necessities? How is it possible that Mars, moving at the inconceivable rate of fifty-five thousand miles an hour, Jupiter with her four great weighty moons thirty thousand miles an hour, and Saturn, with her still larger family of worlds, and with her splendid heating arrangements and great solar belts, at the rate of nearly twenty-one thousand miles an hour—I ask, with all this incessant speed and all these motions—how is it possible that no terrestrial electricity should be evolved from the prodigious mineral resources of the planets, whereby auroral magnetic warmth, and boreal gorgeousness in field and sky, and equatorial vivifications and perfect organic developments, should glorify and characterize these great worlds, which, like the earth, roll noiselessly upon their poles and harmoniously around the sun?

There is one more problem, namely, concerning the analysis of the spectrum of self-lighted stars, and also concerning those planets whose heat and light are supposed to be derived exclusively from the sun.

When you investigate the surfaces of Mars and Jupiter, and subject the luminous rings of Saturn to the spectroscopic slit, how do you separate sunlight, reflected, from the universal stellar light which is absorbed and appropriated and then reflected from other suns? In other words, how can you determine when light is *not* reflected? The replies by science to the foregoing questions will, better than by any other agency, establish our affirmations concerning the possibility of human existence upon the three adjoining planets belonging to our solar system. * But there are a few more considerations deemed essential in this connection. They are these: A slow moving body is proportionally a cold body; and slowness and coldness are the parents of darkness and death. This principle works out the same effects in mind as in matter. You cannot impart an idea to a mind until you first arrest that mind's attention. The momentary arrest of its inherent motions develops, first, *heat*, which is evolved by the suddenly increased action; and, second, its heat develops *light*, which, in ordinary language, is "the idea." Action or motion, then, is the parent of heat and fire. But, in one operation of this principle, the primary motion is, for an instant, *first arrested*. Thus a mass of matter, whose component atoms are suddenly arrested in the sphere or plane of its greatest velocity, will immediately by resistance evolve more or less of light, electricity, magnetism, gravitation, and dynamic force.

Now you will observe that the results depend largely upon the size and weight of the resisting body. Far up in the air, although *nearer* the sun, the cold and the dark are appalling. Because the sun's heat and light meet with little or no resistance; and for the same reason, although further from the sun, the earth is flooded with both heat and light. Thus it is that small globes and world-building bodies millions of miles nearer the sun than the earth, may be comparatively engulfed in

---

* The reader is referred to the " Stellar Key " for some reflections upon the correlation and conservation of force, and to " Nature's Divine Revelations " for a special description of Mars, Jupiter and Saturn.

perpetual night, and may exist in low temperatures; while globes, which are revolving hundreds of millions of leagues further from the sun than the earth, may, because of their greater resisting magnitudes and special motion, be the recipients of proportionally larger instalments of heat and light.

Mars is a peer and representative of the Earth in many physical particulars. But astronomers permit to Mars only half as much light and heat as the earth receives. And yet they discern through the telescope "zones of intense brightness" and belts of "varying brilliancy;" both at the poles and in different portions of the visible surface. And also they discern an ocean of asteroidal bodies moving with extraordinary speed and with many eccentriciticies in the space beyond the orbit of Mars; from which, however they have denied (or overlooked) that Mars should receive by induction and attraction *immense volumes of such atoms* and motions as all planets require for their growth, warmth, development, and perfection. In consequence of all this, it was difficult, as it was unnecessary, for Mars to produce satellites, save a very feeble belt of cosmical bodies.*

---

* Soon after the publication of this chapter it was authentically announced that "two moons" had been discovered near the body of Mars. Concerning these very small new bodies, Mr. Chandler in the *Science Observer*, in substance, said: "Comparison with the light from other satellites gives results that vary from a little less than two to about three and three-quarter miles for the diameter of the outer moon of Mars. The conclusion is that the outer satellite cannot be of over four miles thick, and is probably less; while the minor one, being fainter, is yet smaller. It appears almost incredible that such small masses can reflect light enough to be seen with even the

Concerning Jupiter and Saturn, both immensely vaster than the earth and far greater and swifter travellers, considering the size of their families, I have some recent observations to record.

But first let me remind you of another effect of motion. A world's rotation agitates its waters, and these waters, moving unceasingly and periodically to and fro, taken in connection with the sun's heat and light, also with valleys and mountain ranges, effectuate in what are termed winds, air currents, tornadoes, cyclones, etc. The warmth of the Gulf Stream, as well as its constant flowings in certain directions, have been by some minds accounted for by reference to constantly blowing hot winds and sub-oceanic currents. Let us take this warm stream simply as an illustration. Imagine now, what I have recently observed on the distant planets, that the entire Atlantic Ocean was all the year round as warm as is the Gulf Stream, which, in its warmest place, is about 85°. And then extend a like supposition to the Pacific

---

best of telescopes. Unquestionably, these Martial moons are by far the smallest of celestial objects yet discovered."

The question naturally arose : "Why did not the clairvoyant observer see these two moons ?" The true reply is this : They *were* seen by him, but only *incidentally*, or as by a glance, while fixing the perceptions exclusively upon the planet itself. And the above brief passage by the author, embodies all the importance those minor masses seemed to possess in comparison with the magnitudes and wonderful sceneries of the body of Mars, which, bear in mind, were the objective purpose of the author's especial observations. (This subject is further considered in the Appendix). From three separate and more recent observations, I am forced to conclude that it is improper for astronomers to term these cosmic bodies, "moons;" they are *not* satellites in the same sense that our moon is one; for it will be found that they were not derived from the body of Mars.

Ocean, and to all the great bodies of water. Then fancy overhead an atmosphere so atomically constituted as to absorb and retain from the sun and from surrounding bodies the purest light and the most delightful degree of heat. Now imagine no very high mountains; no deep valleys; no rapid air-currents; no violence among the winds; in consequence of which, no rapid evaporation ever occurs. Then suppose no putrefactions; no cold and poisonous vapors; no stagnant pools of water, no undrained lands, no unventilated or neglected places between the two poles; no weeds, no flies, bugs, worms, snakes, fish, very few animals, and an abundance of floral vegetation, fruitful vines, and various trees filled with beautiful singing birds. This picture, crude as it is, is an outline of Saturn, and it is not very far from being correct of Jupiter.

If our warm Gulf Stream can convey between hundreds and thousands of miles of cold water and icebergs, fragments of tropical vegetation, and fling them upon the bleak shores of Norway, what could not the entire Atlantic and Pacific oceans accomplish toward diffusing a tropical warmth and an Italian luxuriance of sky and atmosphere throughout the globe? Summer warmth would linger all winter in all our northern lakes, and also in the polar atmospheres, if it were not for the rapid loss of heat occasioned by our discordant and swift air currents. Violent winds very rapidly extract both warmth and moisture, and leave behind them electrical coldness and half-dead masses of fluids and solids.

Now I observe that all bodies of water on Saturn are warm, although the tides thereof are consistent with her axial rotation ; and, with the exception of one vast ocean north of her equator, the same remark is true also of Jupiter. And all this is true, and much more of far greater interest; because of certain solar, and planetary, and motional influences, which I have either hinted at or generally explained.

All this digression seemed indispensable to a just understanding of what is to follow. We will now resume our subject: The high-minded inhabitants of the exterior planets.

It has already been shown that the internal of the outer world is a spiritual world. In Jupiter and Saturn this reality is an every-day observation and experience. The people there, owing to their exceeding refinement, purity and interiority, are in constant fellowship with what we erroneously term "spirits," *i. e.*, with individuals who were once in physical bodies, and who, by the triumphal gateway of death, have entered upon their celestial pilgrimage. The atmospheric rarefications are perfect and most delightful to this end ; by which the most interior breathing is universally experienced. And the social elements and enjoyments are as high and harmonious as they are in many portions of the solar-system side of the Second Sphere. A soft, hazy, magnetic atmosphere, like that of the fairest Italian skies, and something remotely like our golden October, covers the landscape with an unutterable loveliness. But, seen internally, with clairvoyant eyes, all this is a thousand fold more lovely and attractive.

And now, for the first time, I have acquired knowledge of the verity that there is a spiritual population upon Jupiter and Saturn consociating and harmoniously intermingling with the almost spiritual, yet natural, inhabitants thereof. And here let it be recorded that a similar consociation will, in the future good time coming, be an actual experience on earth. But this is a prospect hardly comprehensible by our thoroughly materialistic and now exceedingly skeptical humanity.

The diagram No. 5, connected with this chapter, is designed to illustrate, however crudely, the appearance of the Summerland to the natural (yet interior-seeing) inhabitants of the planets under consideration.

It is but recently that I discovered that the orbits of these triune worlds pass through the heavens *over* the northern edge of the spiritual zone. Mars moves in an orbit which, when at his greatest distance from us, conveys him through the upper sky directly over the shore of the zone nearest to the earth. (In the accompanying diagram these planets may be imagined at the right hand side.) Its inhabitants, looking out upon the wonders of space, would see the Summerland somewhat as it appears in the accompanying representation. Planets in our system beyond Jupiter and Saturn, like Uranus and Neptune, together with all their remoter and more volatile relatives, are each visible like suns when in the aphelion of their orbits. To all the people who live upon the inhabitable planets, the Summerland is what "sunny Italy" is to an American; only the celestial Italy is millions of times more understandable and accessible in point of time.*

It has been remarked with what lightning quickness a telegram may be received from some spiritual person-

---

* (See p. 173 "Stellar Key;" also read what is said on p. 163.)

7

(No. 5.)   THE SUMMERLAND BELT, AS IT APPEARS TO THE INHABITANTS OF MARS.

age in response to a mental wish or prayer! If the flight of light is admitted to be about one hundred and eighty-six thousand miles a second, and that it consumes less than seventeen minutes to fly one hundred and ninety millions of miles—or as far again as the vast distance between the earth and the sun—if all this be admitted, then we ask: What time does the tide of the celestial magnetic river require to flow from the earth to the furthest point of the orbit of Mars? This is the distance traversed by earth-born and death-born voyagers to the nearest locality in the Summerland. One hour and twenty-five minutes is the shortest, and four hours and one-half is the longest time I have any knowledge of; and this, then, must at present be my only reply to this question. But the voyage of four hours and thirty minutes had, as I well understood at the time, a destination very far removed from localities frequently and mostly sought by persons going from earth.

If you can conceive of the universe as the perfect expression of an all-loving Mother and of an all-wise Father—if you can make a part of your daily existence the noble conception that the more perfect your intuition of principles the nearer you are to the heart and soul of things—then, naturally, these revelations of the Univercœlum will appear to you not only as possible and probable, but as *certainties*, like the shining of the sun and the twinkling of stars.

CHAPTER VIII.

REALITY OF LIFE IN THE SUMMERLAND.

HAVE I not sufficiently stored your mind with conceptions of magnitudes and distances? And may we not now intelligently approach nearer to the *actual* beyond the tomb? The gates between the stars are ajar, the ever-flowing river is prepared to convey you in perfect safety to the higher shore: Why, then, may you not accompany me to an exalted, interior place of observation? Come, let us look and see! and let us listen and hear !

But, first, let us inquire : Why should men's minds thoughtlessly surrender all ideas of a spiritual existence to utter obscurity, or to unreasoning faith ? Or, rather, why do not mankind use as much reason, and why are they not as logical, when thinking about the next world, as when thinking of the present ? In yet other words : Why do you, involuntarily, exert your mind to make the spiritual, *unnatural ?* The true answer is, first, because the mind is ordinarily inclined to mystify, and, second, because you have been taught to think of the after-death life as something supernatural, and, therefore, as an existence absolutely unhuman and inconceivable.

Swedenborg, laboring under the prepossessions of supernaturalism, although often a telescopic seer, but mainly and habitually an impressionist, and in contact with both worlds at the same time (which is impracticable), taught that time and space in the spiritual world *differed* from all human experience of them in this world. *Distances* after death, he said, were caused by dissimilarities in the life and affections; and time was longer or shorter, according to vital and affectional changes in the individual; thus annihilating both time and space, except so far as they are a part of subjective, not objective, appearance and experience. But in other respects Swedenborg recognized the perfect tangibility and naturalness of the spirit-land. He even went so far as to perpetuate, beyond the grave, the individual's special earthly surrounding circumstances; also his habits and daily associations; so that, he affirms, many a man, after death, does not yet know that he is dead, but seems to be living on exactly as before. Thus Swedenborg, for thirty years, mingled the natural and the supernatural—the reasonable and the incomprehensible; because (see the chapter on " Consciousness," in the first part of this volume) he undertook the impossible task of practically and constantly living in and reporting both worlds at the same time. This resulted, as such a mixture always must result, in projecting and interblending one world with the other.

The simple truth is always reasonable and sublime. And, concerning this question, the truth is, that, as to logical coherency, the Summerland is this rudimental

Earth-land continued. But, being far more interior and infinitely more refined in every form and in each external particular, it follows that parts of it resemble Saturn's scenery more than ours; while other sections, unspeakably more perfect, exceed in harmony and loveliness anything known or imagined upon this or any other planet in the universe.

Nevertheless, as regards the questions of distance and duration, or space and time, all interior or metaphysical thinkers will concede that there is a special sense in which they are exclusively expressions of states and changes of the spiritual consciousness; even as there is a sense or a degree in which "whatever is, is right;" but inasmuch as you cannot conceive of the origin of something out of nothing, or the existence of effects without preëxistent causes, or of a physical world of matter which is "no matter," but only a sensation or an illusion of the mind; so you cannot conceive of "another world" without its own appropriate sceneries, continents, climates, societies, brotherhoods, religions, governments, and where the inhabitants can have no other sense of eternity than the flowings of "time," and no other sense of infinity than the successions of "space."

Concerning this problem of time and space and numbers in the spiritual world, I am moved to ask the reader's attention to the last chapter in the volume, "Death and the After-Life," wherein is an account (by J. Victor Wilson) of the great pear-shaped "Isle of Akropanamede," and also of the wondrous temple of antiquities called "Aggameda." The Isle is described as most beautiful, and as populated by the "Brother-

hood of Plana de Alphos," whose members are engaged
in greatest works of benevolence and art. There is a remarkable description given of the architectural form and dimensions of the temple. It reminded me of the great temple of Solomon; yet it is exceedingly unlike it. But inasmuch as the Order of Masons and Christian scholars have figured out the shape and size of the ancient King's temple; also as some have given us the dimensions of Noah's Ark, etc., the thought occurred to me one day to ask my friend Loomis, a mathematician, to kindly favour me with a calculation of the Isle and the Temple, on the basis of the (to me) vague and complicated description imparted by the communicator. And the following is the result of his calculations: The temple has twenty-one wings, and in each wing seven mansions, making a total of one hundred and forty-seven. From this estimate it is shown that of domes and avenues, including central figures, there are twenty-one thousand six hundred and nine; the number of square furlongs covered by the entire templed structure, is four hundred and fifty-three thousand seven hundred and eighty-nine; and the dimensions of the vast Isle itself, in English square miles, are nine billion seven hundred and five million nine hundred and twenty-nine thousand and five hundred and one; and the numbers of men, women and children composing that noble Brotherhood, are one billion three hundred and eighty-six millions five hundred and sixty thousand seven hundred and eighty-six.

In regard to these figures, my friend in a note says: "I hand you these computations about the Isle of Akropanamede, which I think are *nearly* correct, although they may be considered more curious than useful." My reply was: " Your computations, if nearly correct, are useful as a means of *enlarging* men's minds concerning the immensity of the next human world, ' not built with hands, eternal in the heavens.' " And in order to emphasize this point, I asked him to favor me with some familiar comparisons; and he furnished me with the following calculations: " The Isle is considerably more than two thousand five hundred times the size of Europe, or more than eight hundred times the size of Africa—over one thousand times the size of North America, or about six hundred times the size of Asia. It is a country more than ninety-eight thousand miles square, or is equal to a Circle over one hundred and ten thousand miles in diameter.

" A line to measure the diameter would pass more than four times around the Earth, and this is measuring *only one Island* ' of an unnumbered host that diversifies the geography of the Summerland ! ' "

" The above comparisons," adds Mr. Loomis, " with familiar continents and with square and circular territory, are approximately correct, and the result of considerable care. I think that the dimensions of Isle and Temple deduced from Victor Wilson's statement is correct." *

The flashing rivers of light flow out of the darkness of distance. They surge, with pulses of undying music. Far away they flow among the flower-covered lands in our Heavenly Home. Overhead behold the forever rolling suns, and the ceaselessly turning planets.

---

* The outline of the domes, etc., of this great temple is quite imperfectly set forth on the left hand of diagram No. 5.

Through the boundless dome forever sweep the dazzling comets, enveloped in glowing splendors, like the flaming angels of God. Like a glorious dream arise the fragrances of millions of the loveliest flowers. A delightful crystalline light, subdued by the shadows of overhanging trees, spreads everywhere from the bosom of the rivers. Broad and grand is the landscape on every side. Mountains filled with immortal splendors; among them the homes of unnumbered Brotherhoods. Stars rise and set, like suns and moons, over very remote lands. Beautiful birds, bright representatives of affections, pour their music through the soft summer air, making even the sweet-breathed roses tremulous, and sending musical throbbings through the fragrant hearts of whitest lilies. Mounts and streams glow with the warmth of overflowing love. And the laughing rivers shine with the deathless light of divine wisdom.

Behold! there is something of importance, situated on the right hand, near the river that flows earthward. "Invisible!" you exclaim. What impression do you receive? Oh, the beautiful warm world! The fruit-laden trees and the heavenly groves are dwelling-places for the children of God; and the velvety moss-covered ground is a life-imparting floor beneath their beautiful feet. And yet, listening, do you not hear? There is there, a high school, a college, a university. There is a vast congregation of persons associated with artistic, literary, and scientific attractions. They are bound together by grateful and profound recollections. Mental freedom, graceful moral culture, scientific knowledge, and free discussion characterize this august organization. There

7*

is an inner group among them whose use is to report tidings frequently received from a more interior universe. A beautiful and accomplished goddess is the presiding divinity.

Centuries ago most of them lived on earth—in Greece, Rome, Germany, England, France, Scotland, Italy. It is a very ancient association, and yet see how youthful the wisest appear! Ah! there are recent arrivals from the earth—clergymen, editors, artists, writers, lawyers, statesmen—who, strange as it may seem, really appear *older* than those who lived in the days of Plato and Pythagoras. The new arrivals seem heavy—of the earth, earthy; some of them jerk and jest; some display actual folly and great inferiority by manifesting importance and highmindedness and authority, in the presence of their superiors; and thus most of them easily take outside rank in this celestial University.

Now you behold the gracefulness of best-mannered and most unfolded people. Persons you observe naturally act from their thoughts; thoughts spring out of feelings; feelings arise from their private spiritual condition. Graceful manners are more beautiful than handsome faces or glittering garments. What a charmed Association is this heavenly host! They gracefully aid all visitors and the new-comers; and with equal grace they help mankind universally.

Children throng and play among the blooming groves in the rosy background. Their tender imaginations are fed and nurtured in this natural home of pets and poets. There you behold many associations of mothers watching over and waiting for their unascended children. They lean their faces with sweetest touching affectionateness against the laughing little beauties; and they seem to be half-listening for infant tones and looking for dimples in faces long remembered. But yet (oh, how wisely!) they love and laugh with these happy hearts; and, although thinking most lovingly of *their own*, they nevertheless unrestrainedly join the glad groups with joy and song. The rich significance of the woman soul, as angel friend and mother is poured like elemental wines into every child's bosom. But behold! Every childish face and eye is now lovingly, yearningly looking with a touching, adoring familiarity (as the highest angels are supposed to look at God!) toward a lovely lady whose very presence is a beauty and a benediction, and whose beaming face is quickened and radiant with a divine illumination. * * * "Ma-Abo-sha" is the name I have just heard. Did you not hear it? What does it mean? "Mother of the gods!" is whispered through the tranquil heavens. Angel mother! I behold your holy families all along the distant slopes of the musical mountains. Where *you* are, there are no lost little ones; where you are, *there* are no orphans and no one is homeless; all are free and happy.

A gathering of remarkably familiar-looking women and men you see at the rear of the great association. And there, with three strangers, is one woman I have certainly met years ago. For I recall the fluent glance of her blue eyes, and the delicate, yet downright and sturdy, perceptiveness of her temperament. She stands near her husband, and she also stands for woman. She is graceful, intense, severe and fearless; yet quite pleasingly social and exquisitly feminine.

Hark! There is a conversation. * * * (The last sentence was written about thirty minutes ago.) * * * The woman's husband is a man whose great childlike face you may have seen in New York; he was not long ago one of the busiest of popular editors. Standing behind him is his golden-haired son. In an off-hand, earnest, conversational manner, he is now addressing the group.

"There are objections to such eleemosynary institutions," he says; "and for nearly forty years I used my pen and voice against them. Institutional schemes perpetuating poverty float over society like a solemn cloud that leaves a sense of thunder. I have discussed this question with my divine paternity pastor; who is still at it in one and another way. New York could support its poor in luxurious idleness out of the money derived from licenses granted for the sale of intoxicating liquors. A million men, women and children in the metropolis taxed and kept in misery to sustain seventy-four hundred drinking saloons. The island, from end to end, is threatened with moral darkness and consequent social madness. Alcoholic hells blaze with the punitive fires that may blight religion and overthrow an admittedly corrupt government. Charity is an evanescent pity expressing itself hastily in alms. Build hospitals for the increasing army of non-productive mendicants, and cover the idle and ignorant and drunken with benevolent institutions, and the result will be the poor and the indolent will forever remain on earth. Had I to repeat my busy life, I would rather consign myself voluntarily to a penitentiary, or work with lamp and pick in a coal mine, than lose an opportunity, if I had one, of putting a stop to the manufacture and sale of those poverty-generating beverages. Ignorance and violence, incessant wretchedness in cold, hunger and rags, pecuniary embarrassments, miserable dependence, involving heart-rending sacrifices of wives and husbands, children and homes, often ending in bloodshed and pestilence, or famine—all follow the daily use of Alcohol. Let them discuss the duty and the beauty of charity, either private or eleemosynary—it will do no lasting harm. It shall be my duty, however, to suggest and to insist upon an organization of the industries, with farms and manufactories for Associations of the homeless, idle, ignorant, thriftless." * * * * * (A few sentences in the foregoing were lost in the act of listening; but the main part of the conversational speech as above reported was psychophonically heard.)

Looking southward do you not observe, beneath the fruit-bearing trees, an assemblage, a nucleus of some vast congregation, of very different characters? Does it seem possible that they were once of the earth earthy? Can you believe that time was when each of them walked upon the burning sands of Egypt? Would you think they had once heard the desert's call and the river's ripple in the Oriental part of our earth? It is true. They lived before Homer taught in song; before were built the hundred gates of Thebes; before Pompey's pillar was erected; before Cephrenes and Cheops planned the pyramids; before the magi of the earliest kings acquired the power of holding converse with spirits.

They lived in the dawn of the pyramid-building age. Osiris, Apis, Isis were reigning divinities; and the star-strewn sky was the field of their contemplations. They were the first of earth's astronomers.

Behold that central figure! He is an embodiment of youth and beauty. (Yet older than the pyramids!) His right hand holds the most ancient symbol of universal harmony, the lyre; his long hair flows back, and a sacred wreath adorns his fair brow. His adorable person is religiously regarded as specially divine. He is the prince Apollo among the many recognized authorities in this particular brotherhood. He is the recognized leader among many peers in this celestial association—a prince, a discoverer, a prophet, a warrior against wrong, a saviour of wanderers, the bountiful and quick promoter of Light, Health, Poetry, Art, Music.

This angel-prince, with his associates, first aided Poland. They helped that now mournful country to become (four hundred years ago) one of the noblest and most cultivated countries of Europe. *Köpernik* (who by the Latins was called Copernicus) was born and cultured under this prince's special guardian superintendence. Under his inspiring and magnanimous influence the youthful Polander made rapid growth in a spiritual direction. In 1503 he divided his time between the duties of the ministry, in acts of charity, and in studying the system of the stars. As Moses loved and sought the solitudes of Sinai, so this spiritual man loved the retirements of the Carpathian mountains. He at length erected a tower for the double purpose of interior communion and astronomical research. And now commenced the manifestations and benefits of this prince's guardianship. He succeeded in so illuminating the reasoning faculties of Copernicus (or Köpernik) that, before the invention of the telescope, and in advance of the inductive demonstrations of Galileo, he plainly unfolded the substantial truth concerning the underlying principles of planetary revolution.

"Ha-pri-a-nos" comes into my ear, and into my thoughts the meaning—"Morning Ambassador;" which is the true name of this august spiritual prince.

Continuing to observe this beautiful company, I discover that they still have beneficent designs upon Poland and Russia. They stimulate astronomical research and all the finest branches of educational advancement. They are angel-ministers out of the sky to whomsoever can receive aid from them. Ambassadors of peace among professional warriors; bearers of glad tidings to the bowed down and mournful; messengers of good words, passing to and fro between heaven and the people of the North. Their system of religion is sidereal. The starry realm, overhead and all around them, is the temple of the Infinite. Their ideas of heaven, like their views of hell, are profoundly astronomical. A local heaven or a local hell, they say, is "impossible." For they reason that the universe is as profoundly deep as it is high; that in every direction it is equally boundless and inter-coherent; that nowhere is there any place wholly and exclusively appropriated to either the punishment of vice or the reward of virtue.

These are some of the doctrines of a people who lived and died on earth prior to the immemorial pyramids! There is among them *not one* "undevout astronomer!"

Far away westward (see diagram No. 5) you behold

the dim outline of a great forest. It is the heterogene-
ous wilderness of an almost innumerable multitude of
Diakka, who may be said to have no religion, and to be
structurally deficient or weakened in their sense of
moral responsibility.*

Some of them are quite learned, quite intellectual,
and polished in certain manners. There! listen, and
you may hear what one of their brightest orators is now
uttering: "The non-existence of matter in space is
a fixed fact. It is another fixed fact that there are no
facts. Unable to conceive that mind is everlasting, or
that it has any power to resist dissolution in time, sensi-
ble men wisely accept as their destiny a final quietus.
A formless, unknown mass of mentality is their notion
of God; and to be at last *lost in it*, is the sole aspiration
of the biggest intellects. Gigantic attempts of little
giants in Monotheism are charming; so are the panthe-
istic failures of devout pigmies. It is fun for twenty-
five centuries to make an intellectual simpleton to imagine himself an immortal God with a universal mission.
He is immensely happy! So are we, for we are his in-
structors. He obeys our will by out-growing in a single
day all the majesty of Cæsar and all the wit of Charle-
magne. Shakspeare can't hold a candle to light his pen
in poetry. Our pupil talks sonorously about science,
and stridently of philosophy. The mysteries of creation
flee at his approach. He, like us, grows egotistic and
pluckily independent! Self-denial for any purpose, a
conscience with a spur, or love poised upon virtue, he,

---

* For a description of these peculiar independents see the Author's
work entitled " The Diakka, and their Earthly Victims."

with us, rejects as even more useless and absurd than Jonah's gourd which grew and perished in a single night."

You observe that this oratorical Diakka is continuing to discourse to the increasing multitude about him. But it is the utterance of one who sees nothing nobler, purer, higher than the gratification of evanescent impulses. Although in the Summerland, and although all who compose that great wilderness of independents and egotists were once in human bodies, yet it is true that they realize almost nothing of the divine loveliness and angelic purity which surround them and work for their advancement on every side. What a field for missionary labor is here prepared for those who will erelong leave the earth to unite with like disposed persons in the supernal associations, to exercise their benevolence and most powerful influence to reach and convert these brilliant and cunning spiritual gypsies!

*　*　*　*　*　*　*　*

An hour ago we terminated our seeing and hearing; and now, having returned to the ordinary condition, our chapter is ended. In the next I shall record many more things upon questions recently awakened.

CHAPTER IX.

A NATURAL HOME NOT MADE WITH HANDS.

THE physical heavens are literally loaded with perspective anomalies. Paradoxical scenes are visible on every hand, and (apparently) inconsistent motions are in every point of the radius displayed. Moons seem to be revolving about their primaries in the wrong way, and with varying, fantastic velocities ; while great sun-stars, with their countless trains of planets and inferior bodies, appear (or *seem*) to be wandering away into the empty abysses of space.

The Milky Way Galaxy, for example, presents itself to the human eye as a figure closely resembling the letter Y stretching across the sky at almost right angles with the position of the general system. Space-islands and empty air-abysses, surrounded with stars, are visible in some directions ; and elsewhere you see vast fertile star-islands, surrounded by oceans of unoccupied space. All this gives the impression that the universe is empty and sterile in places, whilst in other localities yielding an abundant crop of worlds.   (Something of these anomalies are indicated in the accompanying diagram.)

Let it be understood that the external appearance of the sky, to an inhabitant of earth, is largely a perspective illusion.   Men pertinaciously adhere to the mis-impressions and the consequent deceptions which they derive from the crude use of their senses.   It is not easy for a man to believe that stellar contradictions frequently arise from the *appearances* impressed perspectively upon the ordinary spectator.

For illustration, the Y-shaped Galaxy is an appearance only, made upon our eyes because of the exceedingly sidewise position we on earth occupy relatively to the great star-belt.   We here exist upon the confines of the universe composing the sixth circle.   Therefore, although light is a fleet traveller, we have not yet lived long enough on earth to receive a ray of light from the more interior circles of suns which occupy what to our bodily senses and telescopes are but yawning chasms of utter nothingness!   And it is because we contemplate the exceedingly remote Milky Way cluster from a side position, that it seems to be divided in places; and it is also because of this that it nowhere suggests (what it really is) a part of a girdling system of suns and inhabitable worlds.

In order to give some faint idea of relative proportions and distances we must present a section of the Summerland as a strip of indefiniteness, stretching horizontally beneath the immeasurable, overhanging circles of constellations, or star-fields, which contain many clusters of constellations.   On the extreme right hand you observe our Sun (S.) and the dependent planets and satellites scattered about; while on the left you behold the great solar mother, Alcyone (A.), toward which our system is now travelling.

To an inhabitant of any one of the myriads of worlds possessed with the adequate telescopic vision, the spiritual belt appears to be thick, or thin, or straight, or spherical, each appearance being in accordance with the perspective phenomena generated from his point of observation. For example, the space occupied by the Milky Way seems to mankind to be comparatively narrow and thin, with stars in places; yet there are in those thin places bright bodies whose diameters, not to imagine their circumferences, are not less than one hundred and twenty billions of miles! Let this be remembered reverentially when you gaze upon the thin-looking Milky Way. And you will also bear in mind that the flashing light consumes hundreds of years in reaching the earth from the Pleaides; and that our sun, which speeds through space at the rate of eight miles a second, requires eighteen million and two hundred thousand years to journey *once* around its parental centre (A.), which is visible in the firmament above. It may also be profitable to remember that if a man could walk one hundred miles a day, from the moment of his birth to that of his death, he would consume eighty years in walking once around our familiar sun! These serious reflections will prepare your mind for the entertainment of enlarged views of the extent and possessions of our Heavenly Home.

A word more concerning perspective observation. Objects nearest you appear to move rapidly, while remote objects appear very slowly to alter their positions

—the furthest appearing to be almost absolutely stationary. For example, walk in a field beside a grove of
scattering tall pines. As you advance, keeping your
eyes upon them, they seem continually to be altering
their relative positions. Those standing nearest you
seem to be moving rapidly, and frequently intersecting
and sometimes eclipsing similar trees behind, while
those at the greatest distance from you seem to be
almost fixed. And their top branches seem to sweep
over a large expanse of sky. But in reality the trees
are stationary, and you alone make the movement and
changes.

The earth's distance from the Spiritual Sphere alters
according to its orbital position in its annual journey
around the sun. Sometimes the space is only about
fifty millions of miles across. At other times, when the
earth is near the opposite end of the ellipse, it is nearly
four times more distant. But over our greatest distance
the sunlight can travel in sixteen minutes. And although, as I have already shown, the tide of the celestial river sometimes flows as fast as light, and in certain
localities even faster, yet the shortest time occupied is
one hour and twenty-five minutes in a bodily journey
from earth to the nearest shore. Of course to localities
more remote—which by affinity belong to, and are
sought by, the earth's inhabitants after death—the distance is proportionally increased, sometimes to nearly
two hundred millions of miles.

We have now and thus arrived at an important answer to many strange facts and curious questions. It is
a fact, for instance, that we rarely obtain intelligence
directly from persons who lived in the most ancient

ages of human history. It is a fact, too, that many modern philosophers have not given, since their death, an atom of evidence that they even now exist. They have departed this life, and not having spoken, with conclusive power and with manifest presence, they seem "dead" in the literal sense of that appalling term. Millions and billions and trillions of persons once on earth *seem* to be literally lost in space or annihilated. For they have made no sign of life! These are really startling facts.

I might now appeal to the dry science of mathematics to enliven this progressive problem. But the human mind does not comfortably live on conceptions of distances and magnitudes. If it could live on such a figurative diet, if it could refresh itself upon the weary wastes of mathematical calculations, I could now furnish every hungry mind with an inexhaustible feast. And this great feast of figures would answer many of the questions raised by these fearfully suggestive facts. But we will not spread the table with oppressive estimates. Instead, we give you a few affirmations based upon figures already presented.

You remember the estimated and accepted distance in miles between the Pleiades and our solar system? And you recall the almost eternity of time consumed by our sun in travelling once around that remote constellation? Remembering and recalling all this (although you and I know that no human mind can *realize* the fact), you will now try to imagine another fact, that *that* inconceivable distance is one of the favorite journeys taken by many of the brightest minds who have lived on earth. It is accomplished both by land and stream, and also by atmospheric excursions. It is, so to speak, the grand fashionable trip across the heavenly Atlantic and through the continent of the celestial Europe. And it is very frequently undertaken from very similar motives—to gratify taste, curiosity, the eternal love of newness, and, incidentally, for ends of best uses and culture. Here, we say that three thousand miles intervene between the two shores of the ocean. Time is consumed in the journey, and more time is required to write letters, and to communicate with loving friends left behind. Five hundred years are occupied in the trip of *light* between those not very remote clusters and our human eyes! What do you think, then, is the length of time required by leisurely or industrious artists, astronomers, florists, geologists, investigators of all branches, theologians, poets, magicians, lovers of nature, conjugal lovers, missionaries, teachers of every religion, and the leading minds of every country and government—yea, how much time (how much of eternity!) do such persons and such mentalities require to make a single journey through some of the distant mansions of the Father's infinite temple?

"But," you exclaim, "does a SPIRIT require *space* to exist in? And *time* to go from place to place?" Absolutely, *yes!* "Thoughts" concerning a subject may be said to be inconceivably rapid. But this is not true; for they take *time*, and the very seconds thereof can be and have been correctly numbered. But a spirit is not a thought. Spirit is not an IDEA. Spirit is the *nucleus* of a man, or of a woman—a personal, bodily, substantial existence; and like every other body, *space* is indispensable to its presence, and *time* is required for its movement from one place to another. What men term Attraction and Repulsion, Gravitation, etc., are but the names of specific *motions* in what is called "matter;" so the term Spirit is but the name of an invisible "substance," the nucleus for the organization of less refined elements about it, poised upon the pivotal will-power, and thus becomes an individual as natural and as human after death as we are after birth. (In other connections I have given other answers to some of these questions, but none that is inconsistent with the foregoing.)

Let us digress for a few moments, just here, to fix with immense emphasis, if such an effect upon your judgment be possible, that in these chapters language is used, for the most part, with its fullest and most *definite* significance.

When I say that the interval between our sun and the star-cluster Pleiades is "inconceivable," that is exactly what is meant. No intellect can possibly contain the stupendous fact as a *realization;* although it may be computed accurately, and presented in figures. This denial of your incapacity may shock your pride, but it will enlarge and strengthen your candor; and it may give you some correct impressions concerning what is meant by the terms "eternal progression." When I say that this or that is "incomprehensible," the term is used with its exact meaning. Think a moment, and you will acknowledge that, while you may say from memory that the apparently empty space between the earth and the sun is ninety-five millions of miles, your mind does not contain the statement *as a consciousness.** It

---

* In this volume no attempt at strict calculations of times, magnitudes, and distances, is made ; because there is as yet no positive

is solely and mechanically a matter of intellect, which works among facts and figures as a mechanic works with his tools; next, the statement enters into your memory, which is a mental writing-desk well supplied with pigeon-holes for the safe-keeping of important memoranda; but your consciousness cannot intuitively accept it as a self-evident realization. All your soul receives from the intellectual statement is a feeling of an oppressively immense "distance." And this feeling is capable of an indefinite expansion, until it begins to urge the intellect to contemplate the incomprehensible.

The incomprehensible is a thought which passes in society under the name of "infinity," which starts (in the child mind) with a few inches or a mile, and then progresses with experience until thousands grow into millions, millions into billions, billions into trillions, &c.; or until numbers multiply beyond the possibility of mathematical expression, and then, when the word is rightly used, the intellectual result is called the "in-finite."

From this digression I return to the subject of human occupation, travelling, and progression, in our next natural Home among the holy stars.

We sometimes read—especially in some of the earlier newspapers and pamphlets devoted to "communications" with the departed—of intelligence being received through mediums from spirits in the fifth, sixth,

---

knowledge among astronomers; some say that the sun is less than ninety-five millions; others that it is more distant; but the greatest discoveries concerning the nature and speed of light, and, therefore, as to the magnitude and distances of the sun and planets, are erelong to dawn upon the world.

8

or even "seventh sphere." *　But how does this claim seem to you while you fail to *realize* the interval (of both time and space) between the earth and our sun's great mother, Alcyone?　What do you think when you are told this truth, namely: The stellar distance just mentioned, when compared with the whole magnitude of the Summerland, is the distance between New York and Buffalo compared to the earth's whole circumference?　Now think how many thousands, yea, how many millions of human beings are born, bred, matured, and buried within the limited space which separates these two American cities!　How many men and women—some of them very high in society and culture—who live a long life without travelling three thousand miles from Paris, London, Liepzig, St. Petersburg, or even one hundred leagues from the country and localities in which they were born and nurtured?　Suppose now that, instead of dying at the end of three-score and ten years, these same men and women had lived through as many centuries: In what respect, or from what new causes, · would they become greater travellers?　How *far* from the home of their childhood did the earth's early tribes or races journey during hundreds and thousands of years?　America, so to speak, is a discovery of yesterday!

And while I write, although the earth has been inhabited tens upon tens of thousands of years, and real human progress has been steadily realized during all these vast stretches of time; yet no human feet have ever stood upon the globe's north centre, and many

---

* In the Appendix this question will receive additional attention.

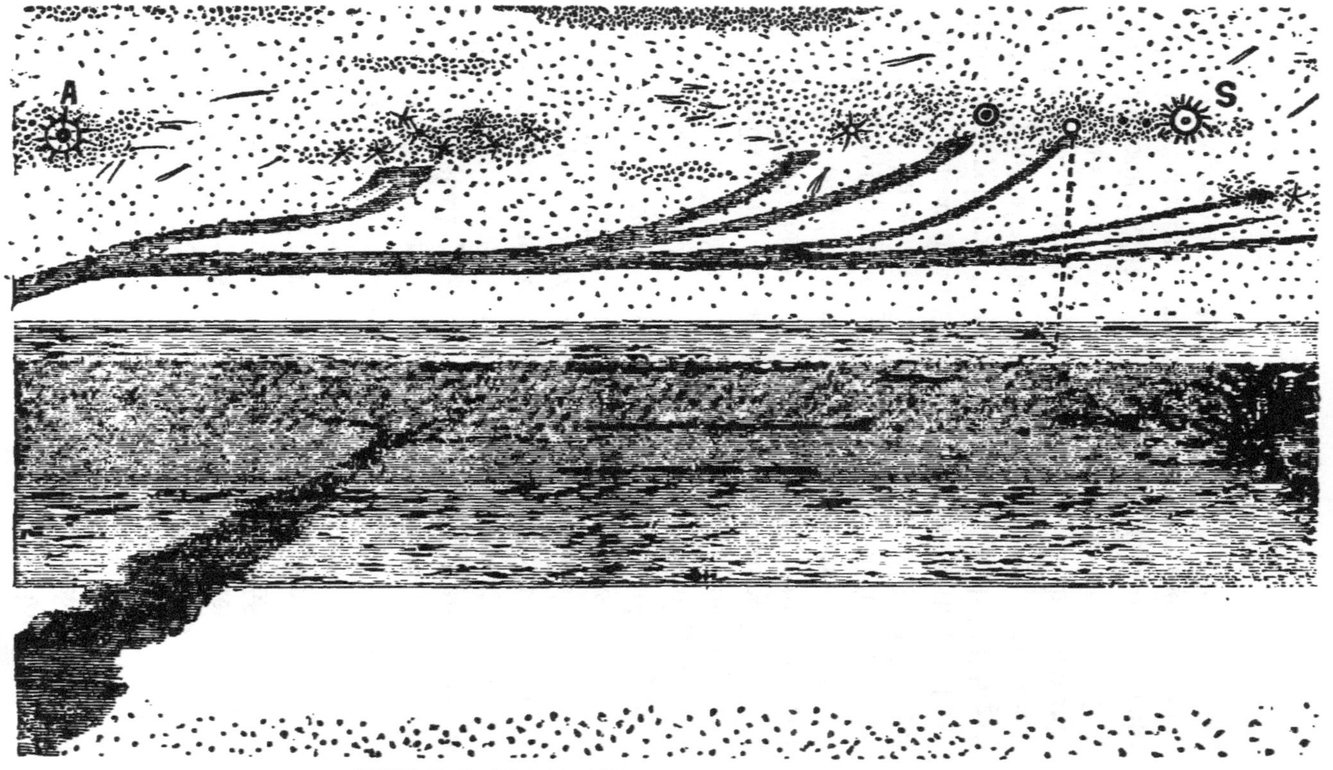

OUTLINE OF THE SUMMERLAND WITHIN THE MILKY WAY.

mountains have never yet been climbed by man, and millions of square miles of our common earth are yet to be sought and explored !

With these fundamental facts in human nature and in human history, and from which human nature as long as it shall exist will never radically depart, I ask (those who question me) what think you of your proclivities and opportunities to be sufficiently "entertained" and "occupied" and "advanced," after you shall have become a resident of the Supernal Sphere?

You now very naturally ask: "What shall we do when we shall progress, become perfect, and *know* it all?" My reply is: Your question originates in a lack of comprehending thought. *You shall never reach the era when your mind can comprehend itself!* You may *now* realize only ordinary mental weakness and intellectual emptiness. Or, if you be a physiologist, or a phrenologist, or a chemist, or an anthropologist, or a scientific explorer and an expounder, why you may even to-day affirm, in all candor, that " you know it all." I tell you, nevertheless, that, in very truth, *you think and talk like a child.* You manifest a child's folly and a child's unblushing conceit. And I tell you further, that, after you have lived your best life in the "Second Sphere" for as many centuries as this earth has been inhabited, you will " put away childish (foolish) things " out of your affections and understanding ; and then, having really become " a little child," in the heavenly sense of the word, you will say : " Come to me, comfort me, O Mother of the Universe! lead me to thy magical mirror, wherein I may behold at least the reflections of my ignorance. And, O Father of the Universe, assist me and strengthen me, direct and control me, and let me forsake my littleness, and show me how to seek for true knowledge and wisdom.   I would love all loveliness, and I would take delight in the truth.   Come to me, O Friend of my earth-life! O Life of my youth! show me the sunlight. and the starlight as they exist in you.   Lead me into the sacred shade; dwell with me in the fountains; stay with me in the sunshine; wander with me through the mansions of glory; walk with me in your boundless gardens; teach me to lift up the despairing; and to strengthen the weak. Vast is my knowledge of my ignorance.   Oh, lead me out of this darkness!   I have magnified myself until I realize my commonness and my littleness.   Oh, let me not dwell in this darkness while the universe is flooded with light."

Astounding revelation to make to the reader, who, being a full-blooded impatient American, intends to enter upon a headlong life of lightning progression immediately after death!

Ah, I now discern the cause of your astonishment. It is because of your *real* ignorance concerning what is meant by eternal progression.   Now, being an American-born reader, I know this assertion of your "ignorance" will be hurled back with a great force upon me.   You think that you are bound to "get all you can;" and that your mental treasury is so constructed that you will be always able "to keep all you get."   And by this straightforward accumulativeness you will at some time, in the great future, acquire all the love, and wisdom, and knowledge existing in God's universe—in short, that your mind and God's mind will, in possessions and attributes, be equals and compeers! Of course, logically speaking, as there will be no further possible progression, and as there will be nothing further to "entertain" or to "occupy" your full-blossomed powers, and lest the "time" may begin to hang too heavily upon your perfect spirit, why, to make the story short, you conclude to plunge into the bottomless vortex of central life, and to commit an eternal suicide! This destination, expressed in many forms of language, is what millions of mankind vaguely dread; and it is an "absorption" of the soul which thousands firmly believe, and religiously regard as the acme of perfect happiness.

Eternal progression of the individual, when justly comprehended, is—to speak paradoxically—a truth beyond all comprehension; which is another way of saying this: Eternity is an impossible conception, except as it is divided up into "times," just as Infinity is incomprehensible, except as it is divided up into "spaces." Therefore eternal progression means to a man's mind, and always must mean, an endless succession of periods, eras, or ages, through which his mind makes pilgrimages, retaining and maintaining his identity by memory of only the substance or essences of all his experiences; but perpetually losing memory of the details of every experience; thus forever keeping the universe new, his spiritual appetites for universal feeding forever healthy, and his aspirations eternally youthful towards the whole, and away through into all its countless parts and varieties. So the human mind, like the sun, has its aphelions and perihelions; it travels to the extreme of its orbit in one great Sphere; then it retraces its steps back to its centre; and then, planet-like, it starts immediately out upon another journey through the boundless fields of an unfathomable Univercœlum.

This chapter should give you the impression that no human mind can comprehend a millionth part of what there is to *see*, to *meet*, to *feel*, to *hear*, and to *know*, even in the next or Second Sphere; and that, so far as is yet known, no person born on earth has ever advanced beyond its inconceivably vast boundaries. But the Love, Will, and Wisdom focus of the Summerland is in sympathetic correspondence to the Great Positive Centre of the infinite whole. This is a focus of essential principles where all, when mentally prepared, may go for universal information. It is a focus of mental progression and spiritual truth; which must be *sought by love* and absorbed by wisdom; from which very extensive and correct knowledge of the possessions of far higher spheres may be derived.

To this spiritual sun, to this centre, I go for information; and by contact with it, while in the superior condition, I receive IMPRESSIONS.

CHAPTER X.

WONDERFUL SCENES IN THE SUMMERLAND.

THE principal object of these " Stellar Key " volumes is, first, to discuss the possibility and to demonstrate the certainty of an inhabitable zone *within* the starry heavens adapted to mankind's existence and progressive happiness after death; and second, by a few brief generalizations, to show the process whereby the constitution of that zone was evolved and incessantly fed by what I am impressed to term " humanized atoms ; " by which I mean those earthly materials which, having been suitably refined " in the mills of God," the highest of which is the human body, ascend to and become the actual foundation and formative substance of our Heavenly Home.

At this point a questioner appears with these problems :

" On page 107 of the ' Key ' is the following statement : ' Innumerable atoms arise and continually ascend from the bodies of persons composing the human family (not less than 800,000,000 tons *per annum*); atoms that float out into space in the rivers of ether, and enter into the constitution of the Summerland.   This process has been long known to seers.'

"It is also stated in the same work, p. 135, that ' the second sphere is the daguerreotype of earth ; the refined matter which ascends is prone to assume the forms from which it was liberated on earth. The scenery is more beautiful and ethereal.   Trees, fruits and flowers are not individualized ; that is, their emanations do not ascend to the spheres in an identified form, but their particles are more prone to assume such forms than any other.' *   *   *   *   *   *

"It is not stated how long the emanations from human forms and inanimate substances of the earth have been ascending to the spheres ; but if they are ascending now, the process must have been going on for an indefinite period—many ages—in the past.

"Assuming that there are 1,000,000,000 of human inhabitants on the earth, of all ages and sizes—probably not far from the actual number—and that their average weight is one hundred pounds each —probably a liberal estimate—their combined weight would be fifty million tons of two thousand pounds ; just one sixteenth part, if my estimate is correct, of the emanations annually given off from human bodies, to be floated away to the spheres.   How is this vast and rapid waste of human bodies supplied?   *   *   *   *   *   *

"Again, it may be reasonably assumed that the emanations from all other earthly substances, brutes, fowls, trees, flowers, minerals, etc., are at least equal to those from human bodies.   This would give *one thousand six hundred million tons* of substantial, though refined, matter annually transported from the earth to distant spheres and appropriated there ; a vast amount, even compared with the entire substance of the earth.   Is this waste supplied or returned to the earth in any manner?   If so, how, and from whence?

(Signed)   A. T. S."

Answer.—Let us first understand one another.   In the book "*Stellar Key*," when speaking of the atomic emanations ascending from the "human family," I did not intend that the reader should think that reference

8*

was made solely to the population of our particular earth. For the truth is that all of the races of men who are living on the several globes in our "island solar system," are equally and unreservedly *taxed*, physiologically speaking; and thus all human natures everywhere throughout the earths of the sixth circle are compelled, under the prompt demands of chemical laws (for these laws are merciless tax-gatherers), to deliver up with every tick of the watch a portion of their atomic substance. These universal and incessant emanations, like the ethereal dewdrops of insensible perspiration, in total weight cannot be less than eight hundred millions of tons per annum. And the speed and precision with which these taxes—these humanized atoms of elements in the human body—fly off to their celestial destinations, is far more wonderful than any miracle reported in Christianity. A series of chemical changes thus incessantly occur between every human body and the physical constitution of the Summerland! To my eyes they seem like a fire running along countless trains of gunpowder. And yet so perfectly and absolutely natural, so still, so inwrought and undeviatingly common (or ordinary) is all this, that not a person, unless sensitive as a medium or seeing as a clairvoyant, is at all conscious of any such wondrous chemical transactions in the universe about him.

Concerning the problem of "waste and supply" in Nature there is an immutable law, which should first be consulted. The rate at which nervous motor sensibility travels in your body this moment is about one hundred and eleven feet per second! Of course this rate of motion is different at different times in the same person; and in different individuals the speed is variable, owing in all cases to the prevailing temperature, and to the nature and extent of the exciting cause. (Therefore *thought*, which is the result of sensation, is *not* inconceivably rapid.) In some circumstances the vital force can travel over a nerve at the enormous rate of three hundred and fourteen feet per second. Now couple with this another fact, namely, that the universal familiar energy called electricity can speed away as stilly as a baby's breathing at the frightful rate of eighty-nine thousand five hundred miles per second, or more than three times around our great globe in a single beat of your pulse—with this fact, added to the first, can you not understand that it is just as easy for billions and trillions of tons of matter to hasten from the inexhaustible resources of the infinite immensity to the earth and to other earths, to the human family here and on other globes—just as easy, to say nothing of the scientific rationality of the proposition, as that a like quantity of refined and purified matter should emanate *from* the earth, and from the human family in general, and enter into the composition and deathless constitution of the supernal sphere?

In connection with this problem of waste and supply, I am frequently stopped with the questions: "How do the people—commonly called spirits—personally look, or appear, to an observer? Are they always *dressed?* And in what style? And, again, do they *eat?* If so, what is their food? and how do they perform their functions? And do they prolificate, bearing children," ect., etc.

Answers to many of these questions have already

been published, which I will not here repeat.*   But I have some important physiological facts to record, just here, which will cover a large field of curious vital truth, and may be of value in this world.

And first, in general, as to the law of progress or growth in matter and mind. Later teachers use the word "evolution." Take this law to guide you, and you can begin with a seed and follow it through successive evolutionary changes until it has ultimated into a full grown tree; or you may trace the series of progressive developments which occur between the primal cell, or ovum, and the perfectly unrolled physical organization.   This doctrine of universal spiral evolution, after waiting thirty years, is advocated by the ablest intellects.

In the progression of Nature, as I have before said—from the lowest living substance to the complex and final organization of man—everything follows the principle of evolution. The lowest is radical, because it is the root; the highest is fruition, because it is the perfect unfoldment. In the germ, or "protoplasm"—as the primal substance is called by the scientific Huxley—is deposited the properties and potencies necessary for the development and regulation of that particular organism, in its various progressive steps up the spiral ascent of Nature. The visible process is that of progressive development. And as all below man is thus regulated and unfolded, reason asks: "Why may not the *body* of the spirit follow the same divine principle?" If the

---

* See " Answers to Ever-recurring Questions; " also the " Penetralia," and several works by authors on Spiritualism.

material universe ripens up into the full-orbed organization of man, " Why may not man's spirit be likewise invested or clothed with the ultimate organs of evolution, with all defects eliminated ? "

Reason puts no questions which she is not capable of answering. The interior Sphinx puts no riddles she cannot herself solve. Reason, when in her superior condition, and the universal common sense of the world, affirm, that the continuation of human existence after death is no more improbable or wonderful than its continuation after birth. And moreover that the principle of progress is immortal; and *evolution* is its mode of action throughout eternal spheres; which, therefore, must yield the true explanation concerning the appearance of the *body* of the spirit in the Summerland.

Physiologists know that there are parts and organs in man's body, like certain cæcal appendages to the intestines, and like the spleen itself, which do not perform any important offices; in other words, they are the remnants of a *lower* stage of organism through which mankind have passed. And the time will come when, by the operations of the evolutionary law, these and other parts of the existing human form will be diminished and overcome and utterly destroyed. For do you not know that the animals are organic stepping-stones upon which minerals and vegetables ascend to the development of the physical man ?

> " See dying vegetables life sustain,
> See life dissolving vegetate again."

It is well known that since mankind's advent, many

species and varieties of animals have become extinct.
Now is it not as reasonable to believe that when the
human race shall have become sufficiently refined and
spiritualized to no longer need or feed upon animals,
they will all disappear from the globe? And may not
internal *parts* of the human body likewise disappear?
Animals are to the erection and completion of the
human kingdom what scaffoldings are to the construc-
tion of a dwelling. When the structure is finished the
builders remove the various instrumentalities, so that
other and higher artisans may proceed with the finer
works ; and after the gardens are prepared, the decora-
tions completed, and the furniture arrayed, it is then
natural to expect and welcome the angel of the house.
And if animals are man's indispensable predecessors
and subordinates, are they not fully entitled to human
sympathy and uniform kindness?

In the Summerland some of the vital organs and
other portions which are no longer needed, do not appear within the spiritual body. There are no fluids requiring kidneys; no negative or broken-down blood requiring pulmonary air cavities; no physical digestion
requiring such organs as stomach, liver and intestines ;
no propagation requiring the external organs of generation ; consequently, the body of the spirit appears,
both male and female, in the most perfect bodily shape,
preserving all the symmetry and intrinsic excellences
and ultimate likeness of our best-blossomed human
form ; which is sometimes clothed and sometimes not,
in accordance with the customs of the society, or the
peculiarities of the latitude in which they find their
habitations. But the ultimates of all the organs are

preserved in perfect form; and they perform spiritual uses corresponding to the natural body.*

With regard to their foods, and how they eat, etc., your attention is asked to the difference between a mortal body and the body incorruptible. The ultimates of the natural only exist in the spiritual. All incompleteness, all imperfection, all that is not of eternal use, is eliminated. There are hundreds and thousands of feet of threads in the mortal body, which are called *nerves* and also *cellular tissues*. These tissues are the natural protectors and the natural feeders of all the membranes, and of all the vital parts ; and to this end they also exist universally beneath the skin ; which is the seamless garment covering the entire living temple.

Now, having said so much as a basis, I come to my cardinal affirmation—that, throughout all the ages of eternity, all human (or angel) feeding and all breathing among the elements of eternal beauty and youth, is accomplished by and through the mediumship of what in the physical body we erroneously term the " nerves " and the cellular " tissues." Youth and health are eternal; because there is a perpetual exchange of these elements, causing and continually maintaining an everlasting equilibrium between the body and the spirit. Sickness, old age, death, can never be known where exists this perfect and just interchange, and this unalterable equilibrium.

In evidence of the possibility of what I have said, your memory and judgment are referred to a few ter-

---

* In the Appendix the reader will find the author's answer to an esteemed correspondent on this question.

restrial instances of cellular and nerve feeding. The
Seeress of Prevorst was a remarkable example, who
was under the protection of her heavenly guardians.
But do you not recall instances in our day and country,
where young women (because their nerves and tissues
are far finer than man's) have lived days, weeks, and
even months, without eating anything substantial, and
sometimes, also, wholly abstaining from drinking? Their
breathing, however, went on all the same, but, in some
cases, all the bodily functions were permanently suspended. And yet, because the patient partook of spiritual meat which only the angels know, the physical
body did not rapidly waste away, and the physiological
wonder grew among men, greater and greater, day by
day. These cases on earth are crude illustrations of
eating, drinking, and breathing, in the Summerland.

* * * * * * * *

Concerning wonderful scenes and structures.—Re-
suming our celestial observations, we pass beyond the
Diakka Reservation, where congregate the bright-witted,
the striving, the skeptical, the darkness loving, the sun-
set-haunted. We look beyond the color-line where the
dark luxuriance ceases and the reign of light and
loveliness begins. You behold a vast continent of what
may be called *Religiousness.*

We stand almost beneath the path in which our sun
rolls on its journey toward the Pleiades. The charac-
teristics of the landscape surprise you; for these realms
are unlike anything terrestrial. The far-away fields of
mossy green and twinkling gold, flowers, and the immense mansion-like chapels and pavilion-looking cathe-

drals, decorated with myriads of shadowy vines, remind you faintly of scenes upon the planet Saturn. Bright, billowy topped trees, and velvety, white paths between, and solemn, anthemnal music filling and thrilling the whole with a feeling of unutterable sacredness; and processions of thoughtful men and women, and long lines of persons who (you can easily see) were once halt and sick and maimed and deaf and dumb and blind, and groups of singing and worshipping children—all impress you as a new world created in the heavens, designed for those who are wholly devoted to " the love and worship of God."

The castle-like chapels and the cathedral-looking temples are the dwelling places of grave and dignified hosts, who were once Popes, Prelates, Bishops, Cardinals, Priests, founders of Secret Orders, Saints, and Dignitaries from every kingdom and principality that ever existed since the foundation of human history. Embowered and sheltered, throughout a vast continent of great natural beauty, and pervaded with a feeling of solemnity, these ecclesiastical associations are glorious and well-nigh irresistible. Here you behold the immemorial holiness and awfulness of what, in religion, is called " very ancient." The sacred clouds of the world's many past ages hang over the gates of every half-hidden sanctuary. Here you recall the poet's line —" The splendor falls on castle walls, and snowy summits old in story ; " but you substitute for " snowy " the literal word *shadowy ;* for the slumbers of ten thousand centuries seem *packed away* in these structures.

There is a painful, oppressive pleasure in contemplating these impressive, these massive, these harmonious aggregations of solemn antiquities. I look at them with a feeling like that awakened by standing beneath great oak trees of gigantic diameters, with tops lifted majestically away up into the calm, clear sky, compared with which one's own dwarfed and insignificant stature is as a grain of sand lying silent at the foot of the mighty mountain. The effect is instructive and benignly ennobling. Annihilation in God, or the momentary and delightful loss of one's personal existence in the ocean-spirit of the Infinite, is the feeling now suggested. There is a strain of mournful music stealing through all these wonderful time-crowned structures. The domes of vast cathedrals, the turrets of temples, the spires of consecrated homes, impress one with the feeling that "there are many mansions" in the supernal Home.

From the examples of sacred precedent, and from a slowly broadening system of ecclesiastical government, these great societies of Religiousness exert very wonderful influences upon the human family, whether on earth, in the Summerland, or upon the nearest approachable planets. In their united strength they send forth upon the golden and purple seas of human life a fulness and a diffusiveness of religious warning and aspiration—an influence that moves millions, as if it were a breath from the very mouth of God himself. Their great empire stretches from northeast to southwest, pervading a country almost as large as the entire dry land of earth. And their history is coëval with that of the human race. Individual freedom—the gratification of the private will—occupies a trifling point; the unification of mankind "in one faith and one baptism" is their settled mission; and the steady progress they make from age to age sufficiently attests their earnestness and success.

"What!" you exclaim, "is all this *in* the Summerland?" Truly all this is in the world after death; where freedom for every sincere conviction is universally assured.

"Why do they not open their eyes, use their reason, aud see their errors?" you ask.

For the same reason, I reply, that they did not open their eyes, or use their reason upon themselves, while they were in this world. They believed while on earth, and they still believe, that what they did not then have, or what they do not now know, is practically unattainable and unknowable. The spirit of love, the sprit of beauty, the spirit of wisdom, and the spirit of worship, they believe they alone possess in true form and in largest abundance. What better can they do than as missionaries, and as heaven ordained ambassadors of the everlasting truth, to reach out their philanthropic hands full of salvation for mankind wherever found? Do *you* think that you can "convert" any one of them to the acceptance of your convictions? If so, suppose you begin to-morrow upon your nearest ecclesiastical neighbor. When you cause him, in the full blaze of the science and reason of the ninteenth century, *to open his eyes*, and to see with them what and as you do, then you may with more consistency inquire why there are sects in the Heavenly Home. (You will remember that the opening of the spiritual senses, as an immediate consequence of death, is not necessarily followed by a corresponding opening of the affections, will, and understanding.)

Behold the religious habitations of the representatives of every imaginable sect scattered all over another great section, which is as large as the continent of Asia. Look now far away to the southeast of the renowned and solemnly magnificent associations and brotherhoods which we have just contemplated.* The heavenly country in this section is ineffably glorious! The plains, and valleys, and groves, and fountains, and sparkling rivers of living water, exceed in degrees of beauty and holy loveliness all verbal expression. The different sects are fraternizing, and seem animated with feelings of mutual affinity, being engaged in a common purpose, namely: In the great work of saving mankind from endless desolation, and in promoting, thorough grace and regeneration, the desirable ends of universal purification and refinement.

It was a perception of this, doubtless, that impressed Swedenborg to affirm that, in all the heavens, the " word " was recognized and read in its true spiritual and celestial sense, and in the ancient language of correspondence; for there, in yonder vast northeastern continent of most advanced sectarian religions, you behold profound veneration for what upon earth is called " God's truth," or " Bible truth; " and, most remarkable to relate, some of the assembled congregations are this moment receiving instructions from men who on earth were distinguished clergymen, discoursing upon themes involving a figurative translation of parts of the New Testament! Camp-meetings and grove-

---

*Allusion to these sects may be found in the volume, "Death and the After-Life."

gatherings of the different forms of religion, all upon a Bible basis, seem to be almost the only thought and purpose of the countless multitudes.* "Religion is the chief concern" of immortals who, not enlightened upon great and most interior principles, and finding that they yet have *time* given them to "make their election sure," give themselves up to the most incessant industry among each other, also as missionaries to all accessible earths in their universe. Beholding all this splendor and gorgeousness in the country of the "house of many mansions," and especially realizing how intellectually contracted, and how spiritually honest and faithful withal, all sectarians naturally are—even after death, when many men and women become very beautiful spirits and angels in the sky—you inevitably acquire a foretaste of the fields of usefulness which will forever open before you, as a philanthropist, a philosopher, a scientist, an orator, a traveller, and a lover of mental freedom and eternal truth.

If you believe that the time will ever come, in any of the future cycles of eternity, "when every knee shall bow" at one and the same time, and if you believe that "every tongue shall confess," and "every eye see," and "every mind comprehend," THE WHOLE TRUTH and ALL BE AS ONE, "knowing the Lord from the least to the greatest"—without requiring the intervention of an incomprehensible miracle, which an unchangeable God never can perform—if you believe this, then you have little knowledge of human nature, less comprehension

---

* In the concluding portion of this volume the "Bible-basis" will receive further consideration.

of the inflexible laws of everlasting progression, and most limited information concerning the harmonious system of government which flows from the hearts of Father God and Mother Nature.

CHAPTER XI.

REMARKABLE PLACES IN THE SUMMERLAND.

"One morning my dear father came to me, and said : ' Daughter, arise ! go out upon the hills with us.' . . . We prepared. . . . We went out upon the hills. . . . The *Seven Lakes of Cylosimar*, . . . disposed at regular distances form-ing a crescent-shaped curve amid the overfolding margins, and beneath the far-off lofty heavens, . . . appeared like the setting of brilliant diamonds."—*Extract from Katie's communication in the Penetralia, New Ed., p.* 278.

AFTER many days we return to contemplate the mani-fold glory and harmony of our Heavenly Home.

I have in the meantime enjoyed four very interior experiences; to detail which would require a large volume. I have observed a glory that surpasses the brightness of twenty suns like ours. It was the enchant-ing supercelestial effulgence that emanates from still higher and more interior Spheres.

In 1854, twenty-three years ago, I received what is recorded in the *Penetralia*, an extract from which is quoted at the head of this chapter; at which time " she could not exactly tell *when* she, with the large party of friends, would return from the northern section."

Many times since I have wondered why she did not bring to me something further relative to her life in the Spheres. But by acquired knowledge concerning the inconceivable magnitudes and the immeasurable dis-tances of the regions or worlds in space, to which the celestial people make prolonged pilgrimages, all sur-prise at her continued absence, as well as all anxiety about the utter silence of scores of others I would be very glad to meet, have perfectly gone out of my thoughts. And in all this I hope the reader's mind is also enlarged and at rest.

Brighter than the brightest crystals is the scene, which is only partially indicated by the map, embracing the Seven Lakes of Cylosimar. Lovelier localities cannot be imagined.* Beautiful aromal emanations surround and pervade three of those lakes; while the remaining four seem to inhale the fragrance and to absorb the very light of the heavens; impressing upon the mind a picture of Paradise which only the pure and the noble would be qualified thoroughly to enjoy. Naturalness, spontaneousness, beautifulness, perfection—are the only words that enter my thoughts. I would remain here and contemplate forever; for here I could forever adore and worship. Hither, amid the glories and super-abounding goodness of Divinity, I would attract all whom I tenderly love. Beneath these bright skies, and beside these soft-flowing golden streams, listening to the voices of angel-people, blending with the sacred songs of beautiful birds, I would dwell and dream away all the ages of eternity.

* * * Looking far away eastward you behold a hill-belted country where live the after-death inhabitants of planets like Venus and Mercury and several of the satellites. Drawing closer, you seem to feel that the people are steeped in sunbeams. Dreamingly, sleepily they look out upon the sky and over the distant spark-

---

* See some references to and descriptions of them in "Death and the After-Life."

ling fields.   An indescribable beauty floats among them, and a drowsy and delightful fragrance fills the atmosphere, to which these remarkable people seem to be blind, and unattracted, and insensible.   Ah! I behold what all this means.   They are a materialistic, a heavy-minded, and a half-developed population.   And while I look there arrive many death-emancipated from our earth—from all countries, especially from the far South Sea Islands and Africa—who float along like inanimate bodies carried, idly and helpless and indifferently, by the sovereign law of that attraction which determines destination.   But behold! the Paternal Divinity never forsakes such dependent children.   In every shady sequestered nook you observe a man or a woman—embodying a matchless union of parent, friend and guardian—who, with warm hand and white arms outstretched, stands ready to receive all guests, and willing to begin the unfolding work upon the new-comers. What a contrast!   Amid these throngs of dumb and dark and dreamy and feeble children, to see such fresh hospitality and such gentleness of nature manifested by those leading, shining Summerland beauties.   It seems like melting, unresponsive snow upon the warm bosom of self-sacrificing affection.   The scene is lovely with unconscious goodness and unrestrained love.

Hither come half developed children, who, owing to some pre-natal accident or maternal weakness, were born imbecile, or idiotic, or deaf and dumb and blind. Little chaotic minds that never evolved a rational thought; feeble, embryonic hearts, unfinished in form and structure, which never felt or responded to the sympathetic touch of love; sealed ears that never heard

" the sweet music of speech;" blind eyes that never opened upon the light and beauty of nature; mute lips that never uttered an intelligible sound; with the senses all closed, and with the whole being more than half unborn—behold! how they float into the hospitalia of this heavenly world. Beautiful charitableness, unrestrained benevolence, sympathy, and all-healing tenderness—how these spiritual virtues glow and blossom with fadeless bloom in this happy land "beyond the clouds and beyond the tomb."

* * * Self-luminous, independent of all star-shine and solar-light, is the Summerland. Its shores are inherently radiant; its streams and rivers and fountains glow and glitter with their own immortal light; its unalterable mountains and undulating landscapes are ever green, beautiful with diamond effulgence, and more "delectable" than the purest pilgrim ever dreamed; while the firmament above is forever glowing with suns and planets, with clusters within clusters, and constellations within universes, far beyond the power of mind to conceive or the resources of language to describe.

* * * Looking eastward of the land of charity and hospitalia, you observe a great multitude beneath the feathery-foliaged trees listening to an orator. He is deep-minded, witty, cultivated; without sentiment, speaking in a foreign language, sounding like ancient Hebrew; and his theme, treated philosophically, is "The Echo!" Let us listen, also; let us catch, if possible, a few of his sentences:

"Reaching beyond the horizon in history," he eloquently says, "we enter the temples of slumberous sounds; responsive to voice, the haunting cradle of

A-o-ma-ba.   Search the air, scale the mountains, sound the sea, explore the heavens, penetrate the forests; it is yet *deuel*—as empty as the word of *Eliaka*.   Lo! it is all belief!   Doubt is Echo; the restlessness of faith, questioning itself." * * * (He is still speaking, but we must away.)

Here is a man of powerful talent, not long since a citizen of this earth, debating like an aged philosopher the questions of faith and knowledge.   An impression comes that he has been approached by a missionary Passionist; one to whom even the *picture* of the "cross" "is a light set in the sky by the Almighty Hand."

The cross, to this Passionist, is the central figure—the symbol of trial, suffering, sacrifice, contest, death, conquest, and the resurrection.   Between heaven and earth, between God and his creatures, it signifies the certain end of the world and the inauguration of eternal life.   All this was said by the Passionist to the Hebrew orator.   The latter replies that it is "Echo."   Pictures, signs, symbols, language (he replies) are younger and less sacred than human existence, which is very, very ancient.   The origin of the cross (he says) will soon be seen and known of all men; it is a part of earliest hieroglyphic language derived from the human body; and out of it, or from what it signifies, have in truth arisen most of human vices and sorrow, trials and suffering, contests and triumphs.   This, in substance, is what the Oriental orator is proclaiming.   But what it all means time alone will fully bring to light.

* * * Surpassingly delightful is the scene to the southward—a great harmonious temple of wisdom.   It is denominated a *logosal* country of beautiful gardens

and groves, abounding in graceful luxuriance of plains and valleys and streams—the Empire of celestial love and supreme mental illumination.   Into the sacred circles of this most noble brotherhood come the wisdom and love of higher and more interior spiritual universes. Here the seekers for true wisdom find perfect repose of soul.   As the sun imparts warmth and illumination, life and development to the forms of earth, so does each higher Summerland impart its love and knowledge and aspirations into souls composing this innumerable host of expanded and expanding minds.   What a privilege only to behold them !

By the divine impulse of attraction you find, drawn into a single group, such minds as Humboldt, Herschel, Columbus, Galileo, Newton, Franklin, and scores of like mentalities of whom you have never heard.   Behold the imperishable furniture of such minds!   Only the natural, the cohesive, the harmonious, the useful.   They deal not at all with subjects involving the "infinite," and ignore all thoughts of the "Eternal."   They do not touch or think of either "doubts" or "beliefs."   Instead of dreaming sentiment, instead of intellectual idleness from a sense of sufficiency and repletion, they know practically but *five* words: Truth, Industry, Exploration, Discovery, Accomplishment.   They are as youthful and enthusiastic as are boys and girls at a picnic!   Intuitive truth they do luxuriate in ; it is spontaneously breathed forth from their faces and lips and beautiful lives.   But it is a fact that they do not look into mirrors ; consequently, never admiring themselves, they map out whole continents of truth, one after another, for future excursions and investigations ; not counting as of any lasting value their past or present possessions.

This great heavenly empire of wise souls renders bright and glorious the very sky above it, and seems to enlarge the infinite world that boundlessly expands around it. And oh, such sweet lessons! Wordsworth says: "'Tis Nature's law that none—the meanest of created things, of forms created the most vile and brute, the dullest or most noxious—should exist divorced from good."

Actuated by this principle, behold how the angel-ambassadors, empowered by this society, speed to earth; to aid those who design and commit crime through a bad organization, and to impress hope upon those who continually do evil from the faults of association or circumstances. They attempt the overthrow of hypocrisy; they meet face to face with fraud and dissimulation; they instil despair into the consciousness of the insistent transgressor; and they aid in awakening a consciousness of those punishments which necessarily follow "deeds done in the body." Under the administrative jurisdiction of this brotherhood, the meddlesome *Diakka* (but frequently *unknown* to them) are necessitated to perform many important missions of downright *good* among the most needy of mankind.

"The temptation of the devil" means, in human life, promptings from evils inherited and suggestions from evils attracted. Of these promptings and suggestions some persons know almost nothing. A healthy, harmonious nature, for example, flows through life like a peaceful river through groves and green fields. But a nervous, irritable, discordant temperament is a daily vexation to itself, whilst it is both a demon and a hell to all about it; and it is to meet and master such that the best angels descend and labor, and it is for such that the noblest of earth are often stoned and sacrificed and nailed to the cross. But prevention, the day of deliverance, will yet dawn.

Yea, altogether glorious is the country devoted to the local uses and fixed habitations of this most noble brotherhood. It covers as much space as both France and Italy; and thus it seems to be a perfect world, a miniature paradise, within itself. The geographical glories of this beaming region cannot be portrayed in words; and it would consume years and fill large volumes to travel over it and relate its diversified possessions; and it would require the eloquent pen of a true poet to give a history of the musical groupings and rhythmical distributions of its population.

Nezzar is the great river flowing nearly east and west. And upon its northern borders you meet the residences of the most gifted of females and men ever known in human history; while on the southern margin congregate in harmonious families all those inter-affiliated inhabitants born upon Mars and Jupiter and Saturn. A glorious stream of living water called *Lustrade*, with its four beautiful tributaries named (1) *Gedor* (meaning a mountain city), (2) *Palesto* (meaning a country of the east), (3) *Esus* (meaning the goddess), (4) *Al-namon* (meaning unrestricted communion)—giving the impression that this country, which holds in its very heart this "river Jordan" and these streaming fountains of "Eden," is in very truth the holy land of the most happy immortals.

From this wise Brotherhood—whose numerous associations and consociations are distributed over such an expanse of celestial country, the Earth's inhabitants have received the greatest benefits and most bountiful blessings. These have been showered upon mankind continuously, from their very earliest beginnings. Delegates and members of this Brotherhood were constituents of "The Spiritual Congress"—the most illustrious friends of one universal humanity—whose names and "Exordia," you will remember, were and are recorded and published in the book "*Present Age and Inner Life.*" But it is humiliating and a great sorrow to be compelled to record the fact, that during the past fifteen years (owing to causes which you can read in "*The Fountain,*" chapters XIII. and XIV.), the most distinguished members of this Brotherhood have been frequently constrained to suspend their personal intercourse with those who should be their most loyal and trusty earthly friends. But now we must turn our eyes and thoughts in other directions.

* * * Continuing our observations very far east of all we have yet seen, you behold the mountain encircled valley called *Ara-Elm-Haroun.* Haroun is the original of the name "Aaron ;" and the prefixes signify " the land of," or the Valley of the Stranger. And how appropriate is this singular name ! For do you not observe the remarkable personal appearance of the inhabitants ? Let us meditate :

O home of the doubting heart ! O vale of the silence of despair ! Here come angels of tenderness and mercy to meet and minister to the constantly arriving suicides, and also to many who have been insane.

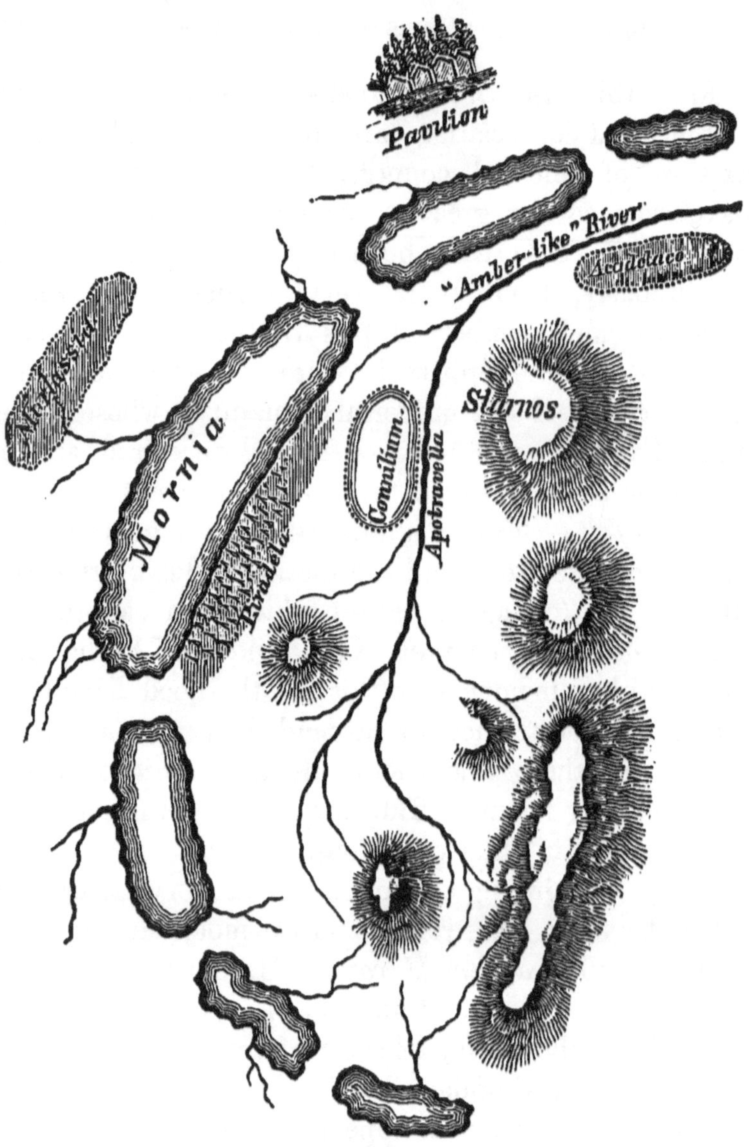

(*No. 7.*)   THE SEVEN LAKES OF CYLOSIMAR.

They breathe and smile upon these unhappy human flowers. But these flowers seem heedless, for are they not enveloped in mental darkness? Angel-voices call the wretched and wrecked wanderers. But, alas! they do not hear the *saving* music of those voices. Lifelong beggars on earth! O ye careless slumberers for years on life's bleak and stormy shores! you do not, because you will not, hear the voice of your Redeemer! You have arrived in this Vale during your profound sleep; and you are in your own proper station in *one* of the many mansions of the Parental Home in Heaven. Tranquillity broods over the Vale of Haroun. The gently rising mountains all around yield only music and floods of pure light and love and happiness. A rich summer gladness fills the bosoms of the birds, and it thrills through all the landscape about you; but you see it not, neither do you hear anything; therefore you cannot accept and enjoy the goodness and beauty that wait upon you.

Oh, what know ye, unhappy suicides, what know ye of the sweetness that is strained from acts of self-denial? Your irrevocable past is your own; and its multifarious effects are your only personal property. You suffered tortures, and you continually lived in misery. But did you not know that there are hundreds like yourselves, living daily in like circumstances, whose ill-conditions and unhappiness you might have alleviated? *Giving*, you would have received; *befriending*, you would have found friends. It is now too late! With violence, by self-destruction, you have *forced* yourself into the Vale of Aaron. Here you find virtue, service, happiness, beauty, angels of purity and mercy,

9*

and yet *you would hide yourself!* with shoulders bent and downcast eyes you would flee to yonder mountains ! Why would you, O suicide ! why would you *conceal* yourself from the contemplation of the fair-eyed and sweet-faced angels who lovingly bend over you ? I will answer the question : Because only the *pure in heart* shall " see God ! " The violent, the impatient, the *impure* are blind and dumb and ashamed; although they may stand in His very presence, they behold and enjoy nothing.

And you, oh unhappily insane ! why do you, too, enter the Vale of Aaron ? Ah, you did not know whither you drifted with your guardians when you left the earth. You came hither to gather a foretaste of the secrets of harmony, did you not ? Discords, operating upon a law of their own, have *driven* you into a heavily shrouded experience. All thoughts of ill, all evil deeds, which you of necessity now have in memory, must be displaced and eradicated. By slow degrees you may be able to lift your eyes to see the soft light of the summery mountains ; and, after a period, you lift them toward the starry skies above you ; and thus begin to learn the pathways of purity, and finally to obtain a conception of the gloriousness of a divine existence. Eternity is nothing to you now or hereafter ; your *internal state* is the all in all.

But O suicide ! and O ye insane ! answer me : Why do you not *rest* in the beautiful land beyond the tomb ? Why are you not " at home " in the very lovely Home of the Angels ? Why are you so *chilly* where eternal summer boundlessly reigns ? Why do you *not* dwell with profound contentment in the balmy fields of God's Elysian ? Why do you seek to retire from the habitations of the beautiful maidens? and why shrink from the touch of the youthful men of the material heavens? Ah, you do not answer. But, instead, you break through the barriers of good manners, and hasten away back to earth. To your old earthly haunts, to the friends you left behind, you eagerly desire to manifest yourself. With burning eyes, with quivering lips, with the trembling hand of friendship—thus you present yourself. Now, why did you wander impatiently back to earth? For you I will answer: *Because your work was not finished!* Because your life had not truly blossomed with the fulness of such terrestrial experiences as were in your own natural pathway. Remember! only the full-grown human life is happy after death. Here we behold the secret of your burning unrest. Let this lesson never forsake you. Be ye forever faithful.

* * * Our observations for to-day must here be terminated.

In the next and concluding chapter other scenes will be recorded. But from what we have seen thus far, while in the superior condition, we can extract a great practical principle to govern our life and actions on earth. It seems that ordinary philosophy may calm the passional tempest, that truth may exalt the purposes of life, that personal excellence may glorify and dignify our daily existence ; but behind all this, and as a foundation for it all to rest upon, it seems that we must sweeten and *purify life* at its fountain-springs, by habitually letting the spiritual in us dominate the natural, and by permitting the highest in us to govern the lowest, for it is only thus that the divine *light*, which is above, can effectively penetrate and shine into our darkness.

CHAPTER XII.

HEAVENLY BENEFITS FOR MANKIND.

—Peabody.

PERFECT JUSTICE and boundless GOODNESS, upon which the infinite Temple of the Father and Mother is constructed and inflexibly upheld, are the everlasting principles of a true, universal, and all-satisfying Religion.

This eternal and perfectly natural Religion is intrinsically adapted to all phases and necessities of universal humanity. And it is the *only* system that is capable of being universally adopted, and of becoming inseparably identified with the eternal intuitions and needs of restless progressive human nature. All classes, and all temperaments, whether intelligent and buoyant, or ignorant and down-trodden, demand of *true* Religion that it shall bring them (what every soul sooner or later needs and yearns for) true Consolation, true Courage, undying Hope.

A true revelation of the immeasurable sublimities of the Univercœlum, while it momentarily exalts the intelligence of the spiritually philosophical, and fills with unutterable delight the ideality and intuitive sensibilities of the true poet, fails to administer sweet consolations when life's trials oppress the heart, and thus proves itself inadequate to the soul's hunger for sympathy, and courage, and hope. Therefore the reverential philosopher and the superficial-minded alike, in certain seasons of heart-broken sorrow and loneliness, plead, each in his own way, for the enfolding love-arms of Providence, for the wise and affectionate guidance and goodness of a Heavenly Power. Prayer breaks forth from the very pious and the poetically reverential; meditation is the medium of the spiritual philosopher; penitential weeping opens the smile of Heaven to the infantile heart; the tragedy of the cross, and the spectacle of the triumphant resurrection, after enduring all degrees of suffering, are a comfort to the sincere believer; but, whatever the form of the appeal, or whatever the expression of the internal need, the only true Religion is that which *embraces* the universe, reveals perfect *justice*, breathes boundless *goodness*, fills the reason with *light*, the affections with love, the sorrowing with *consolation*, the down-trodden with *courage*, and the despairing with the golden beams of eternal *hope*.

Responsive to every real human need, the infinite sources of love and wisdom perpetually flow into and flood the individual receptive spirit; and the innumerable hosts of the heavenly spheres freely shower their fondest affections and their most resplendent thoughts into the common life of the terrestrial millions. Therefore there is no one utterly forsaken; no bleeding heart that either lives or dies wholly alone and unknown; no unrequited life in this universe of love; no possible

estrangement from the redemptive power of the universal Presence. All humanity moves within the orbit of
the spiritual sun. There is no gravitation superior or
equal to the attraction of the interior universe. |Your
feet now point to the centre of the earth, your head
toward the Summerland. This is true all over this
rolling world. Do you not read the infallible prophecy
of this scientific fact? It means that your body will
return to the earth whence it came; and you, *yourself*,
will advance to another mansion in the Heavenly
Home. |

* * * After an hour of interior observation we proceed to relate results.

| Domestic enjoyments, based upon true conjugal
unions, and interwoven with the fondest affections of
children and kindred, you behold in the upper conntry.
Uncompanionated natures on earth, lonely hearts long-
ing for unchangeable kindred love, here find their own.
Did you not observe, during the one hour of our investigation, that five weddings occurred in the neighborhood of the Zellabingens? How long those two men
(angel youths now) waited for the coming of their
mates! How loyally patient those three angel maidens
(once wives and mothers on earth) waited for their dar-
ling husbands to come to them through death's triumphal arch! These ten persons were truly mated and
happily married, four in St. Louis and six in London,
but they had each known sickness and accident and
poverty, and many another earthly trial. Strange fact!
there are a great number of conjugally *true* marriages in
the human family before death; but, whether true or
temporary, justice and goodness eventually prevail, and so

what should occur *does occur*, and the glory and beauty thereof shine into everybody's eyes.*

* * * Another day has passed since the foregoing was written.

Again your attention is asked to the perfections of the structure of the universe; to contemplate with becoming reverence the magnificent system of energies and activities, of uses and beauties, of directing, guiding, supervising causes and their corresponding infinitude of effects; asked to contrast this Harmonial Religion, which "lives through all life, extends through all extent, spreads undivided, and operates unspent," with those special creeds and limited schemes, which, under the name of religion, exist in the theological and church-building world about you. You are hereby introduced to a Father and to a Mother who, as Divine Wisdom and Divine Love, with infinite presence and with infinite power, fill matter with all its known properties and forces, and govern all things with an unalterable homogeneousness of government. From the ebbings and flowings, from the actions and reactions of the tidal life-principles of this dual Supreme Being, you behold all those transformations and metamorphoses in the universe of substance which philosophers call " phenomena." †

---

* If the reader would know exactly what is here meant by the " true " *versus* the " temporary " marriage, and learn of the delightful evidences of the one and of the direful consequences of the other, he is referred to the " *Great Harmonia*," Vol. IV. ; also to the author's re-statement and recent agitations of the question in his smaller work, " Genesis and Ethics of Conjugal Love."

† In the second volume of the " *Great Harmonia* " there is an account of the operations of the Divine Spirit in man's constitution. See the chapter " What and Where is God ? "

In this Religion man is seen, by the eyes of merciful love, as a power with dependencies and extenuating circumstances on every hand; and thus for every evil act of his limited and hampered life there are somewhere healing hands and a forgiving heart; but, on the other side, in this Religion, man is also seen, by the eyes of justice and wisdom, as a wondrous, self-determining power, amply endowed with intuitions of right and wrong, and with the principles of action, reaction, and inaction dwelling in the very heart of his consciousness; and thus for every evil act in his life he is regarded in the moral universe as a transgressor, requiring the administration of retribution, implying self-denial, self-sacrifice, and progressive purification as a self-instituted, regenerative process; and this, too, whether he remains the full measure of his days on earth, or early ascends to reside in a supernal Sphere beyond the Sun.

* * * High thoughts visit us from the heavenly Alps! Pure and deep are our contemplations of heaven. A thousand stainless societies are visible in the Summerland, whose inmost life is in rhythmical movement with the concerted harmonies of far more celestial and supercelestial universes. The effulgence ·of these holy and harmonious centres exceeds the glory and brightness of a thousand suns. Streams of perfections spread everywhere from these loving fountains. Oh, perfect life! Let us measure and govern our existence by the even step of this progressive army.

What response was that! " Not yet! not yet!" Why may we not? Why not *now* enter upon the true life of the kingdom of heaven? We would feel the rapture of that sinless resplendence. We would sail out of our terrestrial discords upon the musically rolling waves of sublime thought. We would reside in the shining dwelling-places of the pure and the happy. "Not yet!" Why not *now*, O ye of the heavenly homes?

"Thy purpose is worthy," I heard a voice exclaim. "Aspire worthily," it says; "and the shadow of thy darkness will vanish. * * * Here thy sight would be dimmed; thy feet falter and refuse to step; thy lips would not speak; thy heart cease to throb with the waves of feeling and thought."

Ah, now I think that I understand *why* the voice said, "Not yet!" My nature is not in harmony with the standard prevailing in those supercelestial consociations. Their light would fill me with blindness; their thoughts would overwhelm my understanding; their affections could not flow through my heart; their supreme style of life would be a strain and a torture to me; their harmoniousness would fill me with discords; their very existence about me, with its resplendence and unapproachableness, would possibly excite in me longings for the dreamless rest of annihilation.

The heavenly lesson is wholesome and familiar, namely, Never trample down or negligently overlook the blessings and opportunities existing at one's very feet in the foolish ambition to scale the "ever-green mountains" before the right time; or, in still plainer terms, never attempt to burglariously enter "the kingdom of heaven by violence."

Thus we are admonished to aspire, to make progress, to grow larger and purer; and at the same time we are told to cover and adorn one's whole life with the graceful garments of gratitude and contentment. This, as it is now made fully manifest, is the true path to reach what all men seek, namely, *real life and real happiness*. But the most of mankind in their blindness prefer the popular "gate" that is "wide" and the "way" that is "broad," both of which lead to a spiritually false life, and to a vast harvest of real misery. "Strait is the gate and narrow is the way" which leadeth to the highest and truest style of life; and this is the simple and only reason why "few there be that find it."

* * * Yesterday we closed our communion with the quotation from the exalted and spiritual, and, therefore (to most persons), supernatural and vague discourse of the person, of whom the officers said: "Never man spake like this man." To the materialist, to the learned Jew, and to the unspiritual multitudes of his time, as of any and every other time, *all interior teaching* seems to be either "supernatural," or else incomprehensibly *unnatural* and "mysterious." It is no new suggestion that "history repeats itself." If you know *how* to read history aright, you need never be deceived by "false prophets;" nor driven from your centre of responsibility by the "marvellous claims" of self-asserting *missionaries* or other religious chieftains.

* * * This morning you behold a remarkable manifestation of the principles upon which the several supernal societies are founded and organized. Supercelestial associations, which shine like spiritual suns in the firmament, are, for the most part, modelled upon the plan and principles of the perfect human body: The form or image of the body not only, but also there is a representation of the various internal vital organs,

with their ties of connection; with all the circulations and essential processes; giving the heart its true official station, the brain its, down the two arms to the tip of every finger, and down both legs to the end of every toe: "All are members of one body."

Here we behold what gave Swedenborg the impression that the whole universe was in the form and shape of "One Grand Man." In truth the divine image is spiritually a likeness of the perfect human form; because the human is the *final form*, into which spiritual substance or "matter and spirit" blossom; the coronation of all possible organizational progression.

After this climax is attained in the progress of *forms*, then begins energetically, yet silently, the operation of the progressive law in essences, attributes, properties, combinations, powers, forces; and thus henceforth, throughout all degrees and gradations of individual and communal life, through all the phases of the adjoining Summerland, and onward and inward, with endless ebbings and flowings, from the outer Sphere to the inmost, and from the inmost back again through the new Heavenly Home of another reconstruction of the universe forever and forever; yet never altogether satisfied, because never altogether perfect, growing old in some things and growing equally infantile in others; then reversing the use and exercise of your faculties, and thus becoming a child again in that wherein you had grown golden and distinguished, with the amplitude of your wisdom; and learning and enjoying the spontaneousness of love where for ages your affections had seemingly vanished out of your heart, changing from a man or a woman, with a thousand millions of years crystallized into your personal history, to a glad-some youth or a joyous and graceful maiden; forget-ting what is called "time," and unconscious of what is termed "space;" oppressed by no weight in accumula-tive experiences, guided by no religious institutes of a prior universe; but once more in the aphelion of your orbit, which you cannot travel once around in less than what you would call "one whole eternity;" again in your youth, among the highest mysteries of your ever-loving and wise Mother and Father, "who are in har-mony;" with a memory filled with the indistinguish-able dreams of the past eternities through which you have steadily travelled, in accordance with the princi-ples of spiral progression; with new ambitions, new impulses, new aspirations, new hunger, new thirst, new appetites, new life, with "a new heaven" loaded with stars over your youthful head, and beneath your feet a new Summerland teeming with inexhaustible resources, surrounding you on every side like a boundless uni-verse newly unfolded; with what was once to you only relative now become absolute, and esteeming what was once entirely familiar to you as the now altogether un-approachable and unknowable; looking with amaze-ment and delight out upon the new life, because not dwelling much in the dark depositories of memory, the same as a bright-minded child gazes wonderingly upon the horizon and the sunset, at the moon, and clouds, and stars in the evening sky; forming new associations among your peers and incidental neighbors; and thus you commence to perform *another* revolution in your immeasurable orbit, unconsciously tending every mo-ment *inwardly* toward the inmost Summerland nearest to the Deific Sun, which will be the perihelion of your orbital pilgrimage, involving a period beyond the powers of the highest angel to imagine, and developing an individual experience which only infinity is large enough to contain, but which, because it is obtained and appropriated in wholesome instalments, passes delightfully and beneficially through the faculties as days slip through the hours, and years through the weeks of our present rudimental life, leaving behind them only a general impression of the thousands and millions of events, great, less, and little, which those days and weeks and years brought into your private consciousness and memory.

* * * In the supercelestial societies in the Summerland—which are in constant correspondence with, as they are exact typical representatives of, the entire population and geographical appearances of the far higher and more interior Spiritual Spheres—I observe yet other plans and principles of organization, association, and government. At some time, very far future in human history, it may be profitable to study and copy after these heavenly methods of order and growth.

In lesser brotherhoods and more terrestrial communities I observe, in various degrees of resemblance, organizations based upon the shape and functions of a five-foliate leaf, not unlike the form and powers of the human right hand ; while in other societies the law and results of crystallization are fully manifested. In still other localities I observe social orders based upon the principles of vegetation, as vines, trees, flowers, and fruit. Elsewhere you meet with systems of social life and education founded upon the principles of flowing water, like the " Children's Progressive Lyceum," beginning with the Fountain and ending with the Ocean which washes the protecting Shore ; thence progressively onward, through rhythmically graded groups, until the climax or point of graduation is reached in " Liberty," which is the crowning privilege and high reward of the true children of our Heavenly Parents.*   The structure and principles of the stellar universe are adopted by the members of other associations as the truest plan of systematizing and harmoniously uniting human interests.   Some associations are composed of highest natures, who have " the law written upon their hearts," requiring neither ordinances, statutes, enactments; nor so much as a *thought* concerning their mutual interests or their methods and ends of life.

* * * I might fill a volume with important and most remarkable observations in these departments of the Heavenly Home.   But it is deemed best, in this sequel especially, to condense as much, and to repeat as little, as is consistent and possible with the ends of plain truth.

There is, however, one universal principle prevailing and pervading the Summerland, to which I am impressed to ask your attention, namely, The principle of Use.   It seems to underlie and to overflow every body and every thing.   There is, consequently, the plainest possible evidence of *a design* in everything everywhere —a primal *love* in all affections, a manifest *thought* within every living thing, an intelligent *purpose* in

---

* The Progressive Lyceum plan you will find in the little work bearing the above quoted title.

every organization and movement—so that, unless the spirit of a man is blind or near-sighted after death, as most men are in this world, a *doubt* concerning the existence of a Supreme Intelligence is simply impossible.

The glorious principle of universal Service, of Use, of Design, of Destiny—this principle distinguishes our Heavenly Home from everything known and experienced by mankind on earth. The happiness and prosperity of each member of society are secured, upon the payment by the individual of the inflexible price, from which no true angel ever appeals; which is that he or she contribute a faithful service, in recognized and appropriate uses, to the prosperity and happiness of others. This principle is beautifully and universally exemplified throughout the superior societies in all the heavenly Spheres.

When may we look for the advent of *such* a kingdom of heaven on earth? The reign of Universal Justice through the reign of Universal Love! For the only foundation for such a state of society is the foundation of perfect fraternal and Universal love. When you pray the "Lord's Prayer," let no other thought, no other desire, no other aspiration occupy your mind; if otherwise, your prayer is in vain, and your lip-service, under the form of religion, will come back to you like "sounding brass."

*   *   *   *   *   *   *   *

The time has arrived, and we must close our spiritual perceptions upon the systems of universal space. The fields of splendor, and the "many mansions" of gorgeousness in the Heavenly Home, with their celestial warmth and harmonious light and beauty, we shield from the gaze of an unprogressed, unprepared, discordant humanity.

"Beyond the clouds, and beyond the tomb!" When your time shall have come in its fulness, you will glide forth upon the magnetic river; and, accompanied by faithful guardians, you will find *your own place* in the inner Temple of Father God and Mother Nature.

THE END OF PART II.

EXPLANATORY DISCUSSION OF IMPORTANT QUESTIONS.

APPENDIX.

(1.)

DISTRIBUTION OF COLD AND HEAT ON THE PLANETS.

By explaining the causes of our terrestrial climates, the reader may understand more about the inhabited planets.

Human nature, both physically and mentally, is essentially swayed by the constitution and temperature of the common, respirable air. The subtleness and extent of this aërial influence upon man's bodily powers, upon his intellectual achievements in the arts and sciences, upon his feelings and disposition as a social being, upon his religious developments and governmental systems, almost transcends belief. In the torrid belt, as in the two frigid zones, Nature and humanity are alike arrested and held in check. Supreme indifference to the voice of every energetic passion in the extreme *hot*, and incapability of evolving any powerful mental power in the extreme *cold*, results in bringing together the two extremes; from which, instinctively, the majority of mankind naturally travel toward the delightful temperature and inspiring electricities of the middle zone.

The philosophy of this fact is, as a fundamental law of Nature, that between two extremes invariably grow the grandest perfections. And the science of it is, that the respirable air, compounded of oxygen and nitrogen, as chemistry now teaches, is really a reservoir and a viaduct for the reception and introduction into man's body and mind of the electricities and spiritualities of both heaven and earth. The sun's influences in the temperate zones combine with the inherent principles of life in the globe. Temperature is another name for *motion;* and respirable air is another name for *life.* Motion of the atoms of the elements (or temperature), and the life of the elements (or respirable air), combine and evolve the cerebral phenomena of sensation and intelligence. These products of motion and life, in both mankind and animals, are deficient and exceedingly imperfect in both the torrid and the frigid zones. Hence, in these two opposite sides, or extreme ends, of our globe, Nature and human nature are equally held in check. Less than one-third of the earth's surface is consequently congenial and favorable to great human and natural developments.

The sides of the American continent are washed by three grand bodies of water—the Arctic, the Atlantic, and the Pacific. The wind-currents as well as the ocean-currents, on this immense continent, will be found working together harmoniously, modified and rendered gloriously variable by the great mountain ranges, the Alleghany and the Rocky Mountains, which for human good coöperate with the great lakes and the mighty rivers between the three great oceans. Along the northern shores of the continent, a powerful ocean current sweeps eastward in the Arctic; which is perfectly balanced by a great northward current, along our eastern shores, in the Atlantic; while along our attractive western side sweeps, in the Pacific, a southward current; these three great oceanic flows, taken in connection with the extraordinary effects of mountains and valleys, lakes and rivers, explain the wind-currents, the temperatures, and the peculiar social, political, and religious developments of America.

The human race from the great East is western-bound, under full speed, in the face of the great winds which flow almost perpetually from the West. Asia, in like manner, is pressed into Europe, and Europe is emptying itself into America; and the great West and Southwest of this new world are rapidly receiving vast reinforcements of human nature; thus demonstrating that it is in the horoscope of every family to make progress in the face of the wind!

Circumstances, both geographical and climatic, largely control the forms, faiths, labors, and disposition of mankind. So much of the Asiatic coast as is reproduced upon our Atlantic, so much of ancient Asiatic experience will be approximately reproduced in America. The history of Greece and Rome, of Spain and France, of England and the great North, will re-appear more or less distinctly marked with likeness between the same parallels of latitude in this newly-populated continent. Moisture (which depends upon inland streams and the direction of slopes) exercises a distinct influence upon climate ; but there is something which is yet more influential, namely: TIME, which brings in its omnipotent arms the habits, the religions, the governments, and the scientific accomplishments of mankind. Government is influenced by religion ; religion is modified by society; society is swayed by climate ; climate is greatly affected by moisture ; moisture is a product of waters, slopes, valleys, and mountain ranges; but mark! these elevated ranges of earth will be surmounted by towers, mechanical instruments, and scientific discoveries, imparting correct knowledge of aërial currents and temperatures, and eventually controlling the production and distribution of rain, snow, electricity, and the principalities and powers of the air; so that, in the reflex action of mankind on the planet and the elements, it would be no longer true to say that man is influenced by his geographical and climatic circumstances, for then man's heel will crush the head of his physical conditions, and *he will be master of the globe!*

(2.)

THE PONDERABILITY OF IMPONDERABLES.

The descending and ascending scales given ten years ago in the first part of the "Stellar Key" has been gradually confirmed by the very wonderful progress of modern science.   In the New York *Tribune*, January 16th, 1878, the following editorial sets the whole subject in a most encouraging light :

" We have before expressed the belief that the last half of the present century will always be accounted among the great eras of scientific discovery.   There are so many wonderful results of recent research, that it is difficult to enumerate even the more prominent ones.   Among them are the invention of the spectroscope, with the discoveries reaching from earth to inconceivably distant fixed stars, which have followed in its train ; the determination of the laws of the correlation of forces and the conservation of energy, which succeeded the discovery that heat is only a mode of motion, and created new conceptions of the whole universe as to its past, present, and future ; the preparation of the aniline colors, which has furnished an infinite number of iridescent and varying hues ; the composition, from lifeless elements, of many organic substances, by which false notions about vital force (which had been accounted half-miraculous) have been overthrown ; the discovery of the satellites of Mars, which round out and nearly complete the picture of the solar system ; the invention of the telephone and the phonograph, which enable us on the one hand to transmit our voices to great distances, or on the other, to preserve our utterances for indefinite periods, so that the speech of to-day may be set aside and heard again at any time in the future.

" To this wonderful record a new chapter is now to be added. Within a very few weeks, two European investigators have succeeded in condensing to a liquid form all the gases that had hitherto defied such effort.   In the early part of this century, when certain gases were liquefied by Faraday and other experimenters, the facts excited general interest, as giving a clew to the real constitution of matter. The new experiments were widely tried, and in performing them at Paris, in a public lecture, an explosion occurred which killed one of the operating assistants.   Then, for more than half a century, discovery in this line was almost suspended.   Several gases, such as nitric oxide, acetylene, nitrogen, oxygen, and hydrogen, absolutely withstood all attempts.   Within a few weeks, the compound gases named, and some others, have been liquefied.   Next, oxygen yielded to pressure and cold ; an event of sufficient importance to be

telegraphed by Professor Tyndall to *The London Times*, and to be
announced at scientific centres all over the world.   Now comes the
announcement that the remaining gases have undergone a similar
treatment, and are liquefied: nitrogen, under a pressure of 200 atmospheres; hydrogen, under 280.   The latter gas was only reduced
to an opaque mist, but the air which we ordinarily breathe was converted into a liquid, and poured out in a fine stream.   The cold required for these experiments is almost inconceivable; it is estimated
at 300° below zero of the Centigrade thermometer, equivalent to
more than 500° below, of Fahrenheit's scale.

" The discoverers who have achieved these results—M. Cailletet,
of Paris, and M. Pictet, of Geneva—will receive due honor from their
scientific brethren.   It remains to be shown what the discoveries
teach.   The degree of cold that was required in condensing common
air, though remarkable, is not greater than is estimated for the void
of space through which the planets are travelling; that extends infinitely between and perhaps beyond the stars.   It was the low temperature—not the great pressure—which liquefied the gases; they
took the liquid form while escaping from pressure, and in the act of
escaping the extreme cold was attained.   It follows that, in the cold
of space, unwarmed by the sun, an atmosphere like that of our
globe would freeze first into a liquid, and then into a solid mass, becoming at last a mere rock as hard as granite.   We can now better
appreciate the vast changes which comets undergo in passing from
the frozen confines of our solar system to so close a neighborhood of
the sun that they are reduced to a vapor.   Knowing now, as we do
with certainty, the extremes of form to which all matter is liable,
we may surely predict that the future of our globe simply depends
upon the amount of heat received by its surface.   If the heat dimin-
ishes, all earth and air will be silent stone without the breath of life
upon it; if the heat increases, the whole world will melt in thin air."

(3.)

ALLEGED ERRORS OF CLAIRVOYANCE

The editor of the *Merrimac Journal*, Newburyport, Mass., Sept. 15th, states the "facts" as follows:

"In a paper published in the *Banner of Light*, Andrew Jackson Davis says: 'What a memorable day was yesterday [Jan. 15th, 1877]. It was the first time since the autumn of 1846, that I have enjoyed telescopic (clairvoyant) observations of any portions of the royal planets.' . . . . Then, further along he says, 'In consequence of all this, it was difficult, as it was unnecessary, for Mars to produce satellites, save a very feeble belt of cosmical bodies.'

"Now, if Mr. Davis was in the state he supposed himself to be, and he thought that mentally he was near enough to Mars to see its inhabitants and know their manner of life, then he should have known whether Mars had moons or not. He said there were none; but since that Prof. Hall with Alvan Clarke's great telescope, has discovered two; and some other astronomer has found a third. The clairvoyant telescope is less powerful than Clarke's telescope. We trust that the *Banner of Light* will shed its rays on this apparent inaccuracy of the greatest clairvoyant in the world.

"Next to our earth and moon, men have a better knowledge of Mars than of any other heavenly body. Venus comes nearer to the earth, but it is not so clearly visible. Mars' surface has been scrutinized and mapped, and long since it was declared to be as well fitted for habitation as the earth, but until this year all have agreed that it was moonless. It has been noticed that it was subject to reflected light, but no examination, till this year, revealed any satellites."

There is a self-evident candor in the foregoing criticism, which moves me to ask attention to a few essential considerations. They are as follows: Recently, in order to obtain more information, I have enjoyed three telescopic views of the surroundings of Mars. During each of these views (clairvoyantly) it is a fact that the body of the planet was of necessity almost entirely excluded "from the field of observation," for thus it was with the astronomers who gazed with their telescope; even as it was with the author, in the first instance, the *surroundings* of Mars were almost entirely shut out of the range of vision while the body and superficial features of the planet itself were the chief *objects* upon which the vision was closely concentrated. But, as I have before explained, the mere *glance* at the exterior of Mars impressed the fact that there existed a " *belt of cosmical bodies.*" And you will observe that I did *not* say that Mars had no moons; but I did say, what astronomers have since discovered, that there *are* " cosmical bodies " around Mars ; but that these " bodies " are entitled to be termed satellites, is a question not yet settled. I have already affirmed that, according to my understanding of their origin and constitution, Mars has no moons in the sense that our earth has one.

But just here, leaving for the present the question of " cosmical bodies *versus* moons " around Mars, I desire to awaken one or two reflections concerning clairvoyance ; as to its source, its power, and the laws which govern, or which should govern, its development and exercise.

A clairvoyant's sight is the same, in princip.c, as the sight of the bodily eyes; only the first is internal, or from invisible eyes, so to speak, and is strictly *telescopic* in its far-reaching power of vision. (This is explained in the first part of the book.) The clairvoyant eyes, therefore, must conform to the same laws and conditions which regulate all ordinary sight-seeing in all sensuous investigations. Spirits (as we improperly call the residents of the other worlds) see and hear and feel by and through their bodily senses, just as we do in this world. These interior senses (that is, the principles within our common bodily senses) are just the same after death as they are now within our present constitutions. They are in both worlds subject to limitations; are therefore liable to be misled and mistaken; and hence are susceptible to education and progressive improvement, in accordance with the universal laws of contact, experience, reasoning, will, affection, activity, and growth This explains why it is that, now and then, a clairvoyant may correctly see exactly what his or her vision is concentrated upon; and, at the same time, overlook very many—or not see at all—other bodies or questions which may be in closest proximity.

"A very *feeble* belt of cosmical bodies," is what I perceived *incidentally* to the vision of January 15th, 1877. Naturally enough, when I first heard that "two moons" had been astronomically discovered around Mars, I remarked to a friend: "Well, that shows that one pair of eyes cannot see everything." "Why didn't you see them," he asked, "when you were looking at Mars?" "Because," I replied, "my vision was fixed telescopically upon the body of the planet, and *not* upon its environments."

But since I have had three separate observations of those "environments" (at which times the planet itself was not visible to me), I have concluded that the exact phraseology, "a very feeble belt," etc., is correct, and

10*

should not be changed. I observed that the "two little masses" discovered, are exactly like many other bodies circulating in an almost continuous river near the equator of Mars; which bodies would be visible to astronomers, like the "two" or "three" already seen by them, if they were large enough to reflect light enough to become visible. I am quite certain that, some of these coming nights, astronomers will discover numerous "cosmical bodies," not as large as some of those about Mars, but similar to them in origin, constitution, and conduct, rotating in the same general direction, northeast and southwest, between two and three thousand miles, in the cold and dark space, in the upper ether atmosphere, which surrounds our own earth.

But to return, briefly, to the " very feeble *belt* of cosmical bodies." Of course this remark is only comparative, and resulted, undoubtedly, in great measure, from the *incidental* glimpse described. According to the calculations of one or two astronomers, the one moon of Mars is only "*four* miles thick," while the other body " is yet *smaller ;* " and these, with many other similar bodies, are flying around the planet, constituting the "belt," which was *first* mentioned by the author.

The reader is aware that the terms " cosmical bodies " are used by the author to mean masses of material elements floating or rotating in space, which eventually chemically unite into larger and yet larger masses, and thus ultimate through asteroids, satellites, and meteoric assemblages, into earths, like this on which we live.

In this connection I may introduce Prof. Alexander's astronomical remarks upon the probable origin of the satellites of our neighboring planet. His paper was read before the National Academy of Sciences, last October.

"The question was, ' Whence came the inner satellite of Mars ? ' This satellite, he said, has a greater angular velocity than the equatorial surface of its primary, thus presenting a curious anomaly in the solar system. This fact, said the speaker, led me to seek whether somebody had not met with an accident there and Mars had not appropriated it. I found that the orbits of three comets intersected near the orbit of Mars. About 1813 two enormous comets were very near in contact in the orbit of Mars, and Mars itself was there. However, an examination of the velocity of these comets showed that neither was great enough to satisfy the conditions. I became satisfied that no nucleus of any comet could have been transformed. into the satellite in question. According to solar physics, the body must have had at least a velocity equal to the orbital velocity of Mars, plus the velocity of the present satellite about Mars. There are formulas in which the mean distance of a body from the sun is a function of its velocity at any given period. By combining the equation expressing this function in the case of Mars with the equation in the case of the supposed asteroid, an expression is obtained giving the mean distance of the asteroid from the sun in terms of the velocities of the planet and asteroid. The velocity of Mars and its moon of course is known. By using the proper value of the velocity of the asteroid to satisfy the conditions explained above, a value for the mean radius vector of such asteroid is obtainable, which is somewhat smaller than the average distance of the mass of asteroids from the sun. However, if an asteroid did come under the influence of Mars, its velocity would have been somewhat lessened before it actually was changed into a satellite. If we add to the velocity of the supposable asteroid in the computations at quantity to represent this loss, the resulting value of the radius vector becomes similar to that of several well-known asteroids. Hence the phenomena presented by the inner satellite of Mars are explained by the hypothesis that *one of the asteroids was drawn away from its original orbit and caused to revolve about that planet.*"

Here, you observe, is a distinguished scientist and mathematician exerting his faculties to explain the fact that the so-called " moons " of Mars do not conduct themselves like moons ; because they are in fact only parts of " a belt of cosmical bodies " rotating in the atmosphere of that noble planet.

Scientific star-searchers, with reference to Mars, have encountered instrumental impediments. According to reports so far, the *inner* satellite of Mars has never been *seen* through any of the very large telescopes. Lord Rosse's great six-foot reflector was only capable of disclosing the outer body, but *not well enough to measure it.* But the refractors, with only twelve, or even seven inches aperture, have brought the existence of both little bodies to the human eye. The fact is that the cosmical bodies and the so-called satellites are too asteroidal to render themselves distinctly visible through reflecting telescopes.

(4.)

CONCERNING THE PERPETUITY OF THE HUMAN FORM.

A discussion recently has agitated many broad-minded and truth-loving persons, the subject-matter whereof is very explicitly set forth in the following letter :

"BROOKLYN, N. Y., July, 1877.

"A. J. DAVIS,

"MOST ESTEEMED FRIEND :—" In Chapter X. of your 'Views,' etc., you approach a very knotty and delicate subject, the organization of the Spirit-body. You say, 'In Summerland some of the vital organs' do not exist, and, particularly, 'no propagation requiring the external organs of generation,' etc.

"I need not remind you—for you are much more familiar with the subject than I—that this, your representation of the spiritual body, which is a merely *negative* one, depriving the human form of the conditions which make it the human form, stands in direct contradiction to the teachings of Swedenborg, whose inspiration and seership you do not deny.

"You know that Swedenborg carries the sexual distinction beyond the Spiritland, even to what he calls Heaven, and represents the 'conjugal delights' as the highest in this condition. He gives the Universe the (spiritual) shape of Man, and locates his several spheres or circles of Heaven within the various (spiritual) organs of the corresponding physical organization, mentioning the genital organs particularly, while you abolish these (and others) already in the *Summerland*, that is, in the next stage of disembodied men. It is, of course, consistent in you to abolish these *organs*, since you abolish the *functions;* but I do not see how it is possible to retain sexual distinction, as you do, without sexual organization, of which, if there be any truth in the doctrine of Correspondence, the necessary logical consequence would be sexual *functions*, also. I think that Swedenborg in carrying *marriage*, that is sexual union, through all the stages of spiritual existence, is more consistent; although not being one who is made to 'jurare in verba magistri,' I confess that his *offspring* from heavenly union of the sexes, which he calls 'thoughts' transcends my comprehension.

"If it should suit you to still throw some more light upon this delicate question, you would perhaps oblige more readers of your inspired 'Views,' besides your devoted friend,

"G. B."

Answer.—It will be first of all perceived that the thoughtful and scholarly author of the foregoing letter —no doubt without the least intention—develops the question of the reliability of witnesses—two seers, with a hundred years between them, looking at the same facts, record exactly *opposite* conclusions. For myself, then, concerning this conflict of testimony, I have this to

say : The only absolute authority is Nature; of which
Reason is the only infallible interpreter; of which Intuition is the only inextinguishable illuminator, being
the true inward " *light* which lighteth every man that
cometh into the world."

In this light, governed by these ever-present and
immortal authorities, I ask my questioning correspondent, as I recommend all human minds, to *test* the question which is awakened by this conflict of testimony
And to the end that the principles and facts of Nature
may be spread before the judgment-seat of Reason, I
proceed to offer further suggestions in the form of
affirmations.

Progressive development is a universal principle. By
and through this principle all the kingdoms of animated
and inanimated nature were steadily, though slowly,
evolved. They were evolved from countless germinal
points, and through countless ages or periods of time.

Science will demonstrate the truth of these propo-
sitions. These natural processes being admitted, the
question arises: What is the human form? Also,
another question, *when* was the final (the perfect) form
evolved and established? When was the last animal-
ized transient part eliminated? And when on earth
was the wholly perfect and the everlasting human form
attained and consummated?

Yonder, for illustration, is a young man of uncommon grace and beauty. He commands the admira-
tion of all beholders; winning, popular, conspicuous,
enthusiastic. Well, is he *perfect* in all his parts? Do
you say that he is free from defects in his anatomy,
physiology, and phrenology? Observe him a few years,

and you will discover in his manifestations of character many points of strength and at least a few points of weakness ; in other words, you will discover numerous imperfections in the operations of the organization of the (apparently) perfect young man.

Now if it were true that the human form is an outcome of the form of the pre-existent perfect spirit, then there would be some foundation for the assertion that all the external appendages of the body would appear and continue to exist after death. For they would then be only so many shapes projected from interior structures. But the truth is : The human body is an ultimate (not of spiritual forms, but) of all the *formative* principles, powers, forces, elements, essences, and properties, which begin their progressive labors in the least and lowest departments of this terrestrial globe. Thus the first dry-land creatures were more bird and fish than animal ; the first indications of humanity were far more like animals than men. When the most perfect human body was developed, it was a factory full of organs, full of wheels and hoppers, adapted to receive grists in the form of food, fluid, gases, and principles. And this corporeal mill is adapted to decompose them, and to refine them, and to promote them into ultimate parts and particles, and thus bestow more substance and more energy upon those soul-elements, which eventuate at death in the *body* of the spirit.

Now, if it be conceded that the *form* which a man wears upon his spiritual consciousness after death, is thus derived, the question arises : When does he attain to the point of perfect *formation ?* A mountain of testimony from the citizens of the next sphere looms up on

the side of great organizational progression " over there."
For example, do you suppose that " flesh and blood "
can enter the kingdom of spirit ?   Or, rather, do you
imagine that man's teeth in the next world are made of
lime ?   Do you suppose that his *final* set of teeth appears like the " temporary set " which nature puts in
the mouth of the child ?   Does the dental organism of
the human adult exactly correspond to those imperfect
teeth pushed out for a few years in the gums of the
child ?   But here on earth are we not all children ?   In
the Summerland you will finally receive the *adult* (or
the ultimate) *form ;* just as the adult teeth are superior
to those of infancy.

The human form, when it is perfect, is an exact representative of the formative principles which reside
eternally in the spirit; or, in truer words, the spirit of
man is a totality, a final individualization indestructible, of a perfect proportion of all essences and principles in the Central Sun.

Sex exists forever in the *principles* of the spirit;
male and female, positive and negative, wisdom and
love.   Outwardly, during all the subordinate stages of
evolution, these inherent principles clothe themselves
in appropriate external organs with legitimate external
functions; but when the individual rises into higher
kingdoms of life, the spiritual progress dominates the
material temporary parts (derived hereditarily from our
animal predecessors), and thus, at last, the most perfect
form is reached as a spiritual ultimation.

Swedenborg, you observe, admitted that *only*
" thoughts " resulted from sexual commerce in the
spiritual heavens.   Why, then, does he insist, illogically

and unphysiologically, upon the existence after death of the outward organs of impregnation and child-elaboration? There is no philosophical connection between the causes (the *organs*) and the effects (the *thoughts*) which are the only offspring born of man and woman in the different heavens?

Now, as to the heavenly results (thoughts) I am constrained to agree with Swedenborg; with the amendment of the additional words, *affections ;* a fact which I have many times noticed among the heavenly families. Thoughts are boys; affections are girls; and many celestial parents are blest with a numerous and beautiful progeny. And it is not exceedingly difficult to feed, and clothe, and educate, and direct the steps of such children !

———◆———

(5.)

DIVERSITIES OF SPIRITUAL GIFTS WITHOUT ANTAGONISM.

THE SUPERIOR CONDITION AND THE MEDIUM STATE.

"Now concerning spiritual gifts, brethren, I would not have you ignorant." Thus wrote the fearless Paul to the Corinthians, in the twelfth chapter of his first letters to them. He tells them to their face that they know that when they were materialistic Gentiles, they were led unto dumb idols in the vain belief that they would receive important information from the Gods;

and he intimates that, although they were now undoubtedly converted to the truth of spiritualism, yet that they
were dangerously *ignorant* of the nature and degrees of
spiritual gifts.

Therefore he proceeds to indoctrinate his over-credu-
lous Corinthian converts in these plain words: " Now,
there are diversities of gifts . . . . and diversities of
operations . . . . but it is the same God [Principle?]
which worketh all in all . . . . For to one is given
. . . . Wisdom; to another . . . . Knowledge; to
another Faith, [Intuition?] . . . . to another the gift
of Healing, [Magnetism?] . . . . to another the working of Miracles, [most wonderful Spirit-manifesta-
tions?] to another prophecy [predicting in both prose
and verse?] to another discerning Spirits, [Clairvoyant
perception?] to another divers kinds of Tongues,
[mediums speaking in different languages?] to another
the interpretation of tongues, [the talent of discerning
the meaning hidden within unknown words?] But all
these worketh " by virtue of " the self-same Spirit" [or
Principle?]. Yet all work together for a good purpose
—"many members" [many forms of mediumship?]
"of one body," in opposition to the *old* Dispensation and
for the ushering in of the *new*. . . . . " For the body is
not one member, but many."

But there must be no jealousy in this many-in-one
movement. Paul understood the prevailing ignorance
on all mysterious spiritual questions; he knew how
ignorance and selfishness carried very honest persons
into ambition and rivalry, impelling many to say and do
wicked things to gain place and power; and so, with
true gentleness and unswerving firmness, he argued the

case: "If the foot shall say, Because I am not the eye, I am not of the body." But, hark ye ! "is it therefore not of the body?" What the fleet, progressive, ambition, brainless "foot" said in reply to this conclusive argument we are left to conjecture. "If the body were an eye, where were the hearing?" If the whole were hearing, where were the smelling? . . . . "the eye cannot say unto the hand, I have no need of thee; nor again the head to the feet, I have no need of you . . . . now, "there should be no schism in the body" . . . . "are all apostles? Are all prophets? Are all teachers? Are all workers of miracles? Have all the gifts of healing? Do all speak with tongues? Do all interpret?" Just here Paul counselled his converts to "covet earnestly the best gifts." And yet, seeing the general failure of almost all who sought to become distinguished by "the *best* gifts," the sturdy old apostle, being reminded that to become a Harmonial Man—a whole (holy) man in the Christ-principle of pure love and trust in the Father—was infinitely better than any acquired "gift," so he closed his letter in these deeply impressive words: "And yet *I show you a more excellent way.*"

Now, brethren! do you believe that we Spiritualists are passing through (among ourselves, too !) the identical condition of ignorance, trial, jealousy, disappointment, and schism, which Paul wrote to overcome among the Corinthians so many hundreds of generations ago? We are! There is a general desire for mediumship; and this desire, as soon as gratified, becomes the foundation of numerous ills ; and, mainly, because each ear wants to be also a hand, and every handsome foot yearns to become a beautiful head, and *face*, too! Why? Because the demand of an ignorant constituency is satisfied with nothing less than the great accomplishment of *many gifts in* ONE. "The mediums are, most of them, persons of peculiar and sensitive organization, as to both body and mind, and after all allowance for unfavorable exceptions, they, as a class, deserve more charitable judgment than they are likely soon to receive."

This passage, so wholly true, was written by a minister; and of Spiritualists the same true man wrote: "Among the people who bear this name and hold this belief, there are many who must be classed with the very best men and women that we have ever known. Some of the most perfect and happy homes that now .bless this world are those of Spiritualist families. Of course persons of this class are free from the absurdities and insanities of which we have spoken. They are thoughtful, reverent, and deep-hearted. Above all, they are *true*, they are *faithful*. They love all 'things that are of good report;' they love their fellow-men, and put their religion into their lives. We cannot describe them so well any other way, as by quoting what Mr. Hale says about the 'Harry Wadsworth people:' 'The free-masonry was that you found everywhere a cheerful outlook—a perfect determination to relieve suffering, and a certainty that it could be relieved; a sort of sweetness of disposition which comes, I think, from the habit of looking across the line, as if death were little or nothing; and with that, perhaps, a disposition to be social, to meet people more than half way.' Thank God for all such of whatever name."

During several years past the author has been frequently reported, much to distress of loving friends, as attempting to *deride* mediumship, and, instead, as trying to exalt, as the only reliable state, the superior condition. And do you believe that a very large proportion of Spiritualists and mediums seem to be under this delusion? It has come to me in a great variety of ways. Recantation has been charged as well. A paper is sent me containing the following:

"Mr. Davis has gone beyond us; he does not believe in spirits holding intercourse with human beings through mortal mediums; but in his own clairvoyant integrity we opine he has not a doubt. But we do not forget that Mr. Davis was psychologized or mesmerized by a human operator in the early stages of his career, and that 'Nature's Divine Revelations' was published *as a contribution from spirits*. If he was really, as the book states, psychologized by a mortal, may he not be psychologized by an immortal? After all, it is possible he may still be under the influence or sport of spirits, and made to turn an intellectual somersault for the sake of bitter experience for himself, and stimulus to the lagging faith of others who, as yet, have not suffered the humiliation of recantation."

Not long after the receipt of the above misapprehension, the author was thus addressed by a troubled mind:

"DEAR SIR :—A few days ago I saw in one of our local papers a notice that 'A. J. Davis, the medium, had recanted, and asserted that what he had written and spoken was not under spirit influence.' I have forgotten the exact wording of the statement. Had I placed the least confidence in the notice I should have been terribly startled. For if you have been deceived or deceiving for so many years, where are we to look for truth? I hope you will answer this at your earliest convenience, if it is but a simple assurance of your steadfastness in your beautiful philosophy.

"Yours very truly,
"P. L. M."

Another writes : " Now is not all this strange talk for a Spiritualist ?   And if it is not *spirits* that communicate with us through mediums—what is it; or what does it all amount to ?   Does it mean that we must accept A. J. Davis's statements as conclusive, without seeking to *see* and *know* for ourselves ?   Is he one of those *rare* cases that can communicate with spirits, and common people need not try, but just swallow all he says ? "

Many striking crudities of mistaken criticism have visited the author by mail during the few years past ; and it is fair to presume that the reader is not more surprised than was the recipient himself.   Because I had written against the errors and fatal abuses practiced in the name of mediumship and Spiritualism ; and because (see the *Fountain*) I had most solemnly declared that the abuses to which the holy light has been subjected by selfish human nature are now reacting upon us in the " withdrawal from direct intercourse with earth's inhabitants, of scores of truly great and learned minds ; "   therefore I was accused (and too many yet believe that it is true) of decrying and repudiating mediumship, of denying that I had ever exercised any of its gifts, and of erecting, instead, the standard of the superior condition as alone worthy of universal acceptation.

Of Spiritualism itself, which I have been unjustly accused of renouncing, I have (see *Arabula*, p. 397), affirmed that it is " the first religion that takes facts for its foundation ; that rears its temples of thought on the immortal principles of philosophy; that has demonstrably brought life and immortality to light ; that has overcome death and the horrors of the grave; that sounded the gospel of Freedom equally to woman and man, to old and young, to lord and serf; that has satisfactorily explained the phenomena of matter and mind, in and out of man; which is the last and best development of the sublime relations between mankind and the next higher sphere of existence."

"Now concerning spiritual gifts, brethren, I would not have you ignorant." I have never denied, but have uniformly taught that the law of mediumship is an immutable law; and, progressively, from time to time, I have given illustrations, in my experience, and by quotations from various mediums, of the fact of communication between the two worlds. But because, solely for the sake of the *exact* truth in these things, I have made a distinction, which exists in the very constitution of things, between seeing and being impressed, independently, and the more passive and receptive state of mediumship; therefore arose all this injurious misunderstanding and misrepresentation, which has effectually prevented new converts to Spiritualism from reading my works, besides *delighting* the supporters of the dismal creeds and conservative churches.

In vain, ever and anon, reference is made to the correct explanations in the first part of "Nature's Divine Revelations." That work is on every hand styled the author's first and only great production; and yet, when a question arises which that book alone can answer, it is easily counted of little moment. Who knows all about mediumship? or all about clairvoyance? Not a living man or woman knows *all* there is to be known about the underlying principles and progressive possibilities of these correlated, yet very dissimilar, human mental conditions. Who does not long to know the truth about it all ? Who does not long to behold the windows of heaven opened, so that the facts of a natural *future* life shall become as positive as any facts in science ? Exactly what that state *was*, " by and through " which the first great work was spoken—and by means of which state all the author's subsequent and present information was and is received—is the question now to be answered.

About midway between the two conditions—between the *third* and *fourth* state—the mind loses almost all its sympathy with the external organs of sensation; that is, the five senses are closed; then "the mind becomes free from the organization," except as it is connected by the internal tie (composed of the elements of which, after death, the spiritual body is made); and " this condition stands in analogy to that natural state of physical disunion known as death." (See pp. 36, 37.) " The body at this time is dormant and inactive in all its parts," except the negative vital action which is constantly kept up and controlled by the united forces of the magnetizer and the magnetizee.

This is the condition of independent clairvoyance induced by magnetism. Magnetism seems indispensable when the subject is too youthful and physically too immature and weak to enter the condition voluntarily. This condition attained, what follows ? On page 38 the language is: "The medium existing between thought and thought, between mind and mind . . . is the *only* active, pervading medium which I am dependent on for the conception of thought, and for the *per-*

ception of all things of a refined, ethereal, or spiritual constitution."

But there is a passage in the next paragraph, on the same page, that is more emphatic and unqualified : "I AM NOT IMPULSED OR IMPRESSED BY THE THOUGHTS OR FEELINGS OF A FOREIGN PERSON, though *I am cognizant of them* through the medium above termed ethereal."

Now turn to page 40, and read : "When the mind becomes *free* from the organization "—that is, free of the sense of weight and bulk which arise from the material, which is the freedom of matter natural to the spiritual condition—then the mind " passes into a new sphere of existence."

The explanation follows on the same page, thus : All truth, all ideas, all principles, etc., " converge to one focus. This I call the Fountain, the Sun, etc. This is the great positive Power ; all subordinate existence is negative." Then comes the explanation that there are many circles, wheels, or spheres. Adjoining this, our *first* sphere, is another, the Second Sphere. In this next sphere there is a centre composed of the ethereal *wine of all things* beneath its exalted station in the universe.

Here comes (see page 41) the most positive testimony, thus : " From this Focus [in the Summerland, remember] I receive *impressions* of the many and varied principles," etc. . . . . " When I pass from the body [that is, rise above all the entangling alliances proceeding from a sense of the organs and weight of the body], it is *not* the distance, the indefinite space through which the mind proceeds " [sees], but it is the superior condition attained, or, in the peculiar language there used, " it

11

is the metamorphosis of the principle of mind to its Second Sphere of existence."

Then follows a reaffirmation, synoptically: "To this centre, to this focus, to the great positive power of this sphere . . . I go to receive information."

The question here arises: "Do not individual spirits, at this centre, impart to your mind the information which you return with?" The anwer is given on the same page: "As the mind generates *thought* by coming in contact [through the senses, of course] with external exciting causes in the natural body, so this Mind [that is, the combined mental possessions and developments of the Second Sphere], so this Focus "creates in my mind parallel ideas, which I term IMPRESSIONS."

But you exclaim: "I don't comprehend it at all." Very likely. In the volume under consideration (see page 42) the fact is thus stated: "The ultimate perfection of all substances, the ethereal existences of spiritual spheres, and the means [and method] by which I receive impressions *are evident to me;* but so greatly different [is this experience] from anything familiar to the natural mind . . . that it is impossible at this moment to make these things evident to *your* senses."

You still insist that my mind must be instructed by some particular "band of spirits." If this was the truth, I would be most happy to announce the fact. But you read on pages 42 and 43 this unqualified additional explanation: "When I pass off [that is, rise above the oppressive sense of a physical body] into the independent state of clairvoyance to receive impressions, *I receive them as the knowledge of the essence of the substance which I had a previous desire to investigate. . . .* THERE

I DO NOT HAVE ANY COUNSELLOR OR INFORMER. . . . I do not observe entities as they would be naturally known to exist." One broad and extensive light pervades all the Second Sphere, which "light is the medium of perception and association." Further on (see page 44) you read : "It is impossible by *words* to convey a full and adequate conception of the *manner* in which I arrive at truth. . . . MY INFORMATION IS NOT DERIVED FROM ANY PERSONS THAT EXIST IN THE SPHERE INTO WHICH MY MIND ENTERS; but it [the information] is the result of a law of truth emanating from the Great Positive Mind, and pervading all spheres of existence." In accordance with this Law, "truth is attracted to, and is received by, the mind."

Attentive readers need not be reminded in this connection that the author has many times explained fully what steps are necessary to the attainment of this interior condition. What care must be taken in physical habits, in foods, in drinks, in exercise, in sleep, the best time of day for investigation, how long it should be continued, etc. And the same reader is fully aware that I have also given the explicit laws and conditions under which, and by means of which, the differing states of mediumship may be reached, and safely employed in the interest of truth, for the advancement of our universal humanity. And furthermore, the candid and conscientious reader will bear witness that I have nowhere, or at any time, attempted to exalt the "superior condition" to the disadvantage of the conditions of mediumship. Whenever a *distinction* has been distinctly made and emphasized, it was solely and invariably in the interest of the whole and exact truth, and never with any hope or desire of unfavorably reflecting upon, or in the least, overshadowing any person's sincere experience in things spiritual. To my mind there is a manifest spiritual presence dwelling with many of the more quiet mediums, which brings a peacefulness and a heavenly satisfaction, while it augments, in the religious affections, the natural delight which is often awakened by the spirit of truth, opening up on every side the windows of the firmament, and letting in upon human hearts and homes the golden glories and sweet gladness of immortality.

Believe me, O friendly reader! You assume a serious risk when you seek for, and indulge in, too frequent communication with invisible intelligences through overworked business mediums; and believe me your risk is not less dangerous when, indiscriminately, you practice such intercourse by and through your own unregulated sensibilities.

Before me is a letter just received from a person who has made the last-named mistake. It is a touching appeal for sympathy and counsel in a serious crisis. He says, "It is not necessary for you to tell me that spirits are around me. I have received positive assurance of it! What I wish to know is—*Must I do as they say?* They tell me to act like *a crazy man.* Now must I do it? or must my conscience tell me what to do?" etc., etc.

Need I record here my reply to him? and which is what I would say to all? Substantially, I said: "When a 'spirit' or a 'mortal' tells you and urges you to say or to do anything foolish, weak, wicked, or unreasonable, when judged in the light of your highest judgment, *reject it at once,* and forever expel from your confidence and society both the principal and the confederate (or medium) of such counsel. Follow the *highest convictions* of your reasoning and intuitive faculties. Reason, which, when pure, is unbiassed, is a far better *guide* than either ' spirits,' or what generally passes for ' conscience.' " Because much of conscience, so-called, is too often the result of situation, education, etc."

Such was and is my answer. But, alas! I know too well that pure impersonal Reason, because it is the best light and highest authority, will be the very last which mankind will listen to and obey. Everything else, both cheap and costly, will be first tried. The *truth*, not personal and private benefits, is what you want and seek, is it not? This motive is admitted. Now whether the differing phases of mediumship, or whether the exercise of independent clairvoyance, is the speedier and the safer method for the discovery of truth—which, in short, is the better, the higher, the more reliable, and most desirable—are questions of lasting psychological importance, and believe me, respected reader, these problems are questions which coming generations of more analytical and more impartial investigators can and will settle for themselves far better than we can, while in the heat and dust and excitement of " making history " in our special individual private and semi-dogmatic mills.

And I tell you, brethren, that it is insufferably foolish, because it is weak and superficial, to array the " say so " of one medium or spirit against the " say so " of another medium or spirit; for when you subject these several and conflicting statements to the crucible of pure Reason, you will discover frequently, that they are of the *first* importance *as testimony* and of *no* importance *as evidence.* And, furthermore, it is diabolical to generate prejudicial differences between persons in the same field of usefulness; for there are too many coteries and class-antagonisms in our primary new school of Progression. "One saith, I am of Paul; another, I am of Apollos." But are such friends *real* friends? Are such reformers *real* reformers? We read their condemnation on every hand. "The ways of wisdom are ways of pleasantness;" and all truth-seekers in these paths look peaceful, powerful, reliable, and happy.

Prove all things.—The result of long years of contact with mediumship has recently cropped out in the form of a proposition to "try the spirits." An authority among Spiritualists, and a writer and traveller of much distinction, says:

" Spiritualists must test controlling spirits more thoroughly in the future than they have in the past. And spirits who object to being reasonably tested, reveal at once their moral unsoundness and spiritual unfitness to be the controlling guides of earthly sensitives. Inasmuch as the heavens and hells are both open to earth; and inasmuch as these immortal intelligencies stand behind the screen or, apostolically speaking, behind 'a glass,' that even the most lucid clairvoyants see through but 'darkly,' would any spirit, after séance had been opened with reading, singing, and invocation or prayer, demur at some such test as this:—'In the presence of God, who is here and everywhere; in the presence of the Christ-spirit of love and truth; in the presence of angels and ever-attending spirits; in the presence of these mortal friends now assembled; and in the presence of, and before the judgment seat of my own soul—I solemnly affirm that I am the spirit of the person who, when living in an earthly body, was known by the name of——, residing in——.' "

The administration of this " iron-clad oath " would be attended with a great variety of dangers and demo-

ralizations. As a rule, any man or spirit, or any media·
torial representative thereof, who would submit to such
an oath, would be tempted, by a secret perverseness
natural to the mental constitution, to rebel against mechanical justice and restraint, and *perjury* would be
the first step in such rebellion. Our truest men only
affirm ; they "*swear* not at all." The solemnity of a
Bible-oath is diluted by the insulting doubt of personal
veracity which it implies. Hypocrites and other dignified enemies of pure truth, like the natural moral cow-
ards of society, are the most ready to pledge their
word " on the Bible." What is true in common society
about us, would be more than reflected, nay, it would
be diabolically practiced, by the spirit oath-makers who
would gladly pay this price to be wholly believed by
their credulous admirers.

Fearless criticism necessary.—Again, the distinguished author, whose eloquent description of the "superior condition " is given in the first chapter in this
volume, has manfully opened his batteries upon the
enemies within the household of Faith, in these well-
chosen words:

"I will not disguise the fact that, as a people, we are too much
disposed to accept everything that comes to us in the abused name
of Spiritualism. We have permitted this too long. Our sublime
philosophy has become a packhorse—a patient beast of burden that
staggers under a vast load of monstrous absurdities and moral trum-
pery. The public should be made to understand that we are not
a mere transportation company. We must get rid of our heavy
freight, or the better class of passengers will take another line. The
evils that lie in our way are quite too general to admit of the restric-
tion of a personal application. It is time to stop the child's play of
closing the eyes, opening the mouth and swallowing ; for why should

the function of deglutition in a Spiritualist embrace everything deleterious and unclean? We make use of sieves and strainers in the kitchen, but seldom in the library. We winnow the grain we eat, and filter the water we drink, and why not sift our literatures. We strain at gnats in air or water, and swallow an invoice of scorpions and a nest of adders in a bad book."

The genuine metal and strength of the foregoing criticism are quite as applicable to the claims and disclosures of independent clairvoyants.

For the twentieth time the author affirms his own most sincere desire to possess the truth—the whole truth, and nothing but the truth—upon any of the questions which have agitated his mind and fallen under his pen; and the same fearless, frank, truth-seeking inspection and analysis, which it is proposed should be meted out to any writings in the fold, he again invites and now prays in all sincerity may be as freely and fully meted out to and upon anything which is legitimately and rightfully associated with his name.

For it is time that all partition walls and class-prejudices should be overthrown. It is time that we, of the New Dispensation, should stand shoulder to shoulder, and heart to heart, faithful and loving sisters and brothers, as one mighty army of invincible Progressives; in order that we may assail and *conquer* the vast array of institutionalized forces which are to-day drilling and entrenching for the terrible conflict.

(6.)

A PREDICTION GRADUALLY FULFILLED.

The following is presented, as one instance, in reply to the question: "Do you ever realize the fulfillment of Spiritual predictions?"

In 1853, in the city of Hartford, State of Connecticut, the author (under a spiritualization fully explained in the "Present Age and Inner Life," page 142, new edition), recorded these words:

"Japan, . . . Western nations think thee abandoned to the night of Ignorance—buried in the depths of Idolatry. . . . Nay, Japan! We [her attorneys and guardians residing in the Summerland] behold thee *as thou art*—the Admirer of the Beauties of Mind; the Patron of elegant manners; the Friend of Education. . . . Let the Western nations enter thy gates. . . . Unite, O Japan, in the cry of the world, ' *Love universal and Justice?* ' Let this be proclaimed, O Emperor! from thy lofty places."

To make this plain, some remarkable data and certain recent events are now in order. The above was written twenty-five years ago. The present Emperor, the Mikado of Japan, was then a mere babe, about one year old, having been born in 1852. This Japanese infant, whose royal blood had flowed through one hundred and twenty-two generations, and consequently whose imperial dynasty dated far anterior to any European family of kings, was destined to carry into effect the will of the celestial delegates. He ascended the throne of Japan

11*

before his sixteenth year, in 1868, having received the title of Prince eight years previously, in 1860.

Christians have a delightful consolatory theory that *they* are *the* " chosen people "—the favorites of God, being the only branch of the human family from which the kingdom of heaven is populated. But the existence of such a delegation, whose tender and eloquent address to Japan begins this section, refutes the gracious theory of the modest followers of the meek and lowly one. Now it seems that from the Summerland, over twenty-five years ago, we received the *first* reliable intelligence concerning the actual condition and disposition of the people of Japan. This fact reflects severely upon the historical information spread through the world by Christian writers and travellers in the East. By these we are told of the idolatrous ignorance, of the universal degradation, of the heathenish viciousness, and of the unbridled rascalities of the Japanese population. But, pouring down from the bright skies overhead, there comes the truth—that those same heathen are constitutionally great worshippers of things spiritual —" admirers of the beauties of the Mind ; " that they are naturally a civil and polite people, " the patrons of elegant manners ; " that they are lovers of true knowledge, and opposed to ignorance—naturally " the friends of education. "

All these attractive communications from the celestial envoys and attorneys of Japan would continue to be rejected by Christians, and the misstatements of their own missionaries would still pass for truth in Christendom, were it not for the developments of the past few years, during which the Mikado has " opened his mystic gates" to the Western nations not only, but, what is of paramount importance, he has freely joined his voice " in the cry of the world for universal love and justice," which cry was not long since officially " proclaimed from his lofty places! "

In order that all this may be demonstrated to the common understanding, I will here give in full the youthful Mikado's own address to his ambassadors, at a dinner given to them in his palace, on the eve of their departure to America. The inspired Emperor, taking the lead of all the daimios, and of all the ex-governors who had controlled the provinces, assembled the members of his embassy around a table in his palace at Tokai, and thus addressed them :

" After careful study and observation, I am deeply impressed with the belief that the most powerful and enlightened nations of the world are those who have made diligent effort to cultivate their minds, and sought to develop their country in the fullest and most perfect manner. Thus convinced, it becomes my responsible duty, as a sovereign, to lead our people wisely in a way to attain for them results equally beneficial ; and their duty is to assist diligently and unitedly in all efforts to attain these ends. How, otherwise, can Japan advance and sustain herself upon an independent footing among the nations of the world ? From you, nobles of this realm, whose dignified position is honored and conspicuous in the eyes of the people at large, I ask and expect conduct well becoming your exalted position—ever calculated to indorse, by your personal example, those goodly precepts to be employed hereafter in elevating the masses of our people. I have to-day assembled your honorable body in our presence-chamber, that I might first express to you my intentions, and, in foreshadowing my policy, also impress you all with the fact that both this Government and people will expect from you diligence and wisdom while leading and encouraging those in your several districts to move forward in paths of progress. Remember your responsibility to your country is both great and important.

Whatever our natural capacity for intellectual development, diligent effort and cultivation are required to attain successful results. If we would profit by the useful arts and sciences and conditions of society prevailing among more enlightened nations, we must either study these at home as best we can, or send abroad an expedition of practical observers to foreign lands, competent to acquire for us those things our people lack which are best calculated to benefit this nation. Travel in foreign countries, properly indulged in, will increase your store of useful knowledge; and although some of you may be advanced in age, unfitted for the vigorous study of new ways, all may bring back to our people much valuable information. Great national defects require immediate remedies. We lack superior institutions for high female culture. Our women should not be ignorant of those great principles on which the happiness of daily life frequently depends. How important the education of mothers, on whom future generations almost wholly rely for the early cultivation of those intellectual tastes which an enlightened system of training is designed to develop! Liberty is therefore granted wives and sisters to accompany their relatives on foreign tours, that they may acquaint themselves with better forms of female education, and, on their return, introduce beneficial improvements in the training of our children. With diligent and united efforts manifested by all classes and conditions of people throughout the empire, we may attain successively the highest degrees of civilization within our reach, and shall experience no serious difficulty in maintaining power, independence, and respect among nations. To you, nobles, I look for the indorsement of these views; fulfil my best expectations by carrying out these suggestions; and you will perform faithfully your individual duties to the satisfaction of the people of Japan."

Turn now to page 143 of the "Present Age," etc., and compare what you there find—the unqualified affirmations there made, the work mapped out, and the half-prophetic instructions there imparted—with the above address of the inspired young Emperor, and with yet other facts recently developed, and then conclude in your own mind how much real evidence exists to establish the claim of spiritual intercourse. Bear in mind

the fact, that, during the last ten years, under the pre-
monitory instructions of the youthful Mikado, and aided
by the wealth of the empire, about one thousand young
men of Japan have been sent into our Western institutions to learn of our wisdom and knowledge. The thirst
for universal education thus entered the heart of the
Eastern realm. Our language and laws, our habitations
and habits, our agriculture and manufactures, our engi-
neering and railroading, our public schools and sectarian
religions, our artistic skill and scientific achievements,
our universal love and equal justice to all—our presi-
dential amusements, too! our revolutionary propensi-
ties, our republican institutions, and our methods of
government—all these, and millions of lesser lights in
our civilization, of which our pictures and our literature
are not the least, are now visited by the Japanese, to the
end that mankind may enter upon an era of love, justice,
and brotherhood.

(7.)

ORIGIN OF THE SCRIPTURES.

"Please explain the origin of the Bible," is asked
by a correspondent. Briefly, this is my answer: The
universally adored volume of Christendom was originated and arranged into a (so-called) unimpeachable
authority about two hundred years after the martyrdom
of Jesus. In the year A. D. 218 the Vulgate form of
the existing Bible was established. Of course all Protes-

tants will thank all Catholics for collecting and preserving the manuscripts which compose what is called " The Word of God."

All known bibles were, as to their contents, " given by inspiration ; " and are (or may be made) profitable for doctrine, for rebuke, for development, for growth in spirituality and goodness ; but let no ecclesiastical tribunal exalt *a dead book* above the' divine LIVING LIGHT that is a part of each human mind.

There are, however, prophetic revelations. Before Christianity, so-called, was a century old, the inspired St. John (inspired just as every medium is, more or less) experienced, on the Isle of Patmos, an apocalyptical awakening of his most interior perceptions. The disclosures of St. John in his " Revelation " have entertained and puzzled sinners, ministers, and followers equally for about seventeen hundred and eighty-five years. It is certain that the remarkable visions and predictions of the medium of Patmos can be comprehended and measured, as to their real import and true value, only by and through a careful study of analogous experiences and apocrypha written mediumistically within memory of the present generation.

Looking afar for a blessing, instead of just at your feet, where the richest diamond lies hidden in the coarse sand, illustrates the difference between a fool and a philosopher.

(8.)

SOURCES OF THE WORLD'S WEALTH.

"What was man's first and most natural occupation?" To this I am impressed to reply: Sixteen hundred years before the advent of Christianity, the science and essential dignity of *agriculture* were anticipated. As far back in human history as the age of pyramids, when the Egyptians were successful earth-workers, the profession of husbandry was recognized and exalted as the basic business of mankind.

Triptolemus claimed to have been taught agriculture by *an angel;* instructed by a divinity bending over him out of the heavens, how to plow, to sow, to reap, and to make excellent corn-bread. In the Eleusinian Mysteries, or rather in Oriental mythology, this great scientific *earth-worker* was helped by a goddess (an angel?) to communicate "what he knew about farming." But, owing to the law of progression, it has come to pass that even editors have become like unto the gods, "knowing good and evil." And in these proud and pompous times, the aid of goddesses and ministering angels are by many counted undignified and superfluous; and yet journalists are easily transformed into aspiring candidates for office, while the earth is surrounded by illiterate explorers, and forced to yield to the authority of science.

The sources of the world's wealth are two: first, the

Land, second, the Sea; and agriculture is to the former what commerce is to the latter; but the master science of all material sciences is that by which the earth is conquered and made to blossom as the rose. . . . I can discern a time when mankind will *control* the production and the distribution of rain. Already the signal office of the United States is handling three instruments —the *thermometer*, the *barometer*, the *telegraph*, and (possibly) the *telephone*. And yet other instruments and scientific means will ere long be employed for the special benefit of fruit-growers and agriculturists.

(9.)

EVILS IN THE SOCIAL STRUCTURE.

A laboring brother, one of the leaders in popular "strikes," writes me "for a few words of light on the Labor Question."

Answer.—The incessantly toiling millions in the social organism find themselves, by force of circumstances, in a state of chronic antagonism toward the wealthy and powerful. Their interests, their tastes, their privileges, their prospects, stand in open opposition to each other. Capital tends to centralization; labor, to free distribution. `Wealth seeks *monopoly* as its most natural fortification, and the reins of government as a means of its perpetuation; while Poverty instinctively seeks freedom and democratic independence, as its most natural birthright and the only road to happiness. The first child of communism is christened "Coöperation;" while the first born of wealth is called "Monopoly." The fight between these forces in society generally ends in the defeat of labor; because the centres of Wealth can afford to "rest and wait," while the coöperative societies "strike and starve;" and the contest ends by the surrender of dying Poverty, which then yields everything—brain, bone, muscle, time, rights, principles.

Communism dreams of an equal distribution of the accumulations of generations; so that no one can be rich, while for only a brief period every one would be equally poor. Industrial and intellectual stagnation would be the immediate effect. The equal distribution of poverty is equivalent to paralysis of individual ambition for invention, conquest, and emoluments. Wealth flows into reservoirs as naturally as water accumulates in lakes. The true philosophical remedy for social evils and injustice, and the pains of Poverty, consists in the application of the principles of love, justice, and eternal truth to the Constitution of the general Government, and to the State laws under which society exists and civilization advances. To this end we welcome all these rebellions and threatenings of the working millions. Strikes, processions, communal outrages, international societary combinations against both capital and government—all, all, are steps most indispensable to the reconstruction of Government, and to the reorganization of Society upon principles of universal love, truth, and justice.

(10.)

ORIGIN OF THE DEVIL DOCTRINE.

For scores of centuries, preceding the era of Copernicus, the hyper-metaphysical Orientals believed unquestioningly in the hollowness and stationariness of our globe. (It seems that, in our own bright day and enlightened generation, the " hollow " dogma of the very ancient cosmogony has been revived for the entertainment of our fellow-citizens worshipping west of the Alleghanies.) But, happily, the dogma of old earth's flatness and immovableness has been kindly omitted. The proposition that spirits or.gods construct the worlds of space, and not the reverse—that the worlds manufacture and evolve the gods—is of very ancient root, and holds some fragments of truth, like alchemy, astrology, and the other marvellous developments of mankind's intellectual childhood.

The bottomless pit, wherein Apollyon reigned supreme, was an old eastern fancy called " Hades "—an immense world of darkness, a dread after-death region, believed to be fixed deep under the immovable earth. The author of " Arabian Nights " gives full, picturesque, and tragic expression to this fearful dream of mankind's religious childhood. All fallen genii, according to this writer, had dwelling-places in the bowels of great mountains. They ascended from their dread abodes beneath the world. But, long prior to the Arabian stories, the doctrine of a bottomless pit and of fallen genii prevailed in many portions of the East. The Babylonians and the Chaldeans made heavy contribution to this theory. The word *Satan* was of Chaldean origin. Lucifer is the Latin for a Hebrew term—*Hellel*—employed first by Isaiah in describing the fall of Babylon: "How hast thou fallen from heaven, oh Hellel, star of the morning?" Lucifer, who was originally the morning light, stands now for the Apollyon mentioned by John as the Destroyer, and as the Devil who tempted Eve, circumvented the beneficent plans of the Almighty, damned the human race, and made the theological scheme of salvation a spiritual as well as a military necessity.

But the true vital origin of the doctrine of a hell and devil, is this:

Mankind, like individuals, conceive badly when badly diseased. Evil dreams mean either a physical or a mental disorder. Ancestors live in the cells of your brain. Their imperfections and passions may come to action and to speech only in your dreams at night ; or your own personal defects may of themselves act and speak in your night-time entertainments. Apollyon is the creation of a spiritual nightmare in religion. A fallen Lucifer, "Star of the Morning," is a childish explanation of evil and its punishment. Evil angels, infernal spirits, devils, come to the imaginations of discordant and superstitious persons. Inherited imperfections of either mind or body twist and blister the glass in the windows of the soul, so that seeing accurately is well-nigh impossible ; the consequences are a number of corresponding imperfections in your feelings, perceptions, and religion.

(11.)

THE FIRST DOCTOR OF DIVINITY.

I am asked why so many good and scholarly men are doctoring divinity. In answer, I beg to refer to the great King David, whose special friend had a reputation for wisdom which exceeded that of any other man in the Jewish nation. He was a great counseller and judicial functionary, and among his friends it was said that he "knew the whole mind of God." Doubtless, therefore, Ahithophel was the first regular recognized Doctor of Divinity; of which important class, in America, there are upwards of five thousand, maintained at enormous salaries. But their great original (Ahithophel), when, at last, his counsels were contemptuously *rejected*, got upon the back of an ass, rode home to his family, explained to them the wisdom and economy of suicide under the circumstances, then withdrew into a retired room of his own house and hanged himself. But modern Ahithophels, who are conspicuously unlike their magnanimous prototype, when their dogmatic ideas of "the whole mind of God" are rejected, seem strongly tempted to maintain their authority with dignity, and *hang* their opponents. But these modern times are different; and we cannot expect that our Doctors of Divinity should follow the example of their great predecessor, Ahithophel.

(12.)

THE CHARGE OF ATHEISM.

Correspondents ask me to explain exactly what this term means. Strictly speaking, atheism is a denial by another of the existence of *the* God in which you have been educated to believe. Denial of this kind may be honest, and ought not to subject a person to reproach. But there is, I think, an absolute atheism which consists in a wilful rejection of what you believe is strictly just and true. This is a godless state of mind; being at once unconscious of, and disobedient to, the laws of the eternal good that is within you. A mind in this atheistic condition is of necessity in the world without God and Hope. Its punishment consists principally in the *absence* of light, affection, hope, and happiness. This kind of atheism is not punished arbitrarily in the future state by an infliction of suffering, but rather by *deprivations*, which is a species of spiritual loneliness and starvation—a most natural result of this, the most deplorable and desolate of all forms of negation.

Belief in the positive existence and superintendence of a Supreme Power, is as natural and congenial to the human heart as disbelief in the necessary limitation of the personality of God is natural to the well-balanced human intellect. You perceive the distinction here made between the heart and head; that is, between *Intuition* and *Intellect*. The first, of the heart, is called Deism ; the second, of the head, Atheism.   But there is neither merit nor demerit in either direction. Because no human spirit, in its affections, can deny its fountain source ; any more than any thinking human mind, in its thoughts, can adopt and believe in a God with personality and measurable boundaries.

(13.)

THE LAWS OF DISTANCES IN THE SOLAR SYSTEM.

"What is the present state of astronomical knowledge concerning the distances of the planets from the sun?"

Answer.—The inventor and author of the *Celestial Indicator* (a most perfect instrument for teaching astronomy *) has given the best popular synopsis as follows :

The planets all revolve in slightly elliptical orbits around the sun, having an axial motion eastward like the sun.   Their orbital paths are nearly parallel to each other, crossing the Ecliptic at small and varied angles, and the planets vary of course in the length of their time of revolution, as well as in their axial motion, as their size, density, and distances vary.

Those that are farthest off travel the slowest, and they gradually increase in speed, the nearer their orbits are to the sun.   Mercury being the nearest to the sun is the swiftest in its motions.   Its dis-

---

* Address the "Bryant Celestial Indicator Co.," Hartford, Ct., for further information.

tance from the sun is thirty-five million miles; its periodic time, eighty-eight days; its diameter, about three thousand miles.

The next is Venus, whose distance is sixty-six million miles; periodic time, two hundred and twenty-four days; diameter, seven thousand five hundred miles. These are called the inferior planets, because their orbits are within that of the earth.

Next in order is the Earth, on which we live, whose distance from the sun is about ninety-two million miles; its periodic time three hundred and sixty-five and one-quarter days; its diameter, about eight thousand miles. Of the superior planets (outside of the earth's orbit) the first is Mars, distant from the sun one hundred and thirty-nine million miles; its periodic time being six hundred and eighty-six days, and its diameter about four thousand miles. The next in order are the asteroids, small planets; a large number have been discovered, sweeping in vast orbits around the sun in a region between Mars and Jupiter; orbits somewhat more eccentric than those of the larger planets, and making greater angles with the Ecliptic. They are invisible except through the telescope. They are supposed to have once formed a large planet, which from some unknown cause was blown to atoms. A planet seems to be wanted in this region, in order to satisfy our conceptions of symmetry in the solar system.

Next to the Asteroids is Jupiter, whose distance from the sun is four hundred and seventy-five million miles, its periodic time four thousand three hundred and thirty-two days, and its diameter eighty-eight thousand miles.

Next to Jupiter is Saturn, its distance from the sun being eight hundred and seventy-two million miles, its periodic time ten thousand seven hundred and sixty-nine days, and its diameter seventy-two thousand miles.

Then comes Uranus, one billion seven hundred and fifty-three million miles from the sun, its periodic time thirty thousand six hundred and eighty-six days, and its diameter thirty-three thousand miles. And last and most remote of the eight is Neptune, at the enormous distance of two billion seven hundred and forty-six million miles from the sun, its periodic time being sixty thousand one hundred and twenty-six days, and its diameter thirty-seven thousand miles. And here, as far as we know, is the limit of our planetary system, though numerous comets sweep far beyond it.

What a vast circle this last or outside planet must describe in its circuit around the sun? too far away to be seen except with the telescope, while yet its relations with the sun are such as to bring it through its course in a given time with wonderful precision. . . . . All these planets and their moons have an axial motion eastward in the direction of their orbital motion. How is this? Did they once belong to the body of the sun? Modern science has located the sun in space, and called it a fixed star. Undoubtedly it is; and it is also supposed to be a variable star. Its diameter is eight hundred and fifty-two thousand miles.

Professor Stephen Alexander, of Princeton College, presented before the National Academy of Sciences, last October, the following table relative to the aphelion and perihelion (or the extreme) distance of the planets.

Ratio.	*Planet.*	*Law.*		*Fact.*	*Difference.*
—	Neptune	30.057	mean distance	30.057	0.000
$\frac{2}{3}$	Uranus	20.038	aphelion	20.043	−0.005
$\frac{1}{2}$	Saturn	10.019	aphelion	10.000	+0.019
$\frac{1}{2}$	Jupiter	5.009	perihelion	4.978	+0.031
$\frac{1}{2}$	Asteroids	2.505	near mean value		
$\frac{2}{3}$	Mars	1.670	aphelion	1.644	+0.026
$\frac{2}{3}$	Earth	1.113	aphelion	1.035	+0.078
$\frac{2}{3}$	Venus	.742	aphelion	.749	−0.007
$\frac{1}{2}$	Mercury	.371	mean distance	.387	−0.016

Two-thirds of the mean distance of Neptune is the aphelion distance of Uranus. One-half this is the aphelion distance of Saturn. One-half of this is the perihelion distance of Jupiter. The ratios in the other cases will be seen from the table. The figures in all save three cases are the aphelion distances. Jupiter and Mercury form exceptions. Neptune, a seeming exception, is not really one. It is the starting point, and its distance is not a derived but an underived quantity. Incidentally, the necessity for using the mean distance of Neptune goes to show that it is the outer planet of the system. Jupiter, the master spirit of the whole, requires its perihelion distance to be used. This is the case with the largest members of the systems of satellites. Mercury is a double planet and its mean distance is used. The unit of measure employed is the earth's mean distance from the sun. These ratios are remarkably simple, and the correspondence between the law and the fact is very close. Many investigators have endeavored to find the phyllotachi series of fractions ($\frac{1}{2}$, $\frac{2}{3}$, $\frac{3}{5}$, etc.) in the ratios of the periodic times of the planets. Phyllotaxis is a botanical term and deals with the arrangement of the leaves upon the stem. This arrangement is known to follow mathematical laws, and the law is expressed in the phyllotachi series. Professor Alexander called attention to the fact that the first two of the series are the same as the ratios found between the aphelion distances of the planets. He did not attach particular significance to this, but thought the coincidence worthy of mentioning.

———•———

(14.)

MODERN PHASES OF INFIDELITY.

" Mr. Davis,

"Dear Sir:—Last evening, our minister, the Rev. Dr. S., preached upon the ' Phases of Infidelity.' They were as follows: Atheism, Pantheism, Deism, Rationalism, and Spiritualism. These were defined, and shown to be defective. Concerning Rationalism, he said: 'It teaches that the Scriptures are not from God; that Paul was no more inspired than Thomas Carlyle, Ralph Waldo Emerson, or Andrew Jackson Davis.' He criticised Spiritualism most severely, and said that it 'played the part of the religious clown; it is made up of the odds and ends of all creeds, all absurdities and all characters.' Now, sir, will you please make public your views upon these phases of skepticism ?

" Very truly,

" N. D. T."

Answer.—The beauty of holiness is as admirable in a minister as in any member of his congregation. Telling the plain truth in a sermon is as commendable as writing it in a book. It is true that the phases of infidelity

—which term means a refutation of and disbelief in the articles of various sectarian creeds—are five-fingered, like the almighty hand of Truth. Providence is showing his hand in these latter days, visible to those who have light in their eyes, finely proportioned, with four great strong, beautiful fingers and a powerful thumb; the four are *Atheism, Pantheism, Deism, Rationalism,* but the member of greatest energy, the thumb, is SPIRIT-UALISM.

We hail your minister gladly to our ranks. You say that he is now a Baptist. He will not, therefore, fear to "wade into" the waters of new truth. He criticised the thumb "severely," and alluded to it with emphasis, and described it in language not lawful for man to utter outside of the clergyman's castle. His mistake was that he did not discern that what he unhappily termed "infidelity" is the great, white hand of Providence, having four beautiful fingers and a thumb, just now moving over the world with an almighty grasp.

And, your minister made another mistake! How true it is that mistakes beget misrepresentations, and that immediately from them misunderstandings are rapidly born, in twins and triplets, until every room in one's social and intellectual house is overrun with more unpromising children of darkness than is lawful under the new rule of "fewer and better." His mistake was in the assertion that Rationalism "teaches that the Scriptures are not from God." For a brief reflection along the line of truth would have enlightened his understanding.

Rational-minded persons, on the contrary, everywhere teach that "all scripture, given by inspiration, is profit able," etc. In this statement you perceive the very rational implication which no true minister ever rejected, that there is in the world a great mass of "scriptures" which is not profitable, because such scriptures were *not* "given by inspiration." But a little mistake, like the foregoing, should not be remembered by any one against your minister; for does he not speak the whole truth in the next passage—that in the religion of Rationalism, "Paul was no more inspired than Thomas Carlyle, Ralph Waldo Emerson," etc. Your minister never uttered a truer sentence. It is, in fact, far truer as it stands than the reverse would have been, namely: "that Emerson and Carlyle are no more inspired than was Paul." For every candid searcher after religious truth *knows* in the secret places of his own heart that Paul's best writings do not contain a tenth part of the internal evidence of inspiration from God as do the best scriptures of either Emerson or Carlyle. But we must remember that your minister said that "Paul was *no more* inspired," etc.; which is saying a good deal of unpopular truth for a minister, and we should be grateful for it.

Again: "Spiritualism," he said, "played the part of the religious clown." A kind of electrical flush mantled our healthy cheek when we read this assertion. We blushed because the remark was like the unexpected utterance of a scandal, in which a beloved and pure relative was ruthlessly and hopelessly involved. That relative is commonly known as "Christianity." Now, the very worst that can be said of spiritual manifestations is, that they reproduce and re-illustrate the "wonderful signs" which followed the early disciples of Christianity. Modern *shows* of spiritual presence, inspiration, and power, are parallel, in every essential detail, to the reported "shows" by the primitive founders of our before-mentioned beloved relative. Your minister should not permit himself to indulge in such slanderous imputations. He knows that the mediumistic *show* of "blasting the fig-tree" is not more objectionable than was his stigmatization of the old miracles as the plays of religious clowns. At this very hour, while I write, there are sterling temperance men stumbling headlong over the performance at the wedding of Cana—the unfortunate spiritualistic *show* by which pure "water was changed into wine." These performances upon the boards of the ancient stage did not exalt either the actors or their audiences. And when your minister stigmatized modern Spiritualism as a "religious clown," we blushed lest superficial minds would reject living evidences along with miracles of the early eras, and exclaim, in their foolishness, "There is no God! Let us eat, drink, and be merry, for to-morrow we die!" The proverb of those who "live in glass houses should not throw stones," and a good many other old saws come up for quotation, but we give them the go-by, believing that your minister will think the matter over, and we hope he will openly recant every mistake in due time.

And here we would, if we could, gladly take down our harp from the weeping willows, and we would, if we could, now begin to sing a new song of welcome to a minister who is making such progress. But we are shocked into silence by his closing saying: That "Spiritualism is made up of the odds and ends of all creeds, all absurdities, and all characters."

Possibly there is truth in the first statement: in fact, there is truth in it all; but the inference is slightly un-charitable, not to say unchristian. Now just take an illustration : A magnificent bouquet of flowers is always made up of the odds and ends of the garden. Who wants the rough roots and prickly stalks, when one can obtain the sweet green leaves (the "odds") along with the thrice-blessed flowers (the "ends")which grow upon the tip-top places and upon the outermost branchlets of the flowering trees and shrubs? It would not be unfair—in fact it is truly scientific—to say that your minister *himself* was made (by God, of course) of the odds and ends of physical Nature. He is a compound of gases, liquids, and solids, which were elementary; the very odds and ends of millions upon millions of organized bodies in the lower and lowest walks of creation. Your minister need not feel disheartened and humiliated, because, physically and mentally, he is nothing but an organized bouquet of such *gases* as oxygen, nitrogen, hydrogen, etc.; of such *fluids* as bromine, mercury, phosphorus, etc.; of such *solids* as iron, sulphur, lime, etc. Nay, he should preach truth-telling sermons all just the same, and be properly re-munerated therefor; his origin and constitution, com-posed of odds and ends, not being remembered to his personal disadvantage.

Nor would we in this place array against *his* theology or against *his* Christianity the ten thousand and one absurdities of Oriental mythology and religious specu-lation which have at last culminated in this popular system which passes in society under the pompous title of "Evangelical Religion." Spiritualism, on the other hand, is entitled to be known by a less ancient and less questionable parentage. It is the legitimate child of modern living facts; not the final result, as theology is, of ancient dead fictions. And it is also something worth recalling that "all characters" find shelter under its adoptive wings. Peter! call thou not *unclean* anything which the Lord God has made. Your minister will recall the great story of the great ark. Did it not contain (by the Lord's express instructions and commands) two of every kind of four-footed beasts and a pair of every variety of creeping things? In a word, the "odds and ends" of all creation. And there were specimens of every character. Why, then, all this antagonism to the ark of Spiritualism? We do not want to put to sea in any vessel that is not absolutely seaworthy, and which is not large enough to carry and provide comfortably for *the whole human family;* composed as it is of all characters, of all creeds, of all absurdities, of all and everything, which the law of gravity holds lovingly and faithfully to the bosom of Nature.

And with this candid declaration we bid adieu to your minister, simply expressing the hope, that he will continue to lead his congregation toward the gates of light.

(15.)

CONVERSION, OR A CHANGE OF HEART.

"What do you understand by the religious experience styled 'conversion?'"

Answer.—This term is used in religion to signify "a change of heart."

The effort of Christians to convert the Jews, notwithstanding the millions of money and the great instrumentalities at their command, have singularly failed, because the Jews are very strict in the inculcation and observances of their religion. They marry in-and-in to keep the race pure-blooded, and are taught to reject the theories and sectarian approaches of every branch of Christians; in like manner as all Christian children are taught to look, with the firmest prejudice, upon every other religion, including the liberal interpretations of the Scriptures by Quakers, Unitarians, Universalists and others; so that it may be said, truthfully, that the efforts of free-religionists to convert Christians in their midst, would be as unsuccessful as have been the corresponding efforts by the old sects among the Jews. The Christians say of the Jews, "their perversity in rejecting the gospel is a proof that they are under the wrath and retribution of God." But what shall Liberals say of the Christians, since it is self-evident that their mental condition of blindness and indifference and stupidity and hardheartedness is the same?

Since the immigration of Chinese, especially since their extensive arrangements to dwell and make money among the mild and *exemplary* Christians of California —strong sectarian efforts have been instituted for their "conversion." Conversion *from* what? and *to* what? Answer, from their heathenish form of superstition to the evangelical creeds most popular in this country. All Chinese, like the genuine Japanese, appreciate the advantage of knowledge. They have an intense natural passion for learning all there is to be known; thus presenting, to all respectable Christians, a most important and timely example. They attend school most gladly. Some of them are learning rapidly both to read and write the English language; to sing Sunday-school ballads; and, lately, are striving to take an active interest in the so-called miracles of popular theology; which miracles, because they are so *ancient*, are precious to the Christian believer. A story is told by a lady correspondent, which illustrates the popular idea, and gives a fair report of the success of "conversion."

"Some years ago," she says, "when I lived in the mines, a Chinaman assisted me in my household duties. He was very intelligent, and extremely desirous to learn to read and write, and I took much pleasure in teaching him. One day a bright thought entered my mind. I would make a Christian of Yun Sooi, and he could return to China and preach the gospel to the heathen! I frequently read aloud to him half an hour in the evening. I chose some of the most interesting chapters in the New Testament for my reading. He listened attentively, as usual, but showed no keen interest. Determined to awaken some surprise, at least, I read one evening the story of the raising of Lazarus, altering the words to suit his comprehension. I finished, and there was a pause. Yun Sooi was in deep thought. I saw I had made an impression, and visions of the heathens flocking to hear my convert preach the Gospel, and converted to Christianity through my instrumentality, flashed across my vision. After awhile I said, 'What you think?' 'I don't know—very good.' 'You sabe?' 'Yes; one man he die, another tell him he get up all alive again.' 'Yes; Jesus one very great man.' 'Oh! I don't know; good many China doctors tell me dead man he get up and walk— all same.' Evidently a miracle did not surprise him. They were common events in the Flowery Kingdom! Again he relapsed into thought. Anxious to know what impression was made, I again questioned him. 'What you think?' 'One man die—he lay in the ground four days; one man tell him get up—he stand on his feet.' 'Yes, that's all right,' I replied. 'Well, I think he been dead four days he *smell very bad.*' I concluded that I was out of my sphere when attempting missionary work, and have never since tried to convert the heathen."

Thus the lady wisely concluded; and in a time not very far future, it is believed that her conclusion will be the practical conclusion of every truly conscientious and intelligent mind; at least, such is the prayerful hope of every true reformer.

" But," it is asked by the Christian reader," do you not admit that there is *some* good accomplished by missionaries?"

Answer.—Certainly, friend! No sincere effort is utterly barren of good. But all sectarian missionary effort is, at best, a negative (doubtful) benefit to its recipients. The true missionary is a preacher and practitioner of fraternal love, justice, truth, liberty. He goes to a stranger with the love of a brother in his bosom. For do you not know that the idea of brother was born in the warm heart of universal equal rights? There is in this gospel no sectarianism, no catechism, no creed, no dogmatism, none of the littleness of Christian ignorance and fanaticism. The Father-and-Mother Fountain of the Universe sends the streams of love and life which throb through human souls. "Oh, brother man, fold to thy heart thy brother." Freely and broadly the Divine Bounty pours itself through all living human hearts. When this Divine Love is felt positively, then selfishness surrenders to benevolence; then creeds and private partialities give way to public virtue and universal good will. Fraternal love is the missionary blossom of a spiritual civilization. Selfishness is to the savage what brotherly love is to the civilized state of humanity. Let fraternal, love universally prevail! It is the only infallible remedy for war, cruelty, and crime; it is the triumph of the Father-and-Mother Spirit in the human heart; it means the overthrow of selfishness, and the inauguration of the harmonial kingdom among men.

"Granted!" you exclaim. "But has not each individual soul got something to do to work out his own salvation, to accomplish in himself something like a change of heart, or a "conversion from evil to good?"

Answer.—If you permit me to substitute the more correct word, "elimination," for the hackneyed term "conversion," I answer that every individual has a deep, constant, prayerful work to do for and within himself; and thence for and within the whole human family. Here let me explain to you my meaning, as follows :

The human mind inherits its past; that is, each mentality holds in its constitution the essential drift of everything which preceded it in its own special line of development. Hence, you obtain, by this law of heredity, an explanation of the great number and variety of individual defects, faults, evils, peculiarities, and imperfections. To be truly "converted," to rise superior to these—to recognize and "eliminate" hereditary evils and misdirections, is the mind's highest and grandest achievement. Individual errors must be *eliminated* from the character, must be thrown off, like perspiration from the skin, before the mind is capable of true happiness, and before it is qualified for the perception and expression of "truth, pure and simple." If the tree is crooked because the twig was bent, and if the twig received its wrong direction from surrounding circumstances—just as the common mind is formed by education—then, since the mind is not a tree, but is a magazine of elastic powers, affections, and will, it follows that the mental tree *need not*, like the insensate oak, remain *bent ;* but, on the contrary, the mind may, by the exercise of its own great love-and-will powers, eliminate both the causes and the consequences of its inherited faults, evils, and errors.

Take history (for example), which is full of errors

caused by the special educational and patriotic prejudices of its writers; or take our popular systems of
religion, which overflow with pious fraud, which makes
a considerable portion of both history and religion unreliable. Now, let all errors and misstatements be
eliminated from history and from theology, and the re-
mainder would be exceedingly *small* in amount, and
surprisingly commonplace in quality. You well enough
know by this time that friction in the " mills of God,"
—or what is called " the experiences of life," which
means the same thing—wonderfully, though painfully,
promotes elimination and " conversion."

" Uneasy lies the head that wears a crown,"

because there is in every wrong a germ of retribution.
The erroneous condition—that of a king, for example—
is punished by the principle of Justice. Truly hath it
been written, " A prosperous worthlessness is the curse
of high life." A crown composed of good thoughts and
good deeds is not for the king's head. The elimination
of error and injustice from a kingdom would be sig-
nalized by a revolution—the destruction of the throne,
the establishment of a heavenly form of government,
recognizing the right of all persons to " life, liberty, and
the pursuit of happiness," which would include the right
of all responsible persons to vote for the laws they are
asked to obey. And the elimination of all error from
a person —were it possible—would be attended with a
serious inconvenience; for it would certainly unfit the
mind for contact with its fellows in error. Such a person would no longer be " a little lower than the angels,"
but would have *become in reality an angel;* and, there-

fore, so unlike mankind, that they would probably reject his teachings and nail him to a cross !

———————

(16.)

CATASTROPHIC CONVULSIONS IN THE ORTHODOX HELL.

A perturbed correspondent, whose mind is not yet free of the fears excited by his early Sunday-school lessons, writes thus :

" MY ESTEEMED DAVIS :—On reading the 'Stellar Key,' Part I., about eight years ago, or soon after it was published, I was horribly disturbed by what you quoted about ' Hell,' etc., on page 136, etc. (I am glad you excluded it from all later editions.) What made you print those horrible speculations at all ? I never could see the utility of giving publicity to such inconsistent notions, etc.
" (Signed)   M. G. L."

Answer.—Those quotations from Swedenborg and Harris were introduced to exhibit the great *contrast* between errors in theology and the harmonious truths of universal Nature. For is not the presentation of truth the best antidote for error?

The disclosures of truth in the present volume— manifesting the unity and boundless glory of the 'Univercœlum, all which precludes the possibility of any such places as an orthodox hell or heaven—are deemed a sufficient refutation of all evangelical teachings on these subjects. Knowing what we know, and believing by the necessity of positive evidence what we believe, it becomes difficult to treat those heathen conceptions seriously. They excite feelings akin to irony and playful sarcasm. A fair-minded and eloquent minister (Dr. H. W. Thomas, of Chicago,) has recently, like many another clergyman, rekindled the terrible fires of controversy, thus:

"The awful pictures of hell in the past ages rise up before the prophetic realization of minds in our day, and they see the meaning —the terrible fact set forth, and they are not afraid to ask if such a thing can be true. . . . . Men will rise up and ask if the Bible teaches such things. And if told that it does, they will ask who put such things in the Bible. And if told that God put them there, they will ask, Who is God, that He should say or do such awful things? And if pressed, they will deny both God and the Bible. . . . . Men are ready to believe in punishment for sin here and hereafter —they feel it, they know it—but they are not willing to believe in all the terrible ideas of Dante and Milton; ideas that were possible only in the cold dark age, and that rob the universe of God and all sense of justice or right."

Conferences on this hell-question are now frequent among ministers of every denomination. Such a conference took place in the metropolis on Monday morning, recently. After gossiping over church affairs, they approached the subject near enough to smell the fathomless subject of hell, and to confess how exceedingly slender is the thread of infinite grace upon which they hope to reach the private orthodox Paradise somewhere in the eternal world.

Among them was an agitator whose specific function seemed to be to stir up angry feelings. He filled all with consternation, irrepressible fear and tremblings, and unutterably horrible forebodings, by proposing for

discussion such soul-harrowing and heart-rending questions as:

"Shall the wicked be finally destroyed? . . . . . Will the wicked
in hell finally become extinct? . . . . . Are the future punishments
of the wicked permanent? . . . . . Are the conscious punishments
of the wicked endless? . . . . . Are the punishments of the wicked
in hell parallel to (*i.e.*, of equal duration with) the eternal bliss of
the righteous in heaven?"

These frightful and wicked questions are enough to
overthrow human reason.

On this occasion an elderly clergyman of some note,
who trembled in his every joint, remarked that "the
subject of hell must not be ignored. The *foundation*
of the Church stands upon this question! Why shut
out the light? [He meant the light of hell!] During
the past week," he continued, warming up to the tragical subject, "I have been approached by the members
of my congregation, saying, 'I see that some are
dropping their eternal damnation.' If the punishment
of the wicked is not endless, then the joy of the
righteous is not. One doctrine stands with the
other. If certain views promulgated, be allowed to go
unanswered, it will make me desperate. My very soul
is absorbed. It's an awful thing with me. Therefore
I propose the following: Do the Scriptures give hope
that the wicked shall finally cease to exist?"

One tall, bilious, dejected-looking minister thought
the public discussion of the annihilation of the wicked
would endanger the safety of souls present. But
another, whose breakfast had suited him, said: "During the seven years that I have accepted this theory of
destruction I have converted four hundred and fifty

souls. And I have not lost an iota of my interest for the salvation of mankind."

Here we have the sweet assurance that, notwithstanding his heart-rending annihilation theory, one minister had "converted four hundred and fifty souls!" What beautiful subjects these four hundred and fifty converts would be for microscopic investigation! Tyndall and Dr. Buchner might make a few experiments upon these sulphates of humanity, who have escaped the fate of ultimate annihilation! What prismatic splendors might be obtained by subjecting these four hundred and fifty converts to the action of the heat-beams of the sun! From a true orthodox hell-and-devil convert the brimstone might be eliminated, leaving nothing but the pure, unsophisticated simplicity of faith in the grace of God—*via* the Episcopal or some other Church. The exceeding minuteness of the residuum, after extracting the natural sulphurous qualities, makes it necessary to employ a microscope. Four hundred and fifty converts —if the old metaphysical fathers of popular theology were not mistaken—might sit comfortably, *tête-à-tête*, and promenade about on the point of a cambric needle! And what is more—if some Spiritualist philosophers are not mistaken—an army to the number of millions of these same converted souls might sweep headlong through the granite hills of New Hampshire without impairing the compact crystals for building purposes!

In the heart of New York, amid the benefits of free schools, surrounded by the achievements of science and art, in the last half of the nineteenth century—can any rational mind believe that any assemblage of ministers could be induced to display such wholesale ignorance

of and indifference to the progress of ideas as is indicated by the speeches and discussions reported in the
foregoing paragraphs? And yet we insist upon shout-
ing triumphantly the heroic maxim — "The world
moves!"

Some modern philosophers will here note a gratify-
ing coincidence, irrespective of partition walls and sectarian barriers—in this: That, whereas the above mentioned minister is "desperate" lest the rule which
accomplished the curtailment of the eternity of hell-
torments might reach over into Paradise, and result in
a corresponding abridgment of the eternal joys of the
angels. Indeed, what logic can be at first more taking
than the saying that "a stick that has one end, has two?"
or, that "whatever has a beginning will also have an
end." Consequently, it follows that "if the pains of
hell and the joys of heaven have a beginning, they must
also at some time cease; unless it be discovered that the
fiat of the Almighty, by instituting and keeping up a
perpetual miracle, insures the eternity of the experiences appropriate to the conflicting sides of his universe.
Prove that eternal punishment will, at some time in the
great future, come to an end—in the annihilation of the
wicked, by "one fell swoop" of the wrathful Infinite
Power—and where is your evidence that there will not
also be at some time a total destruction of all the sweet
candidates for eternal happiness? In fact, this branch
of the subject is so appalling, to say nothing of its pathos,
and the terrible tax it imposes upon one's susceptibilities, that the reader will be good enough to pardon me
if I refuse to dwell longer upon it.

Let us, for a moment's relief, turn our attention to the

remarks of another pulpit agitator. He proceeds to say, that there "must be a difference between utter nothingness and destruction. For instance, a house can be destroyed, or a tree, but it is a something. "I am so sanguine of my views," he says, "that I believe the whole Christian Church will sooner or later embrace them. If the other question does not meet your approbation, try this: 'Does the future punishment of the wicked imply their eternal consciousness.'"

This question brings another minister to the red-hot point quicker than one can boil an egg. He thus relieved himself: "We have had too much of this at the last meeting. There is danger! [Cries of 'Amen.'] We are now to startle the religious community for ten weeks to come, when we should devote our efforts to something higher. *The devil is rubbing his hands gleefully;* he has never had a better chance than the present. If this question be adopted, I must read upon hell, instead of warning sinners from the wrath to come. Are we to begin the year with this devilish, or hellish, excitement? I have no objection that this theme be discussed in March. . . . . But I am not in favor of the discussion of this question with open doors."

This sensation extended to another, who said : "There is no use ignoring the important subject under discussion." He thought it was not endangering the salvation of souls! "Rev. John Wesley," he affirmed, "did not hesitate to speak of hell and damnation ; why should we? Perhaps there may be greater ones here than he. I think this question should be discussed for the salvation of souls. If the doctrine of destruction be accepted, I go about carelessly ; but make punishment eternal, and I go along carefully. I do not pretend to be an angel. I am liable to err, but when the doctrines of the Church are assailed, I rise to arms for its defense. You tell me to be calm! I cannot, when that which is *so dear to me* is wronged. I know that the discussion will do good. The reason why we do not get along faster is because *we do not have enough hell in our religion!*"

Many believe that Christianity would get along faster as soon as the preachers infuse "*more hell*" into their beautiful religion. A smile of satisfaction ripples over every ministerial countenance. More hair put into mortar makes it stick better; more yeast in flour makes the bread lighter; why will not *more hell* in one's religion make it more successful among the ignorant and cowardly? Seriously, hell is an invention of ancient Eastern priests, even before the days of Zoroaster.

But is that little bottom-*fact* any reason why evangelical priests in our day, shouldn't have the exclusive use of the invention of their respected ancestors?

"The English word 'hell' is derived from the Anglo-Saxon and Teutonic 'hele' or 'helan,' which meant a covered or hidden place, and the primary and legitimate meaning of the word is the grave, the hidden world, the place of departed spirits. When a man dies they could only say of him that he had passed out of sight, gone into a hidden place, hell. Originally this word hell conveyed no idea of punishment or suffering, but only of concealment or mystery. The thatch of a cottage, the place where the tailor swept his shreds, the hidden corner where the innocent penalty in a game of forfeits was exacted, was hell. Thus the word, from having conveyed the idea of concealment or mystery, has now the horrible meaning of 'everlasting torture.' This change in the word may be legitimate enough, but it utterly unfits the word for use in the English Bible as a translation of the original, because there is no word either in the Hebrew or Greek of the Bible that corresponds with the present meaning of the English word 'hell.' There are three words that in the original language of this Bible are rendered into English by the word 'hell.' The Hebrew word 'sheol' in the Old Testament occurs sixty-four times in the Bible, and it is translated 'hell' thirty-one times, 'grave' thirty times, and 'pit' three times. It should never in a single instance be translated hell, for the Old Testament has no such idea as is now conveyed by the word hell. It means the grave or the place of the dead below the earth. Neither the doctrine of endless punishment, nor even that of future retribution, is taught or even alluded to by the Mosaic law."

A broad-minded preacher (Frothingham) in a recent discourse, said: "The true teaching of Christianity is to reduce to the very lowest point the element of pain and sorrow. To say that there is a Supreme Being, all wise and all good, and at the same time that there is a hell, is a contradiction which shocks all philosophy and all human intelligence. If there were such things as eternal curses and damnation, and God so willed it, then He could not have done more to justify the Atheist in his disbelief and to prove that the devil was master of the world both before and after death. God is love, and through love the whole world will be converted, even Satan himself eventually yielding to its all-pervading power.

"Wherever science has entered," said the preacher,

"all such doctrines as that of future punishment have fled, and when science has completed its work there will be no evil spirits left. It was only by an arbitrary decree of the Church that the doctrine of future punishment was ever entertained, and intelligence, philosophy, science, and the human heart are all opposed to the belief in a hell.

"It is too true that a large number of professing Christians believe in a hell, and many preachers object to agitating the subject for the reason that the doctrine of future punishment cannot be withdrawn without weakening the whole plan of Christian redemption. According to the orthodox theories there must be a hell to balance heaven, because if it were not so, men would have no cause to repent. They would enjoy life, and then lay down to their final rest in peace."

We close our answer in the words of one who, although still a preacher, has long since outgrown the nightmare dogmas of superstition: "I hold that obedience and disobedience will forever produce their corresponding pleasure or pain. I hold that if, in the life to come, men persist in the violation of the laws of their being, they will unquestionably suffer pain and penalty; but there is no evidence whatever that they will, and there are many presumptions that they will not. I do not think that probation closes with death. In another life I can conceive that the experience of this life, which, by reason of man's physical environments and social influences, has not wrought reformation of virtue, may yet in another sphere and under more favorable circumstances bring men to a very much higher platform and standpoint of conduct and of character. We

have reason to suppose that pain and suffering, which
in this world are of an educating nature, will have a
stronger-educating force *hereafter*, and that they will
be continued as long as there is hope of benefit in them.
. . . The continuance of suffering after it is hopeless
in respect to the individual, and needless in respect to
society, is cruelty, and I cannot conceive of any man of a
deeply moral and reflective nature who would bring himself to believe that God will bring into life, as He has,
myriads which utterly outrun all computation, under circumstances in which they not only have no help whatso-
ever to effect moral growth, but where all their surroundings are adverse and perverse, and allow them to continue under such known conditions, to reproduce generations innumerable, and then to place them in a great
hereafter where the principal feature is suffering and
where suffering has ceased to have any moral benefit,
and so continue them there forever and forever.   This is
to create a department of the universe for the purposes,
simply, of *Suffering;* but needless suffering is cruelty,
and any being who inflicts needless suffering is tyranni-
cal. . . . I do not believe that many men could calmly
measure the nature of a single soul, and its susceptibilities to suffering, and the power of Almighty God to
create suffering in that soul, and of a continued existence only for the purposes of suffering through illimit-
able ages, forever and forever, and then multiply that
soul until there are no materials left on which to in-
scribe the figures, until the swarming myriads defy all
measurement or conception of the imagination; then,
overhanging the mighty abyss, contemplate the writhing
anguish, the screaming agony, the hideous and loath-

some suffering, the brutal indignities of sulphurous demons, the carnival of animalism, and yet be able to turn and utter the first words of the Lord's Prayer, "Our Father!" Neither is the trouble alleviated by saying that the penalties are not material anguish, but they are the torments of conscience, of anguish and despair. While we revolt at physical torment, the refined and cultured nature learns to estimate mental suffering as even more exquisite and more horrible than mere bodily torment; and to teach an eternity of conscious mental suffering, after all chance or hope of reformation is gone, shocks that true moral sense which has been educated by the interior love-nature of God, which condemns and destroys such a vision of future useless eternal punishment as a nightmare vision of barbarism."

(17.)

HOW TO PROGRESS IN NEW IDEAS.

Often it is asked: "Why do not individuals make more rapid progress in perceiving and adopting these new harmonial Ideas?" There is an all-sufficient explanation, a plain cause, which, I think, must be self-evident to every mind observer. "Mankind do not advance in truth faster," I reply, "because they do not educate themselves to think deeply and to reason correctly." Let me fully explain what I mean, as follows:

Reasoning from effect to cause is called inductive

philosophy (masculine), which is the reverse of the deductive philosophy (feminine), which means reasoning from cause to effect.

The first method is called scientific or sensuous; the last is the intuitional or supersensuous. Both methods of reasoning are useful in the work of discovering and arriving at truth. And yet these opposite methods represent two exactly different types of mind.

According to Pope, the Supreme Being obeys the deductive principle. Living at the centre, and being, *per se*, the Fountain of Causation, He is of necessity obedient to the intuitional and deductive process. And thus the poet's insight has expressed it—

> "God loves from whole to parts; but human soul
> Must rise from individual to the whole."

Reasoning from causes to effects, or from effects to causes—unless the mind can comprehend and adopt the true system of relations and bearings—will, I am aware, impart but little satisfaction. And yet no real progress can be made either in science or philosophy without profound researches into causes and their effects.

We admit that the different sects are supported by wealthy and sincere persons who do not, cannot, or dare not use their reason upon the origin and elements of their creeds.

Church dogmas and creeds did not originate in the domain of Reason. Hence it is impossible to sustain them by an appeal to Science, which is the busiest child of Reason.

Creed supporters believe things both contradictory

and inconsequential—doctrines of God and of the soul at once absurd and impossible—theories without foundation either in Nature or in humanity.

Suppose we try Reason upon some church dogmas. For example: Reasoning from effect to cause, would convince any candid mind that the *rainbow*—which is, and always was, produced by a natural refraction of the rays of light—is, consequently, a part of the system of Nature, simply because there is a sun in the heavens. But in the churches and catechisms it is unblushingly taught that the rainbow was supernaturally created by Deity as a signature of His solemn promise that he would not again subject the human race to cold water treatment! Reasoning from effects to their causes would hopelessly destroy the doctrine that there can exist three equal, infinite Gods in one personal and local head. Three infinites in one divinity is a docrine which conflicts with God's immutable laws of mathematics. Religionists generally violate the divine laws of numbers and proportions in order to believe what they suppose to be God's Holy Word! Reasoning from effects to causes would overthrow the Church doctrine of the origin of sin and evil; and if these are proved false, what would become of the doctrine of the *atonement*, which is founded upon the first proposition? If you reason, you discover *a false basis* beneath every theological doctrine.

Therefore, if you be time-serving and timid, you will say: "I *dare not* reason concerning these sacred things:" or, if you be weak-minded, you will say, "I *cannot* reason on the incomprehensible doctrines of my church;" or, if you be narrow and opinionated, you will say, "I *will not* reason concerning matters which must be believed on penalty of eternal damnation."

Respected reader! Where do you belong in this classification? Are you *timid?* Are you *weak?* Are you *opinionated?*

In conclusion: If you will but reason from cause to effect, at this juncture, you will easily discover *why* you do not make progress in new ideas.

END.

DESCRIPTIVE LIST

OF

THE COMPLETE WORKS

OF

ANDREW JACKSON DAVIS.

Published and for Sale, Single Volumes or Wholesale, by

COLBY & RICH,

BANNER OF LIGHT PUBLISHING HOUSE,

No. 9 MONTGOMERY PLACE,

BOSTON, MASS.

THE PRINCIPLES OF NATURE:

Her Divine Revelations, and a Voice of Mankind. (In 3 parts.)

Thirtieth Edition, just published, with a likeness of the clairvoyant author, and containing a family record for marriages, births and deaths. This book contains the basis and philosophy on which the whole structure of Spiritualism rests. It embodies and condenses the fundamental principles of human life and human progress up to and beyond the present, and has a steady and constant sale. Price, $3.50; postage 25 cents.

THE GREAT HARMONIA:

Being a Philosophical Revelation of the Natural, Spiritual, and Celestial Universe, in Five Volumes.

Vol. I. THE PHYSICIAN. Contents of Vol. I.—What is Man? What is the Philosophy of Health? What is the Philosophy of Disease? What is the Philosophy of Sleep? What is the Philosophy of Death? What is the Philosophy of Psychology? What is the Philosophy of Healing? Thousands in the United States, and very many in Europe, have read this volume with delight. The author's description of " The Philosophy of Death " is alone worth more than the price of the book. No one can read and remain unmoved. The volume is especially useful to every family as a work on medicine and the science of disease and health. Price, $1.50.

Vol. II. THE TEACHER. Contents of Vol. II.—My Early Experience; My Preacher and his Church; The True Reformer; Philosophy of Charity; Individual and Social Culture; The Mission of Woman; The True Marriage; Moral Freedom; Philosophy of Immortality; The Spirit's Destiny; Concerning the Deity. In this volume is presented the new and wonderful principles of "Spirit, and its Culture;" also, a comprehensive and systematic argument on the " Existence of God." Price, $1.50.

Vol. III. THE SEER. This volume is composed of twenty-seven Lectures on every phase of Magnetism and Clairvoyance in the past and present of human history. Swedenborg's condition is thoroughly examined. Among the subjects treated are, Philosophy of Clairvoyance and Inspiration ; Man's Ordinary State, considered in Connection with the External World and to the Spiritual Universe; Dependencies existing between the Body and the Soul; Action of the Mind upon the Body in Disease; Manifestations of a Universal Sympathy; On the Historical Evidences of the Psycho-sympathetic State; Condition of Ancient Prophets, Seers, and Religious Chieftains; The Phenomena and History of Clairvoyance; The Spiritual State and its External Manifestations; Concerning the Principles and Causes of True Inspiration; The Philosophy of Ordinary and Extraordinary Dreaming; The Sources of Human Happiness and Misery Philosophically Considered; A Brief Exposition of the Satan which Tempted Jesus of Nazareth; The Authority of the Harmonial Philosophy; On the Uses and the Abuses of the Sabbath. Price, $1.50.

Vol. IV. THE REFORMER. This volume contains truths eminently serviceable in the elevation of the race. It is devoted to the consideration of " Physiological Vices and Virtues, and the Seven Phases of Marriage." It covers ground never before occupied by any reformatory writer, and teaches the most important truths upon the most vital questions that can agitate any mind—those of *Marriage* and *Parentage*. It is a work that appeals first to man's consciousness, by a clear representation of existing evils; and next to the higher faculties, by pointing out the " highway of freedom " from all these evils. Satisfying as it does the understanding, it affords valuable aid to the individual in rooting out bad habits and reforming vicious tendencies. It is a safe book for youth, for it has not the least indelicacy of sentiment or expression; and it furnishes just such knowledge, and inculcates such principles, as are calculated to preserve the youthful mind from contamination, and insure the practice of virtue. It is an invaluable book for the newly-married, for it points out the danger and consequences of extremism and inversionism, and imparts that information concerning the reproductive functions necessary to avoid conjugal misdirections. Price, $1.50.

Vol. V. THE THINKER. This volume is by numerous readers pronounced the most comprehensive and best sustained of the series. Read it, and you will become acquainted with all the great central "Ideas" which, aided by the minds by whom they were unfolded, have carried forward the mighty growth of humanity. Read it, and you will learn of the "Origin of Life, and the Law of Immortality." In this volume you will also find very many new and instructive diagrams. Price, $1.50; postage, 10 cents each.

THE PRESENT AGE, AND INNER LIFE:
Ancient and Modern Mysteries Classified and Explained.

The best critics have pronounced this work one of the most classically pure of all the volumes of the author. It abounds with thrilling passages; and no one can fail to be instructed by the systematic "classification" of all the wonderful developments of modern days. The work is, in itself, almost a demonstration of the claims of Spiritualism. Price, $1.50; postage, 10 cents.

THE PENETRALIA.

This work, which at the time was styled by the author, "the wisest book" from his pen, deserves to be brought prominently before the American public. The importance of the subjects considered, and the peculiarly terse and original style in which they are handled, combine to give the book a most noticeable character. While the topics are mainly theological, many questions of practical interest and value are answered, thus rendering the volume an acquisition to the student and philosopher, as well as the theologian. Price, $1.75; postage, 12 cents.

THE HARBINGER OF HEALTH:
Containing Medical Prescriptions for the Human Body and Mind.

This new and rare volume contains more than three hundred prescriptions for the treatment and cure of over one hundred different diseases, and forms of disease, incident to mankind in all parts of the world. The author's prescriptions are given in the light of the "Superior Condition." The Harbinger of Health has never failed to awaken intense interest in the minds of the most intelligent of the Medical Profession, and it is invaluable to the general reader, containing as it does, information concerning methods of treatment hitherto unknown to the world, and imparting important suggestions respecting the Will Power and the Self-Healing Energies, which are better than medicine. It is a plain, simple guide to health, with no quackery, no humbug, no universal panacea. Price, $1.50; postage, 10 cents.

ANSWERS TO EVER-RECURRING QUESTIONS FROM THE PEOPLE.

During the period which has elapsed since the publication of the author's work entitled the "Penetralia," a multitude of questions have been propounded to him. From this list of several hundred interrogatories, those of the most permanent interset and highest value have been carefully selected, and the result is the present volume, comprising well-considered and intelligent replies to more than two hundred important questions. It is believed by hundreds that this work is one of the most interesting and useful volumes that has been issued. It invites the perusal not only of those vitally interested in the topics discussed, but of all persons capable of putting a question. It awakens inquiry and develops thought. The wide range of subjects embraced can be inferred from the table of contents. An examination of the book itself will reveal the clearness of style and vigor of method characterizing the replies. Price, $1.50; postage, 10 cents.

MORNING LECTURES:

Twenty Discourses, delivered in the City of New York, in the Winter and Spring of 1863.

This volume is overflowing with that peculiar inspiration which carries the reader into the region of new ideas. The discourses are clothed in language plain and forcible, and the arguments and illustrations convey conviction. Among the subjects treated are:—"The World's True Redeemer;" "The End of the World;" "The Reign of Anti-Christ;" "The Spirit, and its Circumstances;" "Eternal Value of Pure Purposes;" "Wars of Blood, Brain, and Spirit;" "False and True Education;" "Social Life in the Summer Land;" &c. This volume of plain lectures is just the book to put into the hands of skeptics and new beginners in Spiritualism. Price, $1.50; postage, 10 cents.

A STELLAR KEY TO THE SUMMER LAND.

Part I. Illustrated with Diagrams and Engravings of Celestial Scenery.

The author has heretofore explained the wonders of creation, the mysteries of science and philosophy, the order, progress, and harmony of Nature in thousands of pages of living inspiration. He has solved the mystery of death, and revealed the connection between the world of matter and the world of spirits. Mr. Davis opens wide the door of future human life, and shows us where we are to dwell when we put aside the garments of mortality for the vestments of angels. The account of the spiritual universe; the immortal mind looking into the heavens; the existence of a spiritual zone—its possibilities and probabilities—its formation and scientific certainty; the harmonies of the universe; the physical scenery and constitution of the Summer Land—its location, and domestic life in the spheres, are new and wonderfully interesting. Price, 75 cents; paper covers, 50 cents; postage 5 cents.

ARABULA; OR, THE DIVINE GUEST.

This fresh and beautiful volume is selling rapidly, because it supplies a deep religious want in the hearts of the people. Best literary minds are gratified, while truly religious readers are spiritually fed with the contents of this volume. All who want to understand and enjoy the grand central truths of the Harmonial Philosophy, and all who would investigate the teachings and religion of Spiritualism, should read this inspired book. It contains a New Collection of Gospels by Saints not before canonized, and its chapters are teeming with truths for humanity, and with fresh tidings from the beloved beyond the tomb. The names of the new Saints are:—St Rishis, St. Menu, St. Confucius, St. Siamer, St. Syrus, St. Gabriel, St. John, St. Pneuma, St. James, St. Gerrit, St. Theodore, St. Octavius, St. Samuel, St. Eliza, St. Emma, St. Ralph, St. Asaph, St. Mary, St. Selden, St. Lotta. **Price, $1.50; postage, 10 cents.**

THE MAGIC STAFF:

An Autobiography of Andrew Jackson Davis.

"This most singular biography of a most singular person," has been extensively read in this country, and is now translated and published in the German language. It is a complete personal history of the clairvoyant experiences of the author from his earliest childhood to 1856. All important details are carefully and conscientiously given. Every statement is authentic and beyond controversy. In this volume (including the autobiographical parts of "Arabula" and "Memoranda" which enter largely into the author's personal experiences), the public will find *a final answer to all slanders and misrepresentations.* Thousands of copies of the "Magic Staff" have been sold in the United States, and the demand, instead of being supplied, is increasing. Price, $1.75; postage, 12 cents.

MEMORANDA OF PERSONS, PLACES, AND EVENTS:

Embracing Authentic Facts, Visions, Impressions, Discoveries in Magnetism, Clairvoyance, and Spiritualism.

This volume of transcripts from the observation and experience of Mr. Davis will be welcomed with great pleasure by his tens of thousands of readers, in which they will find a great variety of those fresh and fleeting "impressions" of the inspired seer, carefully set down by his own hand for a period of over twenty-two years, that can not but let them further than ever into his own nature, and the mysterious realms which his vision is permitted to penetrate and search. There is a peculiar freshness about this latest book from Mr. Davis that makes it specially attractive to the general reader. His off-hand characterization of persons of note will strike all as peculiarly apt and effective. In fact, it is a sort of mirror for all to look into. This volume should be read by all who have perused the "Magic Staff." The Appendix, containing the fine translation of Zschokke's tale of the "Transfiguration," will attract all to its perusal, since it illustrates the curative powers of human magnetism, and the spiritual beauty and purity of the superior condition. This book is also particularly valuable to history, because it contains a chapter written by Mary F. Davis, concerning the "Introduction of the Harmonial Philosophy into Germany." Price, $1.50; Postage, 10 cents.

THE PHILOSOPHY OF SPECIAL PROVIDENCES.

This is a small pamphlet of fifty-five pages, but is living with thought. The author considers the question, "Are there Special Providences?" and no one can fail to be instructed and elevated by its perusal. The pamphlet contains Two Visions, and An Argument. Price, 30 cents.

THE PHILOSOPHY OF SPIRITUAL INTERCOURSE.

CONTENTS.—Truth and Mystery; God's Universal Providence; The Miracles of this Age; The Decay of Superstition; The Guardianship of Spirits; The Discernment of Spirits; The Stratford Mysteries; The Doctrine of Evil Spirits; The Origin of Spirit Sounds; Concerning Sympathetic Spirits; The Formation of Circles; The Resurrection of the Dead; A Voice from the Spirit Land; The True Religion. In this thrilling work the reader is presented with an account of the very wonderful Spiritual Developments at the house of the Rev. Dr. Phelphs, of Stratford, Connecticut; and besides these, the work is replete with similar cases in all parts of the country. This work is completed by its sequel, entitled "Present Age and Inner Life." Price, cloth, $1.25; postage, 10 cents.

FREE THOUGHTS CONCERNING RELIGION.

This volume contains short arguments, fresh and vigorous, substantiated by plain historical and geological facts, against the popularly received idea that the "Bible is the Word of God." Infallibility is demolished, and creeds finely pulverized in the mill of truth. Recently enlarged, it is calculated to "stir up thorght" in a bigoted neighborhood. We recommend "Free Thoughts Concerning Religion." Price, cloth, 75 cents; paper, 50 cents; postage, 5 cents.

THE HARMONIAL MAN.

CONTENTS.—How shall we Improve Society? The Influence of Churches; The Necessity of Organic Liberty; Mankind's Natural Needs; The Means by which to Secure Them; The Philosophy of Producing Rain; A Statement of Popular Theories; The Causes of Rain Explained; The Philosophy of Controlling Rain; Answer to Scientific Objections; Plagiarism; Clairvoyance Illustrated; What will People Say; The Pirate's Simple Narrative. The contents of this little work are designed to enlarge man's views concerning the political and ecclesiastical condition of our conntry, and to point out, or at least to suggest, the paths of reform which the true Harmonial Man shall tread. We might add many commendatory notices of the press, but it is deemed sufficient to give the reader an idea of the work, by publishing its table of contents. Those who know Mr. Davis' style of treating his subjects, will not need to be informed that this little book is full of important thoughts. Price, in paper, 50 cents; cloth, 75 cents; postage, 5 cents.

THE APPROACHING CRISIS:

A Review of Dr. Bushnell's Lectures on Supernaturalism.

The great question of this age, which is destined to convulse and divide Protestantism, and around which all other religious controversies must necessarily revolve, is exegetically foreshadowed in this Review, which is composed of six discourses delivered by the author before the Harmonial Brotherhood of Hartford, Connecticut. It is affirmed by many of the most careful readers of Mr. Davis's works, that the best explanation of the "Origin of Evil," and of "Free Agency," is to be found in this Review. Price, cloth, $1.00; postage, 10 cents.

THE HISTORY AND PHILOSOPHY OF EVIL.

The headings of the chapters in this pamphlet give an idea of its purport, viz. :— I. The Unity of Truth; II. The Anti-Human Theory of Evil; III. The Inter-Human Theory of Evil; IV. The Super-Human Theory of Evil; V. The Spiritual Theory of Evil; VI. The Harmonial Theory of Evil; VII. The Cause of Civilization; VIII. The World's True Saviour Discovered; IX. The Harmonial Cure of Evil. The whole question of evil—individual, social, national, and general—is fully analyzed and answered by the author in this compact pamphlet. It has been extensively circulated, and is highly prized by all intelligent readers on both sides of the Atlantic. Price, in paper, 50 cents; cloth, 75 cents; postage, 5 cents.

DEATH, AND THE AFTER LIFE.

This little work contains three Lectures, and a Voice from the Summer Land. The titles are:—I. Death, and the After Life; II. Scenes in the Summer Land; III. Society in the Summer Land; IV. Voice from James Victor Wilson. Thousands of this new and consoling pamphlet have been published and sold. In the sick-room, where spiritual consolations are required, or in the hands of the lonely and bereft this work is effective. Price, in paper, 50 cents; cloth, 75 cents; postage, 5 cents.

THE CHILDREN'S PROGRESSIVE LYCEUM.

A Manual, with Directions for the Organization and Management of Sunday Schools, adapted to the Bodies and Minds of the Young, and containing Rules Methods, Exercises, Marches, Lessons, Questions and Answers, Invocations, Silver

Chain Recitations, Hymns, and Songs. This Manual is a chart to indicate the best methods in the grouping and educating process. Price, 60 cents; postage, 3 cents; for twelve copies, $6.50; for fifty copies, $22.00; and for one hundred copies, $40.00.

THE DIAKKA, AND THEIR EARTHLY VICTIMS.

Being an explanation of much that is false and repulsive in Spiritualism. Cloth, 50 cents; paper covers, 25 cents.

THE TEMPLE: ON DISEASES OF THE BRAIN AND NERVES.

Developing the Origin and Philosophy of Mania, Insanity and Crime; with full Directions and Prescriptions for their Treatment and Cure. The book contains 460 pages, is beautifully printed and bound, uniform with the "Harmonia," "Harbinger of Health," etc., with an Original Frontispiece illustrative of "Mother Nature Casting (D) evils Out of Her Children." Cloth $1.50; postage 10 cents.

THE FOUNTAIN: WITH JETS OF NEW MEANINGS.

Illustrated with 142 Engravings. The young as well as the old, can read it, and study its lessons and illustrations with ever-increasing pleasure and profit. Cloth binding, $1.00; postage, 6 cents.

TALE OF A PHYSICIAN; OR, THE SEEDS AND FRUITS OF CRIME.

In Three Parts—complete in one volume. Part I—Planting the Seeds of Crime; Part II—Trees of Crime in Full Bloom; Part III—Reaping the Fruits of Crime. Cloth, $1.00; postage, 10 cents.

THE GENESIS AND ETHICS OF CONJUGAL LOVE.

This new book is of peculiar interest to all men and women. Paper, 50 cents; cloth, 75 cents.

COMPLETE WORKS OF A. J. DAVIS.

COMPRISING TWENTY-NINE UNIFORM VOLUMES, ALL NEATLY BOUND IN CLOTH, $29.00

In remitting by mail, a Post-Office Money Order on Boston, or a Draft on a Bank or Banking House in Boston or New York City, payable to the order of COLBY & RICH, is preferable to Bank Notes, since, should the Order or Draft be lost or stolen, it can be renewed without loss to the sender.

☞ All Business Letters to be addressed to

ISAAC B. RICH, Business Manager, Banner of Light, Boston, Mass.